ALL BETS ARE OFF

A SAMANTHA TRUE NOVEL

KRISTI ROSE

VINTAGE HOUSEWIFE BOOKS

ALL BETS ARE OFF

Some days, no matter how awful, are not worth a do-over

One wild weekend in Vegas Samantha True and her boyfriend impulsively marry. Six months later she learns three things about her new husband.

1. He's been killed in a freak accident.
2. She's inherited his secret PI business.
3. He had another wife.

Broke and devastated, she dives into learning the PI business—how hard can it be? Following a binge-watching How To session on Youtube, Samantha's ready to take her first case.

When mysterious strangers show up at her doorstep demanding information about her dead husband, she realizes she's in over her head.

Samantha must discover who he really was. But what if the truth puts her in danger, too?

ALL BETS
A Samantha True Mystery
ARE OFF

KRISTI ROSE

FRIDAY

"Miss True, I have some very troubling news." The lawyer, Tyson Lockett, pushed a tri-folded piece of paper across the desk toward me.

The corner hung off the side of the desk.

Wishing I could avoid the paper altogether, I flicked it back toward him using the nail of my index finger. After which, I rubbed the finger down the length of my skirt, wiping it clean.

His expression solemn, he said, "I have more troubling information."

"More troubling news than my husband's been killed?" I swallowed hard; those had been difficult words to say.

What could trump learning of your loved one's unexpected death? My mind couldn't conceive of one thing.

Lockett wiped a hand down his face and mumbled

something that sounded like he was cursing the dead man in question.

He pinched the bridge of his nose and said without looking at me, "I'm not sure how to tell you this, Miss True. If you look at the death certificate, you'll see that the name and date of birth align with the man you knew as Carson Holmes. But if you look closer, you'll notice the cause of death, nature of death, and date of death are wrong." Then he fixed his gaze on me. His stare unwavering.

I shook my head. "I don't think I understand." My mouth was insanely dry and rough, like sunbaked earth. Nothing about this moment added up. I locked onto the easiest of oddities coming at me. Lockett knew to call me and tell me about Carson, though I'd never heard the lawyer's name before today. Lockett also knew I had kept my maiden name. "How did you know I hadn't taken Carson's last name?"

He blew out a heavy sigh then nodded to the paper. "Please take a look at this." Lockett leaned across his steel and glass desk and nudged the folded piece of paper, perfect for a letter-sized envelope, back to me.

With trepidation, I reached for the document. My hand trembled slightly as I picked it up by pinching the corner with my thumb and forefinger.

The sheet had weight, the sort of paper used for official documents or homemade cards declaring love or good news.

Lockett gave me an encouraging half smile and nod, silently pushing me to keep going.

I clutched the heavy paper, one hand on each side, and lifted the top with my thumbs. The inside print declared the sheet to be an official death certificate from Washington State.

"I know this isn't easy and I'm very sorry," he murmured calmly.

Something about his downturned gaze gave me the impression that he was saddened by the news, too. Or maybe he was sad because he was charged with delivering it.

He cleared his throat. "Two nights ago, the man you knew as Carson Holmes was killed in a motor vehicle accident. He was driving through Snoqualmie Pass, crashed, and a tree fell onto his car."

My mind played its own version of the scene just painted for me. "Impossible," I whispered. I directed my focus on the lawyer as I expelled a deep breath. "Carson was in California at a home security convention, not northern Washington, and certainly not anywhere near the pass."

How did I know this guy was even telling me the truth? Yesterday, I had no idea he existed, and today he was lowering this boom.

"Why aren't the police telling me this if Carson is really dead?" I closed my eyes, seeking equilibrium, and rewound the last few moments. "Why did you keep saying the man I knew as Carson Holmes?"

"Look at the certificate," Lockett said. "Look at the date and cause of death."

With steely resolve, I opened my eyes and further

unfolded the paper. I scanned the page for the important words like "nature of death" and skipped the rest. Lockett was correct; the date of death was not today or yesterday or the day before. The date was from ten years ago and on New Year's day. Today was not New Year's or anywhere close to it. The cause of death confused me more. "This says Carson Holmes died from cancer."

"That's correct," Lockett said.

"So this isn't my husband?" A tiny spark of hope pulsed inside, even if I couldn't figure out this riddle.

"No. Your husband used that death certificate to establish a new identity. The man you knew as Carson Holmes was not really Carson Holmes."

"Come again?" I wasn't usually this dense, but nothing this lawyer had said made a lick of sense, starting with his anxious phone call this morning.

"The man you believed you were married to had a different name, a different birthday, and was actually married to another woman. Well, they were in the final stages of divorce, but that doesn't matter. What does is that it wasn't official yet."

And there it was, the *other* bad news. Yes, death was still the worse of the two, but learning my husband was actually married to someone else ranked up there really close to learning he'd died.

The words came to me as if Tyson Lockett was standing at the far end of the tunnel, his voice metallic and fading. His words tasted bitter on my tongue even though I hadn't spoken them.

I had one of two options. I could toss my cookies onto his gray shag carpet or I could pass out.

Neither sounded appealing, but I chose the latter. And considering how my luck was going, I took preemptive measures and stuck my head between my legs. Didn't want to faint, slide out of the smooth leather chair, and end up in some weird position where I showed Lawyer Guy my tiger-striped undies.

But no sooner had I bent over than darkness claimed me.

2

FRIDAY

W hen I came to, Lockett was beside me, his hand on my shoulder as he gently nudged me to consciousness.

"Come on, Samantha, wake up," he murmured.

I groaned in protest. I wanted to stay in this darkness where the truth stood at bay. Sadly, that was not an option. Instead, I sat up slowly and tried to gain my equilibrium. My vision was blurry, tears threatening to spill. I blinked rapidly, attempting some sort of control in an uncontrollable moment.

"Here." Lockett shoved a tumbler of gold-colored liquid toward me. "Drink this. You're in shock."

Lockett was tall, blond, deeply tanned, and likely spent his off-days on a surfboard where he referred to others as "dudes," regardless of gender.

His office and presence reflected the darkness settling around me—pewter-colored walls, a leather couch the color of a storm cloud, and shag carpet that matched his gray suit. Outside the window, the muddy brown of the Columbia River, the bright blue of a spring sky, and the snow-capped Mount Hood provided the only color.

Nothing was making sense. Not the man, his words, or the atypical sunny sky three days into spring in the Pacific Northwest. Outside was bathed in light and new life; inside was dark and depressing and about death. I was desperate to escape but knew I couldn't. These facts would follow me, even into the light of day.

I took the glass and tossed it back. Liquid fire burned down my throat and landed in my stomach, which was a volcanic gurgling of apprehension and grief. I coughed, half expecting flames to shoot out as my insides burned.

Lockett handed me a water bottle, and I took a large gulp, desperate to extinguish the fire. My stomach revolted. I leaped from the chair and ran for a clear plastic waste can, picked it up, and upchucked breakfast into it.

Lockett went into his reception area and returned with the secretary behind him. She discreetly took the waste-basket from me and then held it away from her as she disappeared from the room.

He guided me back to the chair while handing me a monogrammed handkerchief. The gesture caught me off guard. I hadn't figured him for the old-fashioned type.

I covered my mouth with my hands, his hankie tucked between two fingers, and shook my head. How could what he said possibly be true? I was the other woman? I wasn't even Carson's wife? I couldn't believe a duplicitous nature of this magnitude possible from the Carson I knew.

"Does she know about me?" I slumped into the chair, letting my head fall back to rest against the back. My body suddenly heavy, my limbs like wet logs.

"Yes. When Carson died, he didn't have his fake ID on him. That's why you're being notified by me and not the police. His wife later learned of your..." He cleared his throat. "I was asked to look into matters."

My stomach rolled again. She knew about me. Who I was. I knew nothing about her. "What are the chances our paths will cross?"

"Slim," he said. "It would be a fluke if you did."

How was it possible Carson had lived two lives, and I'd never been the wiser? Is that really where he went whenever he was out of town? I'd seen shows like this on the true crime channels but never thought it could happen to anyone I knew, much less myself.

"You said they were in the process of a divorce... Were they still living together?" I needed to know the extent of which I shared Carson. "Is that why he was near the pass when he died?"

Lockett shook his head. "He had a business interest out by the pass, and the divorce was in mediation. He made frequent trips to..."

The unspoken words hung heavy in the room. I wasn't allowed to know where he'd been or what he'd been up to, a right given to any wife. More talk and confusion with no actual information and clarity. More secrets.

Lockett sighed wearily then said, "Miss True, because you and Carson were not legally married, you have no claim to his estate. Anything under the name Carson

Holmes defaults to the estate under his real name and belongs to his legal wife."

Seeking comfort, I reached for the silver necklace Carson had given me two weeks ago, an unexpected gift to mark our half-year married. My hands stilled when I touched my bare neck. The chunky piece of jewelry, two keys connected to a heart, was missing. Frantic, I felt around, hoping to find it had come undone, only to recall I'd broken the necklace a few days ago, having snagged it on my camera bag strap, and split a link.

I laid my hand flat against my bare neck. "It sure felt legal to me. I went into it with good intentions." If one drunken night in Vegas constituted good intentions. Regardless, I took my oaths and vows seriously.

"That may be true, but Carson didn't. I'm truly sorry." He patted my shoulder awkwardly.

If Carson didn't come into our marriage with good intentions, what were his intentions? I didn't like where this was going. A hot wave of humiliation washed over me.

"You're sorry? For what?" I sat up and stared at Lockett, who was leaning against his desk in front of me. "Because somebody duped me? Because the man I believed I married is dead? Because right now I don't know what to make of my life? Why precisely are you sorry?" A thick knot of tears and anxiety formed in my throat, making swallowing almost impossible. "How do I know any of this is true? I don't even have a death certificate. So maybe this is some really *really* sick joke."

Lockett reached across his desk then picked up a manila envelope. He held it out to me.

"What's this?" I recoiled as if he was holding a snake. I couldn't handle anything else that was going to take the wind out of me.

"In this folder are the forms and documents for the real Carson Holmes. Newspaper articles, lots of other information. This is the identity your husband stole." Lockett stuck it next to my bag on the floor.

"Yet, that doesn't answer my question. How do I know you're telling me the truth? There's more than one Carson Holmes in the world. Exactly who was I married to? Tell me that." I air quoted when I said "married."

Lockett brushed a hand through his hair and sighed so heavily the weight of it pressed against me. "I can't tell you his real name. The family asked that you not know."

"I'm supposed to take this in and accept it based on the word of a stranger?" I asked incredulously.

"I don't know." Lockett wouldn't meet my gaze, but instead stared out the window. His jaw worked as if there were more to say but he wasn't sure he should. He swore quietly, then took the seat next to me. He shifted closer as if about to tell me a secret.

His voice low, he said, "Please believe me when I say you're better off not knowing. You have your memories. No one can take those away from you. But anything you have in Carson's name hide it, get rid of it, or sell it. Separate yourself from the name Carson Holmes as fast as you can. Do you share a joint account?"

I nodded. His tone worried me. I was being warned.

He reached for my sling bag resting on the floor, then handed it to me. "Can you access the account from your phone?"

I nodded again and held the bag on my lap.

"Clean out your account *now*," he said.

His urgency created a sense of rising panic. My heart beat madly. My hands trembled as I opened the large pocket. We had one joint account, a savings. I'd kept my checking account separate for reasons I couldn't recall. I'd been socking my pay into the savings so I could quit my job and do something else. I was burned out on photography, but the something else was yet to be determined. The savings were a cushion to give me time to figure it out. We'd budgeted to live off Carson's wages.

I fumbled with the phone to pull up my banking app. If what Lockett said was true, if Carson was dead, then I needed to get what I could, right? I liked to eat. I liked having a roof over my head. My survival instinct kicked in and took over. Not that we had a whole lot of money in the account, but the sum would hold me over until I could get my bearings.

With trembling fingers, it took three attempts at the password before keying in the correct code.

To make the situation more stressful, I'd quit my job a few days ago. The hate I had harbored for my former employer could not be put into words. I was sick of photoshopping school pictures of the children in the Wind River School District. Telling creepy Mr. Toomey to stick it where the sun didn't shine had been glorious. Worthy of a celebration. One I was going to share with my now deceased husband. This time I added mental air quotes around "husband."

The account was empty. Thirty thousand dollars gone. I stilled, suddenly chilled. I put the phone on Lockett's desk. "There's nothing in the account."

He clucked his tongue. "They're moving fast. You'll need to as well. I wish I could ease you into this, but it looks like we're up against the clock." He took another folder off his desk and thrust it at me. "Carson left you his business."

"How? You said his estate gave everything to the real wife." I swallowed that down like a person did a cockroach.

"He put this in your name. The building lease has been paid in full for the year. It renews at the end of January. It's yours to do with what you want. You need to start securing everything you can."

"I know nothing about security systems. I can't do his job."

Lockett looked weary. "His business wasn't just security. He also acted as a private investigator."

Unable to refrain from being sarcastic, I said, "What? He sold security systems *and* solved crime?" Nothing, and I mean abso-freaking-lutely nothing, made sense. My life was currently the definition of bizarro-world.

"Yes." Lockett gave me this look, part sympathy and part pity, that infuriated me.

I snatched the folder and my bag, jumping to my feet. My savings was gone. My husband was not my husband but, regardless, he was gone, too, and now some blond surfer wannabe was annoyed with me because I'd been duped? Nope, I'd had my limit of crap today. "Is there anything else you'd like to tell me about the man I was sleeping with for the last year and clearly did not know?"

Lockett kept his mouth closed.

"No? Good. Then I'll get out of here before you tell me my dad isn't my real dad and I'm actually a boy named Pablo from Spain." I marched to the door, fueled by indignation and fear.

"Samantha," Lockett said.

I paused. Staring at the door, my hand on the handle, I refused to look back.

"Please be careful. Be careful who you talk to. Who you share information with. Just forget you ever knew a Carson Holmes and get on with your life."

I glared at him over my shoulder, appalled he could ever suggest such a thing. I now had a million unanswered questions, and if there was one thing everyone could tell you about me, was that I had an insatiable curiosity.

3

FRIDAY

How I got from Lockett the Lawyer's third-floor office and into my car was anyone's guess.

The day was unseasonably warm, but I was chilled to the bone. I flung my sling bag and envelopes haphazardly on the passenger seat then took the driver's seat. Without air flow, the thick heat in the car was suffocating. I pressed a button on my fob to lower the windows then clutched the steering wheel, my hands at four and eight, as the turmoil of the day surrounded me.

I stared out the window but only saw the film reel of the past year I'd spent with Carson. Image after image captured by the camera of my mind's eye replayed, this time looking for signs. We'd met at the Portland Marathon, having run the last six miles at the same pace, and crossed the finish line together. We'd celebrated our achievement by dumping water on one another, hugging and laughing. I'd never forget how he'd stepped back, surveyed me as if he was seeing a stunning view for the first time, and stuck out his hand as an introduction.

"Carson Holmes, like Sherlock Holmes," he'd said. I supposed that should have been my first clue. His introduction, a whopper of a lie, had likened him to a fictional person.

"Samantha True," I'd replied. I'd studied the soft angles of his face. He was handsome with a boyish charm, an impish smile, and twinkling brown eyes.

"Can I take you to a celebratory dinner?" he'd asked. "I'm new to the area and would like to make a friend."

Everything in my being had screamed yes. In hindsight, it was shocking really how easily I'd been played. There were no warning signs, no red flags. Ever. One dinner had led to several others. He didn't rush me or work me over like those scary news stories about how a woman became a victim. He'd never hesitated answering questions I asked. Never, not once, did I get the vibe he was hiding something.

And it wasn't like I resembled a bridge troll or anything. I'm taller than most women, but only by an inch or two, with long strawberry-blond wavy hair, gray-green eyes, and straight teeth from four years in braces. My complexion was good, with a smattering of freckles across my nose, and I got the occasional zit, usually at the worst possible time. Yeah, I often wore ponytails and preferred shants (pants that unzip at the knees and become shorts) to dresses, but I'd dated when I wanted to. It wasn't like I was hard up to find Mr. Right.

Six months after meeting, we took a Vegas trip, never

intending the weekend to be more than a fun getaway. Several drinks and a buffet later, a polyester-suited Elvis married us. There was no something old, borrowed, new, or blue. But there had been a drunken video of our nuptial kiss that ended with Carson sweeping me off my feet and carrying me off toward a fake sunset. I stupidly blasted it out on social media instead of calling my parents and telling them. My mother had told me the video quality was poor but the message was clear. Oh, and couldn't I, just once, do things like other girls my age?

Hey, I'd gotten married. What more did she want?

"Samantha?" Outside the driver's side window, Lockett was bent at the waist and peering in at me. "I know this is difficult, but you need to leave. It's not a good idea for you to sit out here. It's not safe."

I gave him the view of my back, not caring about his warning. I wasn't too worried about the food truck vendors, the business people, and stay-at-home hippie moms that were bustling to the nearby parks or coffee shops.

Lockett sighed. "Can you call someone?"

Sure, I could. But I didn't want to. I was in no hurry to have the conversation about my lying, cheating not-really-my-husband with anyone.

I had three options. None of them were good. There was my sister Rachel. She lived on the east coast, was an active duty nurse in the US Navy, and a single parent. She liked to boss me around, like older sisters do, especially when she was worried. I considered my parents next. This was going to rip them up, especially my dad. He loved

Carson and Carson loved him. Or maybe that last part was a ruse, too. I couldn't tell my dad that. Last was my best friend, Precious, but with her came more drama, and I didn't have the energy for that.

Lockett shuffled away, grumbling, and I was glad. I continued to hold the steering wheel, rubbing my thumbs over the stitching of the leather as I tried to put the pieces together. How had I judged so poorly? Even now, I couldn't pick out the clues.

I must have done this for some time because when Lockett returned, he had a friend.

"I can't get her to leave," Lockett said. From the corner of my eye, I caught a glimpse of the man's gray pants, his hand in his front pocket.

Lockett's face appeared at the window. "You left me no choice. I'm not trying to cause you more trouble."

Another face came into my periphery, pushing Lockett out of view. "Hey, Samantha. How's it going?" Asked the cop at my window.

I closed my eyes, hoping that when I opened them he'd be gone.

"She's not had a good day," Lockett whispered. "Maybe not ask her that."

The cop cleared his throat. "Samantha, it's Leo. Wanna tell me what's going on?"

As if.

I said nothing.

"Want me to call Hue, and you can talk to him?" Leo held up his phone.

Hue was Leo's kid brother and one of my closest

friends. Leo *was not* one of my closest friends. In fact, we had a past heavy with mutual irritation for each other.

He'd been the star quarterback for our high school team while I'd been the photographer for the school paper. Every time I tried to get a shot, he'd turn away. But only for me. He'd let others take his picture. He was that sort of butthead. To add fuel to the fire, Leo Stillman had borne witness to my most embarrassing life stumbles. Or contributed to it, depending on who was telling the story.

Besides my current one, that was.

I'd gone to college for photography with high hopes of becoming a forensic photographer. During the intern phase in my year, I was asked to photograph an auto collision for insurance purposes. The scene included a dead deer. Trouble was, I had the flu—body chills, clammy skin, queasy stomach, and double vision. One look at the deer's beady black eyes and twisted body, and I'd upchucked everywhere, including Leo's still-being-processed scene. The night had gotten worse from there as the cops had taken a call to respond to a second scene, one where a woman I'd grown up with had been chained to a pole and hit by a car following a robbery.

Seeing the dark underbelly of the criminal world had left me uncertain of my life's plan. Sensing this, Leo told me to give it up and go take pictures of babies dressed like peas in a pod. Sadly, for the last ten years, I'd done just as he suggested. And, no lie, there was a dark side to women and their unbendable determination to have their precious little ones captured just right.

"Go away, *Officer*," I said and stuck the key in the ignition.

I bet Leo Stillman would never marry a polygamist.

Perfect people didn't do stupid things. He stood well over six feet with the wide shoulders of a warrior. His dark skin and steely gray eyes were enhanced by his broad features and the high cheekbones passed down through his Native American roots. He was the walking epitome of the word *strong*.

"Wanna tell *me* what's wrong? You need to talk to someone." He spoke to me like I imagined he would a person on a ledge, contemplating jumping. Like I'd lost my marbles. Asking a jumper to share their woes wasn't a good place to start. It was where you want to go eventually, sure. Even I'd learned that in Criminology 101. What more was there to make a person carry out their plan than to rehash their failures?

I turned the key over one click so the SUV had power then raised the window up, closing it in his face.

Leo ducked his head and sighed so loudly it briefly fogged the window. Then he straightened and walked around to the passenger side, Lockett with him.

"You can't sit here, Samantha. You need to move on." Leo again with his commands.

Apparently, this was his be-stern-with-the crazy-person voice. I raised the passenger window while simultaneously lowering the driver's. I might be in shock, but I wasn't ready to roast in my car.

Leo slapped his leg in frustration and strode around to the driver's side. I reversed the position of the windows.

Eventually, he would get the hint and, hopefully, it would make him go away. How did he like having someone always turn their back to him like he'd done to me? I wanted to point this out, but that would require me to look at him.

We did this song and dance three more times before he lost his cool.

"Dammit, Samantha," Leo said. His words were muffled by the closed driver's window. He banged his hand against the roof of my car and stepped up onto the sidewalk where Lockett waited. I left the windows up and cracked my sunroof. I picked up bits of their muted conversation but couldn't decipher it. I needed to figure out what to do next. Exhausted from the power play with the windows, I let my head fall back against the headrest and my eyes shutter closed, fatigue pulling me into a dark abyss.

The earsplitting trill of a coach's whistle ripped through the air.

I jumped and banged my head on my car's ceiling. My heart raced like a pony out of the gate.

Standing outside my car, purple coach's whistle between her lips ready for another blow, was the large-breasted, big-haired, Amazon of a woman known as Precious. Her real name was Erika Shurmann, and she also happened to be my best friend since second grade. We'd discovered being sent from class for extra help—me because I'm dyslexic and her because of a stutter—that we were stronger as a tribe. We brought Hue Stillman, who also had dyslexia, into the fold. And we'd stuck together for our entire school career and after. Until Hue joined the Marines and shipped off to foreign lands.

The nickname Precious came when another kid asked her what was so special about her that she didn't have to read in front of the class, and she'd responded with, "Because I'm P-p-precious." Yeah, the moniker stuck, likely because it was used a lot to tease her, but over the years that had shifted. She embodied the nickname. The girl treated everyone like they had a gift to give to the world and, in return, she was treated the same.

As a best friend, she was loyal and had the biggest heart. As a professional life coach, her no-nonsense, frank-speaking ways and honesty came in handy. It also didn't hurt that she always looked as if she stepped out of a fashion magazine. Today, she was immaculately dressed in a figure-fitting plum dress with matching nails and lip gloss.

She had one impractical weakness. A deep love for all things Bigfoot. She spent her off-time on the Washington Bigfoot Research Team.

I clicked the key and lowered my window.

"Holy cripes, Precious, I think I wet my pants," I said and squirmed in my seat as a way to check.

"Samantha Jane True, just what in the h-e-double-hockey-sticks are you doing sitting here in this car? According to this tall drink of water over here"— she gestured to Lockett— "you've been here two hours. I get a call from Officer Hot Pants who says he thinks you're high or drunk or something."

I glared at Leo through the windshield.

"I told him he was being ridiculous. But you don't really look so good. You're pasty, almost sickly." She reached into the car and put her hand on my forehead. "Clammy, too."

"This must be the legendary Precious," Locket said to Leo. "Her reputation precedes her."

"Precious," I said. Tears burst forth and ran streaks down my face. Grief? Humiliation? Both?

"Jumping flying crickets, what's happened?" She bent forward and studied me, the purple coaches whistle swinging on the lanyard around her neck.

"Carson," I said hoarsely. Too humiliated to say the words, I picked up the manila envelopes Lockett gave me and waved them in her face. "Lawyer," I forced the word out and pointed to Lockett.

Precious's eyes narrowed. "Are you telling me that slick son of a gun you married has filed for divorce? I will skin him alive. I will flay him to the bone."

"That's the same thing," Lockett said.

"Hush," Precious said and pointed a long finger at him. She returned her attention to me. "I'm sorry, Sam. I always knew he was too good to be true. Men like him are in romance novels, not real life."

Leo crossed his arms and cleared his throat.

"Oh, please," Precious said. "In high school, the only constant in your life was your jock."

"No," I said shaking my head. "Not divorce. Dead." On the last word, I let the tears flow freely. I covered my face with my hands.

"Aw, jeez," Leo mumbled.

The door jerked open. Precious pulled my hands from my face. "Are you kidding me?"

I shook my head and sucked in a ragged breath. "That's not all. Turns out Carson isn't his name. He has a whole other life and a whole other wife. I married a polygamist."

Lockett stepped forward. "Who has some powerful enemies. The sooner you can get her out of here and away from me, the safer she'll be," Lockett said, making shooing motions with his hands.

"Care to explain that?" Precious asked.

"I can't." Lockett gave a sheepish shrug.

"Can't or won't?" she asked.

He shrugged again.

She faced Leo. "Why are you here?"

He jerked a thumb toward Lockett. "He called Wind River PD and asked for assistance, requested someone who knew Samantha. DB sent me."

DB Louney was our police chief, another jerk I'd gone to school with. Only he'd been a dweeb who puberty had been kind to. He'd gone from skinny dork to buffed-out meathead over the course of one summer. Personally, I thought his change was a regression.

I groaned and pointed to Leo. "You can't tell Dweebie what's happened. He'll blab everywhere, and I haven't told my parents."

Leo gave a brief nod. He didn't have a reputation for being a gossip, and I was counting on that.

Precious mumbled something about people being useless. She pushed me over into the passenger seat. "I'll text Bob to come to pick up my car," she said and quickly tapped something into her phone. Bob was Precious's neighbor and a lovestruck Lothario who'd do anything for her. This was the life of Precious. No man would play her for a fool.

"Let's get out of here," she said. "Clearly no one here is going to help you except me. We'll stop and get several gallons of ice cream and some wine. We'll sort this out." She grabbed my hand and squeezed, her eyes moist with unshed tears. "Hold on to your titties, kitty, we're in for a long ride."

I wish I knew then how huge of an understatement her words were.

4

SATURDAY

The next morning, I woke from a restless sleep to find my life was still a dumpster fire. Yesterday hadn't been a bad dream. And to make matters worse, I hadn't gone to see my parents. Hopefully, they were still in the dark about Carson's death.

I needed to fix that, and soon. The secret I wanted to keep was Carson's polygamy. I was okay if no one else ever discovered that little tidbit, but wasn't sure how I could contain it.

My mother, a non-practicing lawyer, was currently the town mayor, and following this term, was eye-balling a position on the school board. My father owned and ran the local paper. The Trues were go-getters. They always did the right thing, overachieved when they tried something new, and were pillars of the community. This description included Rachel but not so much me.

Overachieving was hard when written language was

essentially hieroglyphics. Too much time and energy were spent deciphering, which left no time for overachieving. Instead, I spent my time exploring life. I got busted cow-tipping, got suspended from school for skipping (Precious and I went to follow up on a Bigfoot sighting), didn't finish my master's degree, and now I could add *married a polygamist* to the list. #Winning.

I rolled off the couch where I'd crashed the night before and shuffled to the kitchen.

Bright morning sun streamed through the patio sliding door. It was going to be another beautiful day in the Pacific Northwest. I loved when the natural light filled the townhouse. After our impromptu wedding, Carson and I agreed to start our lives in a new place, both of us giving up our small apartments. This townhouse had been an easy compromise.

The layout was simple. The front of the house opened into a foyer and staircase along the left wall. The foyer fed into the living room kitchen combo. The kitchen ran the length of the far right wall and ended in a small dining room. The space flowed right out onto a large deck that overlooked a wildlife refuge. Island seating for four broke up the space between the living room and kitchen.

I slid onto a barstool and rested my forehead in my hands, looking up through my brow at Precious. She stood in my kitchen, scrambling eggs for a breakfast burrito. Even though she wore the same clothes as yesterday, she appeared fresh as a daisy. I wore yoga pants and an oversized T-shirt and could be mistaken for being homeless. My hair was a mess of errant strands and greasy matted-down spots. There was even a patch of dried, clumpy hair from when, in a bout of tears, I'd dropped my head inadvertently into a bowl of ice cream.

She slid a burrito in front of me. "Eat something. It will help."

"I'm not hungry," I said and ignored the burrito.

"That's grief." She took the seat next to me. "How you feeling today?"

"Numb," I said. "Angry. Sad. Confused." Late last night, I'd gathered from around the house many pictures of Carson and me and burned them in the firepit on my back patio. For an odd second during that exorcism, I felt as if everything was going to be okay, that I'd make it through this one way or another.

Precious shifted on the seat beside me and sighed.

"What?" I asked. Something was on her mind. Being friends for more than two decades taught me this.

She pressed her lips together.

"Just spit it out," I said.

She turned and placed her hand on my shoulder. "You know I don't do inactivity well and I know you need to grieve. You're hurting and confused. I'm going to walk every step of that journey with you. But I can't let you sit here all day wallowing."

"I deserve to wallow. I'm humiliated and... I'd say heartbroken, but I'm too damn angry to be heartbroken. What else can I do?" I said, worrying my hands.

Precious kicked out her long legs. "Yeah, I've been thinking about that. If we're going to hide the truth about

Carson, we need to go about the business the same way a grieving widow would."

I snorted with derision.

She continued, "So, um...given the situation, I'm guessing there won't be a funeral?"

My hands stilled. I hadn't even thought of that. "How do I have a funeral with no...?" I gestured to my body. "One of these."

Precious grimaced. "That's tricky. We have a few options. We could—"

A loud pounding came on the front door. Looking through the peephole showed an agitated Mr. Linn, my landlord. He kept glancing over his shoulder.

Linn, a retired railroad worker, was shaped like an old whiskey barrel, squat and round with short, stubby legs. He didn't believe in money sitting idle in a bank and had sunk his retirement in a row of townhouses.

I made a halfhearted attempt to pat down my hair before opening the door.

"Girly, we've got a problem," he said before I could say anything and pushed through the front door, slamming it behind him.

He held up several sheets of rolled paper. He thrust them at me. "Sign these."

"What's going on?" I asked, taking the papers.

"Some man left a message yesterday, said he represented your husband and that Mr. Holmes was deceased," Linn said, looking at me for confirmation.

I nodded.

Linn ducked his head. "I'm sorry, girly. Kinda figured it

was true when Precious here practically carried you inside yesterday."

"What did the message say? Anything else?" I asked. "Did he say who he was?"

"Richie or something. He said that Mr. Holmes was dead and he was the executor of Mr. Holmes estate. He wanted to know if the lease was in Mr. Holmes's name or yours. Said if the lease were in Mr. Holmes's name, then the estate would like to terminate the lease, pay any accompanying fees, and evict the tenant. I'm to call him back, let him know, and he'll send a company down to pack up and remove the furniture."

I gasped. *How dare they?*

"Are you kidding me?" Precious said, jumping to her feet. "The nerve of these people."

Precisely. This was my home. Who did they think they were? Then I remembered. The estate of Carson Holmes, or whatever his real name was, belonged to his wife. His legal wife who found out about my existence only a few days ago. She probably felt as humiliated and duped as I did. Only difference? I wasn't taking my feelings out on her. Not that I knew who she was, but if I did, I still wouldn't.

"What's going on here? Who are these people?" Mr. Linn asked.

"Oh, ah, they're—" I glanced at Precious. We'd agreed last night to omit some facts about my current situation. Clearly, we hadn't figured out the small details. But one fact that couldn't be leaked was the legal wife.

Ultimately, the less we said the better.

A lie tumbled from my lips. "It would seem Carson owed some people a lot of money."

"But why aren't you the executor of his estate?" Linn asked.

Yikes! A question I hadn't even thought to prepare a lie for. I shrugged and went for something close to the truth. "We hadn't gotten that far, Mr. Linn. We weren't expecting to die soon and..."

Precious interjected. "And Carson never changed it from his old business partner, so here we are."

Dang! Precious was quick. I caught her eye and gave her a mental high five. She winked.

"They're moving rather fast, wouldn't you say?" Mr. Linn looked skeptical. And rightly so.

Precious said, "Yeah, well, apparently the people he owed had already been in the process of collecting. His unexpected death leaves Sam to deal with them. She just found all this out yesterday."

Mr. Linn reached out and patted my shoulder. He accompanied the action with the look of pity I'd been dreading. But better he thought Carson bad with his money than greedy with collecting women.

Time for a diversion. I planted my hands on my hips and leaned toward Linn. "You can't evict me. This is my place. I've been a good tenant. We've paid the rent in full for the entire year." That had been Carson's idea. "And they can't have my furniture. This is *my stuff*. This is *my house!*"

Mr. Linn tapped the papers I'd placed on the island. I stared down at the lease agreement.

"That is why I'm bringing these over. I've no intention of kicking you out. This is a lease agreement with you and only you listed. Far as I know, this agreement has been the only one I've ever had." He took a pen and another folded paper from his back pocket and shook the paper out to open it. He held it up for me. It was the original lease agreement. "Make sure you use the same date that's on here."

I took the pen and the new agreement and signed under the line where Mr. Linn had already signed. "Thank you," I said, my anger banked by his act of kindness.

Linn shrugged. "Can't sit across the poker table and explain to your dad why I evicted you. He'd probably write an article in that damn paper of his and call me a slumlord." Mr. Linn smiled to show he was joking. "Besides, I liked Carson. He was a good guy. I don't know what's going on, and I'm awfully sorry for your loss." He gave my shoulder a squeeze, an attempt at condolences, before scooping the agreement off the table and rolling it into a tube.

I walked him to the door. "I can't thank you enough." Word would soon spread about Carson. It's not that Mr. Linn was a gossip, but he did like to hang out with the other retirees at the local hardware store in our small downtown. "Mr. Linn," I said, "I hate to ask, but would you mind keeping this information to yourself for a bit? I haven't had a chance to tell my family yet. I haven't really processed it myself."

Mr. Linn pressed his lips together in contemplation.

"You better make quick work of it. I'm guessing anyone Carson did business with is getting a phone call."

I nodded. He was right.

"Besides, you still have another issue," he said.

I glanced at Precious, confused. She shrugged.

I asked Mr. Linn, "What's that?"

He gestured to the door. "Looks like your car is being towed. Repo maybe?"

I gasped and ran to the door. Sure enough, a tow truck had hitched up the Jeep, a gift from Carson. The driver was walking to the cab.

"Hey," I yelled, bursting from my house. "That's my car. What do you think you're doing?"

His hands were up as if to say it wasn't his fault. "Just doing my job, lady. I was told to collect this here car because the title was in the name of"–– he glanced at his clip board–– "Carson Holmes."

I deflated. Carson's family was merciless. Precious ran up beside me.

"Give this to the person who hired you," she said and showed the driver her middle finger.

The driver gave a half smile. "I'll pass it along."

I went back to the house, receiving a pat from Mr. Linn as I passed. Inside, I fell onto the couch.

"What am I going to do?" I asked Precious.

She pushed a notepad and pen toward me. "You're gonna need a list. So far, you're a few steps, if not more, behind these people. They've taken your money, your car, and wanted to kick you out of your house. What could be next?"

I narrowed my eyes, glaring at the paper and wrote. *Have a tête-à-tête with T. Lockett.* What kind of game was this lawyer playing? Who were the players and what was their endgame? I'd already lost so much.

"If we're going to the lawyer, maybe you should get cleaned up," she suggested.

Motivated by my anger, I moved to the hall closet where I kept my shoes and shoved my feet into slip-ons.

"No time. Let's go," I told her while reaching for my bag.

From inside my bag, my phone rang. I glanced at Precious as I took it out, afraid of what else was about to happen. Because it was an unknown local number, I answered with trepidation.

"Uh, yeah, so this is Toby Wagenknecht. I work at Holmes Security, and this number was listed as an emergency contact." Toby spoke with a slow, easygoing pace, as if he were in no hurry to get out any words. It took a second for my brain to make the connection, but I was able to place the voice. Toby had graduated high school the year before me and was the town stoner.

"Hey, Toby, this is Samantha True. What's this about Holmes Security?" I shrugged to Precious who was giving me the what's-up look. I made like I was smoking a joint. She nodded her understanding.

"Oh, hey, Sam. I called the emergency contact number and got you. Guess you're my emergency contact." He chuckled and then sucked in a breath.

He was drawing on his vape. He liked to wear his vape pen around his neck, hanging from a lanyard. He might put weed in his pen, but anytime I'd run into him, he'd only been toking on vape juice.

"Emergency contact for what? I'm confused."

Toby snort-laughed. "That's a good one. Usually, I feel like the confused one. Carson listed this number in the company handbook. Guess that makes sense in case I can't get ahold of him. Which I can't. You know where he is? We got a sitch here at the office."

I vaguely recalled Carson saying he hired Toby to do some tech stuff for him. Up until then, Toby's only job had been that of an on-demand private driver. "A sitch?"

"Situation. Someone broke into the office, trashed the place. I tried calling Carson but couldn't get ahold of him. So, I called the emergency number. You. What should I do? Call the police?"

I circled my index finger in the air, signally to Precious it was time to roll.

"Do nothing, Toby. I'm on my way." I ended the call. "There's been a break-in at Carson's company," I told Precious as I snatched my bag from the couch. I flung open the door, ready to dash out, but froze in place. Dash out to what?

"We don't have a car," she said. "Bob collected mine and took it to my house. I guess I could call him."

I closed my eyes in disbelief, and then the solution dawned on me.

I swallowed a chuckle. Deadpanned, I said, "You're going to hate this." I shifted my attention to my one-car garage.

She followed my gaze, and when realization dawned,

she shook her head, groaned, then said, "At least I'm not going to a meeting or somewhere important."

I feigned indignation. "I think a break-in might be important." But I knew what she meant. My ride embarrassed her. "You can stay here."

She rolled her eyes. "As if."

"Run in and grab the folder about the business," I said as I ran to the garage. I flung open the door to expose LC, a 1991 Hunter Green Jeep Grand Wagoneer, faux panel siding and all. The first car I ever bought. LC, short for the explorers Lewis and Clark. He was as moody as Meriwether Lewis and as unrestrained as William Clark. Together, we'd had many adventures. Carson had replaced LC, claiming safety concerns. But when I fired him up, the rumble of LC's engine ran right through me, and I was reminded of two things. First, how something magical happened to me when I sat behind his steering wheel, like the world had no boundaries. And second, LC would need a quart of oil soon.

When I backed out, Precious stood on the sidewalk, scowling. Secretly, I believed she was jealous of LC because I loved him so much, but she claimed the AC never worked properly. Precious didn't do sweat stains.

She climbed into the Jeep and mumbled, "It's like we're back in high school all over again."

"You had a great time in high school," I reminded her. Not so much for me. "Tooling around in LC was a highlight for me. He made me popular. I had the coolest ride of all. Hue's Mazda used to always get stuck in the fields when we'd go out partying. Not LC." Bonfires and beers on deserted farmland had been the primary activity of my graduation class.

"Your popularity, or lack thereof, had nothing to do with this hunk of junk." Precious huffed.

"Says the head cheerleader." I groaned. Bringing up her cheerleading days inevitably brought up my baton-twirling days. I'd been a majorette. At least for half a year. The school cut me and the one other baton twirler from the band, stating funding issues. But we all knew it was because we sucked. When you knock out the band leader with a baton—twice—it doesn't take a genius to do the math.

Precious laughed. "I ran into Chris Watt the other day." Chris had been the band leader. "He said he has PTSD from getting hit by those batons. Every time he hears the school fight song, he wets himself. Can't go to any of the games."

"I'm sorry I brought it up," I said.

"Oh, I'm not." She laughed some more.

5

SATURDAY

Carson's business was on the other side of Wind River. Wind River was bisected by Interstate 5. To the west was the old town with the city center, the river aptly named Windy River, and where my townhouse was located. To the east was the newer side that comprised a strip mall with a bank, Thai restaurant, a veterinarian, Junkie's Bar and junkyard, a gas station, and several new housing developments in their early phases of build. Scattered between were a handful of older, restored houses turned business. One was Carson's.

I peeled out, curious as to what I would find.

LC's fan was on the fritz again, shooting the occasional blast of cold air interspersed with dirt.

Precious slumped low in the seat. "I hate you, LC," she screamed and covered her face with the manila envelope Lockett gave me yesterday.

I flipped off the fan and lowered the windows. "Make

yourself useful and look through those papers," I said, whipping through a roundabout, the Jeep listing in a way Precious hated.

I, on the other hand, was in my zone. I loved fresh air, and the slight nip to the wind was rejuvenating me. The day was beautiful, and the distraction a wonderful reprieve.

I'd spent twenty-four years of my life in Wind River, having moved here when I was six from California after my father, a sports reporter for a big LA paper, broke the story on owners making players use performance-enhancing drugs in the professional football league. He paid the consequences of narking on such a powerful industry, spending three years battling lawsuits, and he even spent time in jail, protecting his sources. Once the madness from the scandal died down, Mom and Dad happily waved goodbye to big-city life and their fast-paced careers to move two states north.

They settled in Wind River, a town of less than ten thousand with no stoplights, only roundabouts and speed bumps. Dad bought the local paper, added news coverage for the two closest towns, and increased circulation. Mom had worked as a local lawyer until a few years ago when she ran for Wind River mayor and won.

Wind River's downtown consisted of an eight-block square, two blocks to each side. The farthest west side faced the Windy River and its marina. We had a farmer's market, and kids painted rocks with words of inspiration and left them all around town. We weren't a town where con men came to play.

But I wasn't so naïve to believe that everyone in Wind River was upstanding. My one-time experience as a forensic photographer intern had taught me that cold, harsh truth. Discovering people I'd known most my life and trusted were scamming auto insurance companies and robbing local businesses had been a pivotal moment in my life. The experience left me with a big decision. Have a life where I saw the darkness or one where I saw the light. I'd picked the light. *Jokes on me, I guess.* Darkness followed me anyway and asked me to marry him.

"What do the papers say?" I asked Precious as I sped through the last of the roundabouts that would lead over I-5 to the other side of Wind River.

"Looks to me like Carson has had the business license and lease for almost two years. It was put in your name right after you married."

Two years? That sounded about right. When we'd met, Carson had told me he'd grown tired of city life and had moved to Wind River, specifically for the small-town appeal. He'd even gone so far as to say meeting me had been the icing on the cake.

Yeah, probably because he'd discovered a patsy in me. I clenched the steering wheel, wanting to rip it from the steering column and beat it on the ground. He'd played me from the beginning.

Precious held out the paper and pointed to my signature on the document. I couldn't recall ever signing such a paper. Blind faith. Look where it got me.

"The license is for a private investigation firm with under ten employees. That's the standard number for a small company and how Washington designates company size." Precious thumbed through more paper as I overtook an eighteen-wheeler headed in the same direction, the pages whipping in the wind. She shot me a frustrated look. "There's a bill of sale to you for the business for one dollar."

I whipped through the last roundabout, taking the second exit toward the strip mall and row of small repurposed houses. The strip mall was to our right, the houses to our left. Carson's was the third house of five. It dawned on me then that I'd never been inside. The times I'd come to Carson's office, he'd met me in the driveway. I hadn't given it a second thought then.

Toby was sitting on the ground, leaning against a car shaped like a cap eraser, a Honda Fit, his vape pen in his mouth.

He tipped his head when I got out of the car but didn't stand. "Were you able to get in touch with Carson?" he asked and blew a light cloud of smoke. It smelled like cherry cola.

The front door of the office had a window, which was smashed in, leaving in its place a gaping opening. I peered through the hole. Scattered on the old wood floor were chunks of glass held together by the vinyl lettering I assumed was once the business's information.

The door was closed and locked. I reached over the broken glass, careful not to nick myself, and unlocked the door. A second later, the lock reengaged.

"The keypad is going to keep locking it," Toby said and

pointed to a keypad on the wall. "That's how Carson set it up. It's a failsafe in case the keypad breaks."

The keypad had also been smashed.

Toby continued, "The backup system will keep the lock engaged until I code in the password." He waved his phone.

I gestured for him to do so. The lock disengaged.

"You'll have fifteen seconds to open the door. That's not the password to keep it unlocked. I have to do that at the main system. Not here," Toby said while pointing to the smashed keypad. "I have to override that."

As if I had any clue what he was talking about regarding the main system. I just needed the lock to *not* reengage. I took a rubber band out of the front pocket of my bag and wrapped from one doorknob to the other, crossing over the latch bolt to keep the lock tucked, hoping it would be enough of a hack to trick the system.

I pushed it open with my foot and gingerly stepped inside, careful not to walk on glass and to minimize messing up the crime scene. TV had taught me that much.

"Don't touch anything," I told the others.

"Duh," Precious said.

We stepped into the lobby. It contained a row of four folding metal chairs and was lit by a large plate-glass window that looked onto the street. *Holmes Security* was written on the large front window in the same royal blue vinyl letters that were on the floor. I stepped farther inside to scope out the place.

Beyond the lobby were three rooms to the left. One was

an office and the other a supply room. The office was as meagerly furnished with a desk and two chairs in front. No filing cabinets. The supply room was just as sparse with two filing cabinets and a card table, under the table was an unopened box of fifty-four-count variety pack of chips.

The rooms were separated by a restroom. In each room, the folding chairs were upended, as if whoever broke in had knocked them down on their way out. Likely in frustration or anger. Toby had said the place was trashed, but I'd say it was messy. Other than the window, it would be an easy cleanup. The filing cabinet drawers were open, but no files had been tossed because there were none. The drawers held reams of paper, boxes of pens, and Post-it notes.

Toby stood in the doorway. "The house is divided into two offices. We share the building with a dance and yoga studio."

"Did they clean you all out?" Precious asked.

The place had the vibe that business wasn't done here, but I could be wrong and the thief had taken more than I assumed.

Toby shook his head. "That's the thing. I can't see that anything was taken. That's why I didn't immediately call the cops." He stuck his hands in his pockets.

He reminded me of Shaggy from the old Scooby Doo cartoon. He wore his hair long with bangs side-swept over his face that had a few scars from acne. He was tall, but his shoulders stooped inward as if standing straight required too much work. He wore camouflage cargo shorts and a T-shirt with a giant cannabis leaf.

Precious chuckled. "I'll admit when you told me about this place, Sam, I pictured a sleek office like Remington Steel or maybe lots of mahogany and lamps with yellow light." She grabbed my arm and squealed in excitement, "This place needs a complete makeover." The girl loved to redecorate.

"Can we get through this first please?" I gestured to Toby and the broken glass.

Precious scoffed. "Please, whoever did this took one look at this place and moved on. Probably cursing their rotten luck for picking such a dud."

She'd nailed it. The office and the break-in were both enigmas. Who would buy a security system while sitting in this outdated environment? Now I understood why Carson had met clients at their home. What didn't make sense was why bother having this office at all? And what was someone hoping to score by breaking in? I surveyed the room. The thief was obviously looking for something and hadn't found it. My gut told me this break-in wasn't random.

Hopefully Toby could help make sense of everything. "Explain to me everything you do for Carson." I waved my hand around in the air as if it would help me understand what exactly the business did.

"Being the tech guy, I research the clients and stuff." Toby made like he was typing on a keyboard. When Carson said he'd hired Toby, I'd assumed it was to manage things like his website and stuff. I honestly hadn't given it a second thought.

"Where's the...?" I made like I was typing as well.

There weren't any computers in the office. "Were they stolen? Do you work normal office hours?" I had no idea how this business ran.

Toby lifted his vape pen to his lips. "I bring my own tech and come in when Carson texts me and tells me to. He did that a couple days ago. Otherwise, I work remotely." He took a puff. "Today I got an alert on my phone that the building alarm had been activated so I came over to check it out."

I scanned the waiting room for a second keypad or something to give me more information. "Where's the alarm?" I asked.

Toby pointed to some wires that ran along the inside of the door. "Here. They're on the window, too. You manage it by using an app on your phone."

I nodded, though I was clueless. I felt as if I'd fallen through a slit in the time-space continuum. I recognized the people, the scenery, and understood the language, but I had no clue what was going on. "You said Carson texted you?"

"Yeah, few days ago. He had a new client and wanted me to do the preliminaries on them."

"Preliminaries?" So much to learn.

"Background check basically."

Precious came to stand by me. "You'll need a police report if you want to make any claims for insurance."

I set aside my questions and slid the phone from my bag. I called the non-emergency police line, reported the break-in, and was told to wait for a responding officer and not to disturb the scene further.

We went outside and waited at the side of the office.

I tried to get a handle on the situation. "Let me get this straight, Toby. You and Carson are the only employees?"

Toby slouched against the outside wall. "Yep."

"Who sits here and waits for customers?"

Toby rolled his eyes. "They aren't customers; they're clients. Carson says that all the time. We work for the client. They are the job. The job isn't helping a customer and moving on. It's helping a client so they can move on."

I blew out my frustration with a sigh. "Okay, so who waits in the office for clients?"

"No one. Carson has his number on the window." He gestured to the broken pane. "Oh, guess you can't see it. They call the number, and he meets them here or somewhere else."

And here I'd thought my husband hung around his office all day unless he was out doing quotes. I was a dumb-dumb. That much was clear.

"The background checks? Was that part of the security business?" Precious asked and leaned against the building next to him.

Toby nodded. "Both, but yeah mostly the PI part. You'd be amazed at how many of the cases Carson got were solved simply by doing some deep web searching." He drew from his vape pen.

"Carson rarely talked about the PI part of his job," I lied.

Toby nodded, not surprised by my statement. "Because we keep that on the down-low. People who buy security systems want others to know they're safe. People who hire a PI don't want others to know they're vulnerable. Carson had a real knack for finding people who needed his service."

I asked, "Did you do a lot of PI business?"

"Couple people a week. Missing people, pets, money shots for divorce, but the money is in Carson's home assessments and setting up security systems. He does those a lot." Toby offered Precious his vape pen, but she declined.

I caught Precious's eye over Toby's head. She arched a brow and looked at Toby. An easy guess as to what she was trying to tell me. Toby needed to know about Carson. I moved to stand next to him and Precious did the same on Toby's other side.

"There's something I need to tell you." I stared ahead at the house next door, focusing on a large spot where the paint was peeling. My throat spasmed as I tried to say the words.

"Carson's dead," Precious said and patted Toby's shoulder. "But we need to sit on this information. Sam only found out yesterday, and she has to tell her family."

Toby slid down the wall then fell on his butt. "Man, are you serious?" His attention volleyed between me and Precious.

"As a heart attack," Precious said.

Toby's jaw dropped. "He had a heart attack? He was so young."

"No," I shook my head. "He was in a car accident."

"A heart attack while driving. That's awful," Toby said sadly.

"No heart attack," I said. "Just a ginormous tree falling on his car when he crashed into it." Said the Washington Department of Transportation article I'd read online last night. It hadn't mentioned Carson by name, but the description of the car on fire had been awful. I shuttered. To think about someone you knew had died a horrible death was awful enough, but when it was the person you'd married and loved. Well...

"You work for Sam now Toby," Precious said. "No one else. If someone else comes around and says otherwise, you call Sam right away."

Man, was I glad Precious was thinking ahead. If the person who inherited Carson's estate was trying to get me evicted, why not try and take this office, too? Our conversation ceased when a large white SUV pulled into the drive.

"Popo is here." Toby stood and made like he was going to split.

I grabbed his arm. "You need to stick around. The police will need a statement from you."

Toby glanced at his watch. "Well, technically, I have the time. I start my job as an on-demand private driver in an hour." He pointed to his Honda Fit. Two stickers bearing the names of two on-demand car companies were in the window. "And look, I had these made up recently." He dug in his back pocket, pulled out a business card, and handed it to me.

One side was his contact for the on-demand driver job and the other was for his IT services for Holmes Securities. I stuck it in my bra since I had no pockets.

"Folks," Leo Stillman said as he strolled toward us. He surveyed me, his attention lingering on my hair before sweeping down my body. He raised his brows. "You call this in? Were you here when the break-in happened? He rough you up?"

"No," I said bitingly. "I wasn't here. Toby is the one that discovered the break-in. I'm here because I'm the owner." I'd said it with a bravado I didn't have and planted my hands on my hips for good measure.

Leo glanced at his watch. He wore one of those manly dive jobbies with a thick black band and large face that could be seen in any weather condition. "I'll make this quick, Toby, so you can get to your other job. Why don't you tell me what happened? Start at the beginning."

Toby recounted the events that brought me here.

"Let's walk through, and you can tell me if anything is missing," Leo said.

I fell into step behind them. Leo gave me a questioning look.

I put my hand up in protest, not giving him a chance to speak. I wasn't about to wait outside. "This is my company. I'm going, too." I gestured for him to start moving.

"Just don't get sick or anything that might jack up the crime scene." His lips twitched in amusement.

I rolled my eyes. "Ha. Ha."

Toby took us through each room. Drawers had been jimmied opened, but apparently Carson kept nothing of significance in the drawers, only the standard office equipment like a stapler in one, paper clips in another. We circled back to the waiting room.

"Where do you keep the files? The ones on the clients? And maybe a schedule of what's to happen when?" I was a paper person, especially pretty paper. I liked planners of all shapes and sizes, and if a planner came decorated beyond the plain white with a flower or scrolled designs, then all the better.

"On the cloud," Toby said in a tone that implied *duh* should end the sentence.

"Do you back up the cloud?" This from Leo.

"Duh," Toby said.

Leo had the patience of a saint. "Where?"

I was wondering that myself. There was only a printer, nothing else. No cords except the power one that fed the printer.

Toby looked uncomfortable. His glance darted between me and Leo, his lips pressed together tightly as if he didn't want to spill the secret.

"Spill, Toby," Leo said. "Carson is dead, and we need answers."

A heavy sigh escaped Toby. "You aren't going to like this," he said and pointed to the ceiling. "It's up there."

Leo and I both craned our heads back and stared up at the ceiling.

"The cloud's in heaven?" I asked, thinking Toby was referring to Carson and the information had died with him, so I'd essentially inherited a building and some old furniture.

6

SATURDAY

Toby snorted. "Heaven. That's a good one."

Leo crossed his arms, narrowed his eyes at me, and shook his head in disappointment. I was familiar with his expression. It was the same look he'd always given me, the one that said he thought I was more annoying than a mosquito. "Heaven? Really?"

Toby still chuckling, said. "I was pointing to the attic. Carson made it a control room of sorts."

"Where's the access door?" I looked down the hallway, thinking I overlooked it.

"We share a small corridor with the dance studio next door. We have to go outside to get there." Toby led us out the front and around the corner to the back.

I paused before turning the corner. The hairs on the back of my neck were raised. Like they did when you knew someone was there but you couldn't see them. I suppressed the urge to look around. Instead, I stepped to where Precious was waiting by my car, messing with her phone.

I whispered, "Can you secretly video the street."

Her gaze met mine, her eyes narrowing. She had an amazing sense of adventure. She didn't need an explanation. "Consider it done."

I caught up with Leo and Toby as they approached the back door to the dance studio. The door was solid wood, the name of the studio affixed to the door using the same type of vinyl letters that Carson's office had used. Toby was digging in his pocket, for a key I assumed.

"Wait," I said and butted to the front. I knocked on the door.

"But I—" Toby started.

"I know," I said.

Leo searched my face, his gaze bouncing to my hot mess of a hairstyle before he looked away. He scanned the area behind me while tapping his small notebook against the palm of his hand. "You see something?" he whispered.

If he picked on me for my behavior at a crime scene nearly a decade ago, how was it going to go if I told him my gut said someone was out there? Learning to listen to my intuition was something Carson had harped on. When he read the paper, he constantly would point out stories of women who had been victimized. He'd even told me to take a self-defense class, something I'd been meaning to do but hadn't got around to it.

I said. "Other than the window being broken, nothing else is damaged. Nothing is missing. What if it's because they didn't get what they were looking for?"

"What if it was a junkie and they were looking for things to pawn?" Leo countered.

"Wouldn't you expect the junkie to take the snacks?"

"I would have," Toby inserted. "Snacks at any time of the day sound good."

Leo nodded once and knocked on the door a second time, using more force.

A young waifish woman with pale skin, straight shiny white teeth, and dreadlocks contained by a light pink Slap cap, answered the door. She sported yoga pants and a tank with no bra. She didn't have much of a chest but still....

"Is something amiss?" She smiled at all of us but brightened when she saw Toby.

Toby said, "Ruby, this is Samantha." He pointed to me. "She's Carson's wife."

Leo cleared his throat and shot me quick glance before returning his focus to Ruby. He introduced himself and said, "I have a few questions for you. The office next door was broken into. I'm wondering if you heard anything or if you might have been burglarized as well?"

"Can we come in?" Not waiting for a response, I stepped into the small foyer, essentially pushing her back.

Her smile fell, replaced by confusion on her face. "Toby has a key. You can come in whenever. This is a shared space." She moved to let the men in. "Did you say the place next door was broken into?"

"Yes, ma'am," Leo said.

"Oh, my Goddess, that's scary," Ruby said, wrapping her arms around her front.

Leo closed the door behind us then pulled Ruby aside to ask her further questions.

In the small corridor were two doors. One opened into the studio and the other was labeled *supply closet*. Toby used a key to open the door to the supply closet.

"What? No keypad?" My question was heavy with sarcasm.

"Too suspicious, Carson said," replied Toby.

Inside were a row of four metal shelves loaded with paper towels, toilet paper, printer paper, and the other typical overflow items. Toby waved me in and down the row. He pulled the shelf with paper towels away from the wall, and behind it was what looked to be an indentation. Upon closer inspection, it became clear the indentation was really a handle painted to match the wall color. It blended perfectly.

Toby pulled the handle and tugged the door open, exposing a set of stairs. Toby reached in and hit something on the wall. A light popped on and illuminated the way. A layer of fine dust danced through the air, disrupted by the door's opening. Another thin layer blanketed the stairs.

"It looks undisturbed," I said.

"It does," Leo said behind me.

I faced him. "Where's the dance lady?"

"Ruby," Leo and Toby said in unison.

Leo continued, "She's in her studio. She's spooked by the break-in. She wasn't here when it happened but she'll keep her eyes peeled for any strangers coming around." He gestured for me to go up the stairs.

The room at the top had a small windowless alcove, furnished with another card table and a folding chair. A light silver box the size of two large shoeboxes sat humming on the table. It looked like five hard drives stacked side by side. Red lights blinked at various intervals and a tiny blue backlit screen sat next to it.

"What's all this?" I pointed to the equipment. I'd never seen a setup like this.

Toby gestured to the small screen. "That's an LCD." He put his hand on the silver box. "For you laypeople, this is our cloud." He did air quotes around the word cloud.

My brain was on overload. I didn't even bother to ask to have that explained.

"I'm going to need a list of your clients," Leo said to Toby then turned to me. "What was Carson doing that required encryption at this level? No offense, but I wasn't aware this was some high-end security firm with deep-pocket, high-profile clients. Most people with a business at this level use a file hosting company. Carson didn't. He kept that in house to the tune of several thousand dollars." Leo pointed to several of the boxes.

I shrugged. This was way over my head. "He was in security. Maybe he thought he should practice what he preached."

Leo looked skeptical then turned his attention to Toby. "About that client list."

Toby hemmed and hawed. "There's a confidentiality thingy. I'm not sure I can do that. That's Sam's call."

I recalled what Toby had said, how Carson had been particular about protecting people's privacy. Part of me wanted to say Leo could have access to everything. I was washing my hands of it. But that didn't seem fair to the clients. They didn't know Carson was...less than upstanding.

The guys waited for me to answer. Toby looked worried, nervous, fidgeting with his vape pen, likely because he was afraid I wouldn't continue to do things the way Carson had established. Leo looked smug. Like he knew I'd give the list to him.

I blew out a heavy sigh. What I wanted and the right thing weren't meshing here.

"I'm going to need a list of clients, too," I said to Toby. Before he could protest, I faced Leo and said, "Let me go through the list and see if anything unusual pops up. Because, correct me if I'm wrong, don't you need a warrant to get my client list?" Carson had gone to great lengths to protect his client list. That much was clear. Those clients didn't deserve to have their dirty laundry aired because Carson died.

Leo's expression hardened. Then he surprised me by not insulting me. "I don't like this Samantha," Leo said, looking around. "Parts aren't adding up here, and you might be smack in the middle of it. I'm concerned for your safety. Hand over your phone. I'm going to put my number in your contacts." Leo's uneasiness warmed me, bringing my attention to how cold and numb I was. I rubbed my hands over my arms.

"Everything will be okay." I said with false optimism, but gave him my phone anyway. "Things will settle down soon enough."

Disoriented was my current state of awareness, like a blind person trying to navigate their way in an unfamiliar land with unknown dangers. Ignoring the state of my life and hoping it would go away wasn't going to happen. Whether I liked it or not, and I absolutely did not like it, this was my life right now. I hated Carson for thrusting me into this.

Leo's expression was skeptical. He surveyed the room, his gaze sweeping over the high-tech computer equipment. He took something from the shelf and handed it to me.

"This is a stun gun. Charge it and keep it on you at all times. I don't like that someone has to be close for you to use it, but with the way things are going..."

"I don't think I'll need this," I said.

He pointed to a shelf that held two palmed-size light gray cubes. "Those are jammers. They block Wi-Fi or phone signals. They're illegal. I thought your husband put in security systems? Made people feel safe?"

I gripped the stun gun. "Me, too. Turns out, right under my nose, he was running a completely different business than I believed." I left it unsaid that somewhere in a different city he had been also living a different life.

7

SATURDAY

Toby and I arranged to come by my house to check my firewall, online security, and show me how to access the cloud and the client list. This would all have to happen after his on-demand private driver job and the time he took off to get high responsibly. Apparently, the hours between 12:30 pm and 4:30 pm he went home to chill, smoke weed, binge eat, and binge watch TV.

"Like clockwork," Leo had mumbled.

After dropping Precious off, I drove to Lockett's office building. I stood in the apex of my open car door, debating if I wanted to go in or not. My gut told me he knew more than he was letting on. He acted as if he was simply the messenger from family number one, but something wasn't adding up. His warnings to stay away from anything related to Carson, to separate myself as much as possible, bugged me. It wasn't as if I could erase the memories of anyone who knew I married Carson and forget this ever happened. Lockett even warned me to stay as far away from himself, too. That didn't make sense. And when Precious arrived, he'd known her nickname. Try as I might, the pieces from yesterday didn't add up, and I wanted to know why.

I slammed the door and made my way into the office building. I avoided the elevator because I didn't want to be around anyone and wasn't fit for polite company, The elevator had mirrors on all sides of the car to prove it. I climbed the three flights of stairs, then paused at the top landing to catch my breath before I entered the hallway.

At the far end was Lockett's office. The floor was quiet, some of the offices empty, something I hadn't noticed yesterday. The lights were off at Lockett's. I glanced at my watch. It was the middle of the day. Had he and his secretary gone for a late lunch? Was he closed on Saturdays?

The door was slightly ajar so I pushed it open to find the office empty. Not only empty of people but *empty* empty. No computers. No pictures on the walls. No pen and pencil holders or staplers.

Had I hallucinated yesterday?

I moved to the secretary's desk and rubbed my hand over the top. No dust. Which didn't mean anything because the building might have a cleaning service come in routinely. But it could also mean that yesterday someone sat at this desk and impersonated a secretary. My spidey senses pinged, and my stomach clenched with unease.

I wasn't crazy, and the only time in my life I'd ever hallucinated was when Carson and I had hiked twenty miles on the Loowitz Trail on Mt. St. Helen's and I'd crawled into my sleeping bag ready to pass out. The bursts of flashing light I'd seen hadn't been a UFO but exhaustion. Yesterday was nothing like that night on the trail. Yesterday was real.

A bang like the sound of a drawer slamming shut came from Lockett's office.

"Hello?" I called and leaned sideways to peek into the dark space.

Nothing. But the hair on the back of my neck stood, and goosebumps shimmied their way across my arms. I wasn't alone.

I narrowed my eyes. It was probably Lockett. He knew it was me and was hiding. Coward.

Just in case, I tucked my ignition key between my index and middle finger with the metal part sticking out like a dagger. My plan was to jab and run if need be. I cursed myself for leaving the stun gun Leo had forced upon me in LC.

"I have some questions for you, Lockett," I said and stepped toward the door.

A large man rushed out from the room. He was dressed in all black and moved so fast he was a blur. He thrust out one arm and flung me out of his way. I lost my footing and wind-milled my arms in a weak attempt to regain my balance. The keys dropped from my hand. I fell backward into the floor, slamming my left wrist on the secretary's desk as I went back. Sharp pains shot up my arm. My bag caught on the door handle and ripped the strap as I went down, separating it from the bag. I caught sight of blurry man's backside as he fled the office. Dark hair, cut close military style. Over six foot. Not Lockett.

After picking myself up off the floor, I peeked into Lockett's office. The man who'd run me down had been going through desk drawers and the filing cabinet. But they were empty. This wasn't Lockett's office, never had been. It had been a stage. Did that mean Carson wasn't dead? Was he in on this? I left Lockett's office in a rush, more confused than ever. Nothing in the last twenty-four hours was adding up or making any sort of sense.

I sat in my idling Jeep, my torn bag in my lap, and scanned the parking lot. All day I'd had this sense of being watched, but every time I looked around, nothing seemed out of the ordinary. Nothing had shown up on the video Precious took while we were at the office either.

I wondered about the man in Lockett's pretend office. Had Lockett played him, too? If so, I hoped my unexpected arrival told him he wasn't alone.

One thing for sure, I wasn't getting anywhere by sitting in this parking lot. I needed to tell my parents before word spread. Denial was a beautiful thing, but eventually people would start talking about Carson's absence. If Carson was alive and these events were some terrible and cruel game, then he could suffer the consequences should he reappear.

Exasperated, I shook my head. Believing all this took more than I was capable of because to do so meant I had to face some ugly truths.

. . .

My father's newspaper office sat on the square in down-town Wind River. Many of the town's citizens were baby boomers who preferred to get their news the old school way so readership wasn't an issue. The paper itself was divided into three parts: straight up unbiased news including sports (sports was totally biased), a lifestyle section that was equal parts events and town gossip, and the classifieds. The Wind River Gazette was housed in a two-story building on the south side of the main square. The paper itself took up the first floor. The second floor, with its separate entrance from outside, was a small studio apartment where I'd resided until Carson and I'd taken the townhouse.

My folks listed the apartment on Airbnb and enjoyed renting to out-of-towners, saying they were doing their part to bring in tourism dollars. But Wind River didn't have a large grocery or fancy restaurant, only a bar and grille and a small market, so people often took their tourism dollars into Vancouver.

An on-street parking spot a block from the paper was open, forcing me to parallel park. Using the corner of an old hoodie I'd forgotten was in LC and a half-drunk years-old water bottle that had been rolling around on the floor, I cleaned off my face and attempted to smooth down my hair. Looking slightly less disheveled but still with dark bags under my eyes that would require a pound of makeup to cover, I made my way to the newspaper.

Inside, Stella MacInerney manned the front desk and performed a bajillion other jobs at the paper. The Wind River Gazette was essentially a three-man show, newspaper delivery guys aside. Dad was the reporter for all sections, paying freelancers by the word for human interest and other articles. Dan Dix ran the IT department which included the website and the layout for the paper. The actual printing was outsourced to a larger newspaper printer in Vancouver. Stella ran everything else.

She was an average-sized, middle-aged woman with long curly brown hair and pale skin. Today she stood staring out the window.

"Hey, hun, how are you this morning?" She scanned me up and down before her attention returned to something outside the large plate glass window.

I shrugged. "I've been better."

"Take Echinacea," she said distractedly. "Or dot Thieves on your pulse points."

If it wasn't an herb, it was an essential oil that Stella believed to be the cure for any ailment.

I stepped up next to her. "Stella, is something going on?" I moved to the window but she grabbed my arm and pulled me away toward her crescent-shaped desk.

"Don't look," she said. "I've been watching a guy out there for the last thirty minutes."

"Is he hot?"

Stella liked her men. She'd put three in the grave because she liked them older. Said they were more mature. Stella was an outdoor enthusiast and would drag the out of shape, stationary beaus of hers out to hike, paddle, bike, or whatever, trying to get them healthy. Heart attack was the usual cause of death, but Dad said they likely died from exhaustion.

"He's creepy," she said, hurrying behind her desk. "Parallel parked on one try and has been sitting there ever since. He watches everyone on the street, and I've seen him look over here a lot. A lot, a lot. Know what I mean?"

"Yeah," I said, troubled. "You mean like he's watching the place."

She nodded while searching through her drawer for something. She came out with a small essential oil vial and dumped some onto her hands. After tossing the vial back in the drawer, she rubbed her hands together then stuck her nose into her cupped hands and breathed deeply. Wafts of vanilla filled the air.

"He's making you nervous?"

Stella said the scent of vanilla was naturally calming. "I have a bad feeling." She did a few more deep breaths. Like me, Stella liked true crime books and podcasts. "Go get a paper and check him out. Tell me what you think."

By the large window were two chairs and a table with the latest edition. I did as she said, and while bending to grab a paper, checked out the guy. He was easy to find as he was the only person sitting in their car.

Tall, dark, and hard to see through the tinted windows of his dark SUV. Fortunately, rain clouds had moved in and were blocking the sun, so I could make out the basics. He was similar to the guy who'd knocked me down at Lockett's, but I'd need to see him from behind to be sure. He did sport the same military precision haircut.

He lowered the window, and his gaze held mine. I forgot to breathe. If this *was* the same guy from Lockett's, he was angry if the sharp and menacing look on his buzzard-like features were any indication. I didn't believe in coincidences, and my gut told me this was the same dude from earlier, but I couldn't explain why he was sitting outside my dad's paper.

"Samantha?" Stella said.

Instinct kicked in. On autopilot, I swiped my finger across my phone's screen to activate the camera, then aimed. I put my finger on the button and snapped several shots. He didn't have to know the glare off the window made his image appear hazy and out of focus.

He gave me a finger wave and a smile that sent chills down my spine, but not wanting him to know he'd spooked me, I finger-waved back and took another picture. Maybe his image would be a clue for the cops should I unexpectedly turn up dead, too.

8

SATURDAY

"Sam," Stella said again.

I snatched the paper, spun on my heel, and walked shakily to her desk.

"Do you know him?" She held out her hands for me to take a calming whiff.

I inhaled deeply, hoping it would steady my racing heart.

"No. Maybe you should call the police, just report you don't like it."

Stella rolled her eyes. "I tried. Pamela was on a break so Louney was manning the phones and addressing the calls. He blew me off."

Wind River was small enough that our police force consisted of nine people, eleven with support staff. After Louney was Pamela Hopkins who ran the front desk and was the day 911 operator. Lydia did it in the evenings, and after ten p.m., the emergency response calls were routed to a larger facility. Cody Hinkle replaced his brother Hunter who had moved on to law school. Cody was the sergeant and Leo Stillman had replaced his mentor, Rawlings, who left for a bigger city to be a detective. Leo was the lieutenant. Six other full-time police officers were on the payroll. Both Cody and Louney had graduated with me and had been tight in high school.

I considered calling Leo, but it seemed silly to do so over speculation. I didn't want to be the widow that cried wolf when one day I might really need them.

"He's staring at you," Stella whispered.

I shrugged, acting more cavalier than I felt. The hairs on the back of my neck were raised. "We're going to laugh when whomever he's waiting for comes out of the market and they drive away."

"I hope so." But she didn't sound like she believed it any more than I did.

The dude was creeping me out, and I needed to get to my reason for coming. "Is Dad here?"

"Russ," Stella yelled over her shoulder. Tucked in the right back corner, second room from the end, was my dad's office.

Dad came out of his office, papers clutched in his hands, his glasses on the lower part of his nose. He was bald on top with a gray strip of hair around the sides and lower back. He sported a matching gray beard cut close. He wore khakis and an untucked light blue shirt with rolled-up cuffs and ink stains on the elbow.

He said my name and opened his arms wide for a hug. This was standard for him. As he folded me into his arms, I swallowed my tears. Not because Carson was dead. I'd shed my last tear for him in the wee hours of last night. No, these were tears of frustration and feeling over-whelmed.

He ushered me into his office, closing the door. I often ragged on Dad for being a hoarder. Piles of books and papers lined the walls of his office. Our family's old brown leather couch with the four-inch rip in the center cushion was the only seating option.

I had a special connection with my dad and Rachel my mom. Maybe because I resembled him (with the exception of the bald head and hair color). Maybe it was because I loved the outdoors as much as he did and never turned down a chance to hike or camp with him. Or maybe it was because I was a tad scattered and so was my dad. Unlike Rachel and my mom who were methodical with planning and execution.

"You should call Mom," I said. "I only want to say this once."

Dad's brows shot up, but to his credit, he said nothing. He called my mom and told her to come over pronto.

Her office was across the street so it took two minutes for her to show up. Dressed in a dull green Hillary pantsuit and with her red hair pulled back, she looked severe and ready to scold.

"Have a seat," I told them and pointed to the couch.

"I have a bad feeling about this," my mom said.

"Everything is going to be okay," Dad said, patting her knee.

I told them the bare minimum. Carson was dead. Car, tree, fire. I didn't tell them about the first wife and not-legit marriage. That would have gone over like a floating turd in the punch bowl. Out poured the same lie as what I told Mr. Linn. I figured this could come in handy should I have to explain any of the other weird stuff. My dad had a keen sense for story that I could do without. Besides, I'd omitted truths before, and we'd all been the better for it.

Dad was the first to speak. "Have you told your sister?"

I shook my head. "Could you tell her?"

Dad nodded.

Mom said. "We'll call her from here. Now, do we need to talk funeral?"

I closed my eyes, dropping my forehead into my palm. Funeral! "Can I get back to you on that? I don't have any information yet."

"Carson didn't have family so it's up to us to do this right," said my mother. "I know you like to buck convention, Samantha, but this is not the time."

"Um...there's the issue of money," I said, playing up the debt thing.

Dad said, "How about a celebration of life instead?" Dad grimaced then continued. "I'm assuming we won't need a lot of space for his body. You said something about a fire." My dad held out his hands a shoebox width apart.

"Oh, Russ," mom said, slapping his upper arm. Then she covered her face.

"It's true," I said and curled my lip, grossed out. I was

mad, mad, mad at Carson and what he did to me, but I hoped he didn't suffer. Much. "Do we have to do anything? Can we just have something private?" Or nothing at all.

Mom stood up and came to hug me. "I must say, you're holding it together...well enough." She stuck a finger through a hole in my shirt and studied my face. She pulled her finger from my shirt and peeled off a bundle of hair stuck to my temple.

"Shock?" I said.

"Sad, really," Dad said, lost in his own musings. "We all liked Carson a lot."

"Lots of people liked him," Mom said.

Dad stood. "I think a celebration of life ceremony is necessary, Sammy. We can give others he knew closure, too. It's the right thing to do."

I was torn and skeptical. "Maybe," I said. Because there was likely no way around this.

"I can put a small ad in the paper. We can have it at the Frontiersman Bar and Grille. People can come, and we'll ply them with drinks. And if Carson's financial troubles come around, well, maybe folks will remember the rousing good time we had instead of that. It's sad his life ended with debt hanging over it like a dark cloud."

He had no idea. "Okay."

Dad nodded. "Sounds like a solid plan. We'll do it in two weeks from Monday, six in the evening. That will give us time to get the necessary parts in place."

Like a fake body, or in this case, a box of ashes.

Dad continued, "The paper prints tonight so I can add

a notice. I'll handle everything. All you have to do is show up."

"Okay," I said again, numbly.

Stella knocked on the door and then pushed in, a bundle of mail and packages in her arms. "Everything okay in here?"

"It will be eventually," Dad said.

"Mail came. I hated to interrupt, but there's a package for you in here, Sam." She deposited her load on Dad's cluttered desk.

"Me?" I said.

Stella dug through the pile, pulled out a heavily taped box the size of a hardback novel, and tossed it to me. The package was light enough to catch with one hand. I gave it the once over, wondering if it would be the right size for Carson's fake ashes and could be used for the celebration of life ceremony. *Mental note, search the internet for how much a cremated body weighs.*

The label had no return address and was mailed three days ago, the day he died. "This is in Carson's handwriting."

Dad produced a Swiss Army knife from his pocket and slit a long line down the tape, separating it from the package.

Mom filled Stella in on the news while I opened the box. I pulled out Carson's backpack folded over and duct taped to a fraction of its size. He never went anywhere without it. Breaking through the tape, I unfolded and searched the pockets.

Tucked in the front pocket were his driver's license

and credit cards in the name of Carson Holmes. I left them in the pocket. I had no logical lie to tell my parents as to why he would send these to me.

I held up the backpack and said, "Why would he send me this?"

9

SATURDAY

Late for my appointment with Toby, I dashed home, Carson's backpack, my new purse, slung over one shoulder. Timing was perfect since I'd ripped mine falling at Lockett's office. I ignored the creepy guy in the car outside the newspaper. He didn't follow me so maybe he really was sitting there waiting for someone. Perhaps he was a tourist and his wife was hitting the few shops we had or grabbing them a coffee. *How Ya Bean* was a popular coffee house and on occasion had long lines. And now some weird-ass girl had taken his picture.

Toby was waiting for me on my porch. From him, I learned Carson had set up an insanely strong firewall for our home Wi-Fi. I could access the business cloud through an encryption program that made me feel like a spy. I was living in a new world where the technology exceeded the imagination and the knowledge of the players was limited.

On the cloud were five notebook icons labeled *Clients, Financial, Business Docs, Home, and Misc.* Inside *Clients* were three other files: *previous, current,* and *potential.* There were over two hundred clients listed in the *previous* file. Carson had done a lot of work in the two years he'd had the business. Most were home security and business consultations. The *current* file, organized by months, was remarkably small considering how many clients he'd had in the past. Only eight clients for this month.

Seeing information on a computer was one thing. Processing it in my brain was another. I did things old-school. I pulled out a notepad and jotted down the client names.

Toby gasped. "Carson didn't like paper. He forbid me to use it."

"Except there was a copier and reams of paper at the office," I pointed out.

Toby shrugged. "I don't think I ever printed a single thing. He did use the printer as a scanner to upload images." He glanced pointedly at my notepad.

"Toby." Knowing how Carson did things was imperative but figuring out how I was going to do those things was going to take time. Toby needed to understand this. "Carson isn't here anymore. I have to notify these people that he won't be completing the job."

"No, paper was really important to him. He said it left a trail."

I nodded, understanding. The person who broke into the office hadn't found a single thing because of that philosophy. "Cut me some slack for now. I'll burn the sheet as soon as I'm done calling everyone on the list."

Toby shrugged, gave a slight nod, then pointed to three names on the list. "These are finished. Part of my job is to send the final paperwork and the invoice to the client. We've automated that. All Carson had to do was add client-specific info into these fields." He clicked on the financial file and on a document inside that said *Final PPWK/INVC* then scrolled to a client's name. "See here, Carson added the info needed. I can now close out the file." He pointed to a date on the form. Carson had filled it out the day he died.

"So these three should be paying us?" I made a notation by their names on my list.

"Yep. As soon as I send these out." He did a few clicks, screens popping up and closing. "Okay, sent. They have ten days before they get an automatic reminder."

He showed me how to check for received payments.

"To which bank do the payments go?" If they were routed to the same bank that Carson and I shared, I wouldn't see a dime. His *wife*—I blew out an angry breath—had the rights to that one. Because of that, I needed to switch from that bank as soon as possible.

Toby did some clicks while taking a hit from his vape pen. The smoke smelled like Tooty Fruity. Several screens popped up, the last showing the name of the bank and the account number. It wasn't the one Carson and I used. I jotted down the information. The ledger in the master file showed the account had money, but I needed to figure out payroll and expenses before I got too excited.

"Are you shutting us down?" His mouth pulled down in a frown. "Cuz this was, like, the best job I've ever had. Carson said I had mad skills, and the hours work for me."

The future of Holmes Securities was up in the air. How does a business stay open when the man with the experience was dead? How does an unemployed photographer keep it solvent?

My answer was a big shrug, the kind where your hands come up with palms out to really emphasis you actually knew nothing at all. "You'll be the first to know once I figure everything out."

The *home* file caught my attention, and I clicked on it. A video popped up. I leaned closer to the screen. The image was of the backside of two people.

"That's us," I said. "Right now." Over my shoulder was the fireplace. I expected to see a camera, but on the mantel were the few remaining pictures of Carson and me I'd decided not to burn and a small Eiffel Tower tchotchke that we'd bought in Vegas the day after our unplanned wedding.

"Camera." Toby was leaning back in his chair, vape pen hanging from his lips. "It's the Eiffel Tower. Carson has a few throughout the house."

My expression must have been alarming because he straightened, the pen falling. He rushed to say, "Not anywhere that would be uncomfortable. Only looking at entries. Like for break-ins."

"A video system?" Yes, we had an alarm system. That was to be expected. But why hadn't he ever told me about this? I mentally scoffed and added this question to my growing list of grievances against Carson.

"Yeah, he had one for the office, too." He picked up his pen and took a puff.

"Wait? What?" I shut down the *home* file and clicked on *office*. The image was in real time. "How do I rewind? Maybe we have a picture of the person who broke in."

Toby showed me. "I watched it already. Guy never looked at the camera."

I leaned in closer and studied the dark image on the screen. Toby was right; he kept his face hidden. I wasn't one hundred percent positive, but the burglar looked to be the same man in Lockett's office and outside Dad's paper. Tall, broad-shouldered, dark hair, and a powerful, purposeful stride. He came up to the window and immediately busted out the glass. This person knew no one was going to be around.

He'd clearly staked out the place, which had allowed him to approach the building with confidence. Or he simply didn't care. Like he knew Carson was dead and wouldn't be there.

I was ready to shut down this new part of my world. A few days ago, I was using Photoshop to remove scars and acne from school pictures, and today I was experiencing the seedier side of life. I'd been here before. Ten years ago when I did my first crime scene photos for a course I was taking in college. Knowing criminals walked among my community, some I thought of as friends, had been hard to accept. So much that I'd picked a life where I wouldn't have to be constantly reminded of the dark side. Yet, here I was again, facing the same truths, only this time the criminal was in my home. I had a tough decision to make. I could bury my head in the sand and hope to hold onto the light side of life, or accept that the universe was once again asking me to choose a path.

"Will this be saved?" I tapped a finger on the image.

"Everything goes to the cloud," he assured me. "But let me set it up so if we have any more intruders at the office or here, you'll get a notification on your phone. You'll need to get the app."

I closed the file, hiding the break-in image from the screen even though it was burned into my mind. Toby took me through a few more of the files and showed me how to access the app. He left after I pinky swore I was comfortable with the cloud and logging in, which I was, and would hide my computer when I left the house. That one made me nervous.

I was out of my element. My pits were wet with sweat.

Precious arrived a few minutes after he left. "I've brought sustenance and courage." She held up both hands, one held a bag of takeout food marked from the fish market and the other gripped two bottles, one huckleberry vodka, the other lemonade. Precious was dressed in flowered Capri pants with a navy twin set, looking fresh as a daisy. My hair, I'd given up on it and had put it in a braid that resembled a greasy rope. She unloaded on my dining table then came to look at my computer.

"Wow, this is some crazy good system. I've been trying to automate my company more, but these programs are insanely expensive. A leak or breach from hacking where someone's info is stolen can destroy a business, especially a small one. I can't even afford the consultation for the system," she said while opening the food.

Precious did well in her job. For her to say she couldn't afford the consultation surprised me. "How expensive are they?"

She pushed my hand off the mouse and moved around the screen, clicking on documents and files in the *Financial Master* file. "They start at a quarter of a million. This one would be more expensive. It's custom. That includes the equipment."

I nearly fell from my chair with shock. "Two hundred and fifty thousand dollars? How is that possible? How is it that a company as small as Carson's has more than half a mil to put into software?"

Precious shrugged. "Looks like Carson had the skills to build it himself. This is one heck of a puzzle, Sam."

"I'd prefer a puzzle that wasn't so personal." I pointed to the bottles. "I might need to start with some courage. And remember when you brought up a funeral?"

Precious nodded.

"My parents want to do a celebration of life party for Carson, and he's invited. I need to find some ashes and an urn."

10

SATURDAY

Precious plopped in a chair, stretched her long legs out before her, and said, "I can get some ashes from my fireplace."

Mine was gas.

Jeez, I loved this woman. She'd had my back since we were kids. Knowing she was going on this journey with me made me weepy.

"Would it be rude to have the ashes in a bag?"

She shrugged. "I think they come like that. But no one is going to look into the urn. You could put a bag of beans in there. Maybe two if you didn't want to use ashes."

We bumped fists.

I said, "There's a bank account I need to follow up on to see if I can access before the others get their hands on it."

Precious narrowed her eyes. "They're vindictive, these *others*. Cleaning out your account. Trying to get you kicked out of here and repo-ing your car." She sighed with frustration. "I'm trying to understand where they're coming from. You know, you're the other woman and—"

"And I was sleeping with her husband." I'd avoided saying that as long as I could because the truth of it made me sick to my stomach. I assumed she was sleeping with him, too. Or else why was the divorce dragging out? Anger from his betrayal *of both his wife and myself* was the strongest of all the emotions I was riding.

Images of Carson going between two women who were unaware of each other made my skin hot and itchy. I was eager to scrub him from my skin and life.

"Maybe she doesn't care. Maybe she hated him."

"And me," I said.

Precious nodded. "Yep. You. You're the homewrecker scapegoat."

The very thought of being the other woman did something awful to me on a primitive level. I dashed to my kitchen sink and prepared to empty my stomach. Only nothing happened but a few stomach cramps and a convulsion.

"I'm guessing you're not in the mood for food," Precious said, taking a fish sandwich from the bag. She turned her attention to my computer. "Listen. I know it sucks. Well, I don't know, but I'm guessing it sucks royally. But it is what it is, Sam. You can't change it."

"I'm in the mood for all of this to go away." In the course of two days, I'd lost my husband, savings, and car. Not to mention I had quit my job prior to all this madness.

My shoulders slumped from physical and emotional fatigue.

"Then throw in the towel. Close the business, go live with Russ and Liz, and lick your wounds. If you don't want to live with your folks, you could always sleep in LC since you love him so much." Precious finished her sandwich and dug into mine. "It would be so easy to let *the others* take the rest of it."

She had a point. It being I could continue with my pity party and lose everything or I could suck it up and fight back. I had a home, a car, and a business. Albeit one I didn't know how to run. Nevertheless, I had the opportunity of money, and I'd lost enough already. I wasn't about to lose anymore. I snatched my half-eaten sandwich from her hand.

"I don't know how to make this business work for me," I said. "I can't run a security system business."

"Close that. Call the people, tell them Carson is dead, and you'll be refunding their deposit."

With money I didn't have, unless some was magically waiting in this business account. I was desperate for an income stream. "But keep the PI portion open?" I shook my head. "Yeah, I need a job and I definitely need money, I'm not sure I have the time it'll take to learn to be a PI."

"If only you had access to someone who could help you sort that out." She rolled her eyes. As a life coach, Precious helped entrepreneurs reach their potential on both personal and professional levels. Her track record spoke for itself. If I were to launch a new business, she would be the one to help me do it.

"I couldn't afford to pay you," I reminded her.

She dismissed my words with a wave of her hand. "You could help me out at my office. I'm short-staffed. As for income, you have those clients. That's money waiting to be made." She pointed to my computer with her other hand. She clicked some keys, then showed me the screen. "These people are waiting for a job to be done, and from the notes next to their name, they're not looking for a security system."

Holmes Securities client list showed eight names. *Could I run the business?* A maniacal giggle, part incredulous and part question, escaped from deep inside me. I must be losing my mind to even consider running a business I knew nothing about.

"Maybe I can hire a PI to do these jobs?" I wondered if the internet would tell me what percentage would be an appropriate cut if I was bringing the work to the PI.

"Why can't you do it?"

"I'm not a private investigator. Or a cop. I know nothing about..." I shook my head in denial as I read a note next to a client's name. "How to do a background check on someone."

"What's it take to become one?" She keyed in some stuff and pulled up a page. "Look," she said showing me the computer. "All you have to do is take a test." She gave me a puzzled look. "Didn't you once study for this? Back in college? Didn't a bunch of you in the forensic photography class talk about getting your license so you all could make it rich taking money shots? Kinda a sign, don't you think?"

"Look." I pointed to a line of text. "A lot has changed in a decade, including federal and state law and...oh...a few hundred other tidbits about this line of work." My tone was heavy with a spectacular amount of sarcasm.

Precious did not like to be bested. "Why are you so afraid to take this on?"

I slumped in the chair next to her. "You weren't there that night I had to take photos of Ms. Trina chained to the pole at Junkies. I can still see every detail of those images." I tapped my temple. Not only did my camera capture clear pictures, so did my mind, and I had the uncanny ability to recall them on demand and see them as if I was looking at the picture in real time. A photographer with a photographic memory. A gift that was both good and bad. "Ten years of taking pictures of babies and puppies and pimple kids has done nothing to erase those images of her and that scene from my mind."

Precious considered me, her brow furrowed. "Okay, so what does that tell you?"

I shrugged.

"It tells you that you have to stop fighting it. Stop trying to mentally look away. Own the image. Compartmentalize it. Or it's going to continue to own you. Ten years ago you decided to not pursue forensic photography because of these images. Are you any happier? Has the image of Ms. Trina diminished any over time?" She gave me a pointed look. "Because I can tell you *aren't* happier."

"I was content," I argued.

"Sure, that's why you quit Toomey's Photography Studio. That's why you were saving money to start up your own business. Because you were content." She tapped a nail against the tabletop. "Crazy as this might seem to you, I think you're getting a second chance to discover what you're meant to do with your life."

We sat in silence for a few beats. Then I said, "I'm scared because this is the real deal. This is more than redoing a picture. This is life and death and heartache and happiness. It's more disappointments than successes. I know because my parents say that all the time."

Precious smiled. "Yet, they wouldn't change a thing."

I tossed the idea around another beat or two. "I just can't magically be a PI. I'd need an internship or something if I'm going to do this right."

Precious smiled big and clasped her hands together in excitement. "Maybe Carson had someone on contract he could call up or something. My business license has to list the number of employees."

I showed her the *Business Master* file. While she scanned the documents, I pushed a French fry around a Styrofoam takeout box, collecting the dried kale seasoning.

Precious gasped then tossed back her head and laughed.

My throat constricted from fear. "What now?"

She swiveled the computer toward me. A business license was on the screen. "Your company is allowed up to six employees. Right now, the company employee roster lists three. Carson and Toby—"

"I'm the third person, right? Because I'm the owner. So no on-call PI? Maybe he had a contract PI instead?"

Precious shrunk the screen. "Oh, there's a PI on the employee list. This image here is the one that's gold."

I leaned in to look at the image. It was another license. A Private Investigators license. *In my name.* I blinked in hopes of clearing my vision.

Yep, my name was on the license.

"You're the PI listed," Precious exclaimed.

"I don't get it."

"Evidently, *you have* taken the PI test and passed. You were awarded this license." She clicked a few other screens. "Carson has one, too. This is the document that shows the current register of employees for your company. It lists him, you, and Toby."

"How? I never took a test."

"Ever sign papers without really looking at them? My best guess is he took the test in your name."

"That can't be legal!" Mind blown. "Yeah, I signed papers, like the lease on this place and some banking documents."

"And you never read every single sheet?"

She knew better than to ask that. The print on legal forms was tiny and speed-bump words were hard to pick out. I ducked my head with embarrassment. Besides, I'd trusted Carson.

Precious leaned forward, her face alight with excitement. "Come on, you can't ask for a better, clearer sign than that."

I snorted. "Let's not ignore the fact that Carson falsified documents. I'm seeing a pattern here."

She pointed her index finger at me. "See, you are already acting like a PI."

I rolled my eyes. "It doesn't take a genius to make that deduction."

"You ready to become Magnum PI and make this business work?" Precious arched a brow, excitement written across her face. She raised a hand for a high five.

"Do I get a Ferrari and a guest house in Hawaii?" Constant sun sounded magical. All that vitamin D and goodness. I smiled at the thought of escaping to anywhere but here.

Precious laughed. "What you get is your beloved LC, all this fresh air, and your townhouse until your lease is up. If you need an escape, then we can find a head shop with some wacky tobaccy that might make you *think* you're in Hawaii." She waved her hand. "Don't leave me hanging."

I gave her a high five. She squealed in excitement.

"Hard pass on the weed," I said. Being in control had a much higher value to me than the idea of forgetting my woes for however long a high lasted. What if something were to happen while I was stoned? Look what had happened to my love life when I had too much to drink?

I continued, "What do I know about being a PI? Nothing."

She rolled her eyes. "No one is asking you to solve a murder. Let's start with looking at what clients are left and what they want you to do. Between doing that and supplementing with jobs I might have, you can totally make ends meet."

She was nothing but positive and confident, and her flippant and easy way of presenting the alternatives made me think I *could* actually do it. Precious believed everyone had the ability to be awesome. Even when you didn't believe it yourself.

"Don't think, just do," she said.

I hesitated and bared my teeth in an awkward grimace-like smile. Then I blew out a deep breath. "First I need to..." I needed to get organized, but was overwhelmed with where to start.

Precious stood then grabbed the hardback journal I kept on my bar to jot reminders and notes. She handed it to me along with a pen. "Go to the bank and see who owns the account. My guess it's you. Then call those clients. You'll have to cancel the ones who want security systems, but some of these are for other services. See how many want to continue with you. You have to tell them Carson is gone anyway. Then the ones that stay, you work their case. Now, I'm going to say to you what I tell my employees." She clapped her hands once, loudly. "You got this! Now get out of my office."

I sprung to my feet.

"Hold on to your titties, kitties, this is going to be an awesome ride," she said in a sing-song voice as I hustled away.

"Or really, really bad," I muttered as I pondered what a PI wore to work every day.

11

SATURDAY

The first three people on Carson's client list seeking a PI decided to seek services with another more skilled private investigator. I couldn't blame them. The fourth person I called was Shannon Kleppner. We'd gone to high school together; she'd been a year ahead of me. Shannon had always been nice to everyone if my memory served.

Shannon taught fifth grade at the same elementary school where Precious's sister, Heidi, taught kindergarten. The picture in her file was almost identical to how I remembered her from high school, only older. Shannon had been a cheerleader, a perky blond cliché. With thick thighs and thicker mascara, she'd landed Sean Kleppner their junior year and held on tight. He was in line to take over his dad's landscaping company, and everyone knew they made good money. The company had contracts with many of the towns in the surrounding area.

She answered on the second ring.

When I finished my spiel as to why I was taking over Carson's case, she said, "I'm sorry about your loss, Sam. Are you sure you're up to taking this case? I asked your husband to get me the money shot."

Money shot was the picture of the cheating spouse with the new honey and used in court to win whatever the jaded partner wanted. This is what us fools in college had thought would be easy money. I learned from YouTube videos on how to be PI that money shots could also be clandestine business meetings, worker's comp fraud, and any commissioned photo one person could use against someone else.

I snorted. If only she knew. "I'm up for it. Besides, I'm pretty handy with a camera. Thanks for taking a chance on me."

"Who else am I gonna use? Your husband promised discretion, and I expect that from you." Shannon huffed, then cleared her throat, her voice thick. "You did my family pictures, remember? That cheating turd. I'm going to cut him out of them as soon as we hang up."

"And you're sure he's cheating?" If so, why did she need me?

"Oh, I'm sure. Lipstick on the collar. Late night hang-ups. It's like a bad made-for-TV movie. Who calls a land-line anyway?" She was fairly shouting.

"I dunno," I said. *Who had a landline these days?*

"It's the phone the kids use, and his bimbo is calling it. My child is picking it up. I want you to get all the shots.

Every possible angle. I need you to help me nail his butt to the wall. You think you can do that?"

I gauged my feelings. Was I in the mood to nail someone to the wall? "Yeah, I can totally do that." Maybe it wasn't the healthiest way to work through Carson's death and betrayal but who was I to be picky?

"Great! Your husband had a list of the places Sean frequents. Let's see, it's Saturday, so he'll likely be at the casino. He loves his roulette. I suspect when he's done wasting his retirement money, he meets up with his bimbo somewhere. If I didn't have little kids in bed, I'd follow him myself and find out where."

The sun was fading, which happened later here in the PNW. My watch said I missed dinner, but the hour was ripe for gambling.

"I'll let you know when I get something," I said. "Um, Shannon. Do you mind me asking? How did you know to hire Carson for this?"

"He put in a security system for the house. We got to talking, and I maybe told him about Sean. He offered to help."

So Carson would do one service then pitch for more work? How very entrepreneurial.

We ended the call with plans for me to check in with her in a week after school.

Dinner was drive-thru with nothing to show for my sub sandwich but the small bit of lettuce clinging to my shirt. Two Winds Casino was in La Keep but on the Cowlitz Reservation, Leo's tribe. In 2002, the tribe finally received recognition from the federal government. The battle for that right had waged from before I was born.

Shannon said Sean would be in his work truck, which was easy enough to find, but a drive through the parking lot turned up nothing. I contemplated my next move. From Sean's company website, I screenshotted his picture and headed into the casino, figuring I'd probe staff and hope something turned up. The lot was full, and I was forced to park at the farthest corner from the casino.

I flung Carson's boring black backpack over my shoulder and headed inside. I was wandering through the place, getting a sense of the layout, when I came across the pit boss, an average height woman with bottle-blond hair, a big smile, and a killer tan, like she'd stepped off the beach today. She was wearing the Casino uniform of navy-blue slacks with a matching blazer and a white button-down shirt.

"Nice tan," I said with genuine envy. No one around here was that sun-kissed. People had to travel south for that, and one place in particular was a favorite. "Mexico?"

She nodded. "My brother runs a fishing boat out of various foreign ports. Comes in handy."

"I need a brother like that," I said.

She laughed. "How can I help you?" In her ear was an earpiece, the microphone clipped to her shirt, the curlicue cord visible from the side. Her nametag read Lisa Harper.

I said, "I'm looking for a friend, a guy who likes to come here and gamble." I laughed and slapped my forehead. "Duh, I guess that's almost everyone in here."

She chuckled. "Pretty much, yes."

"We were supposed to meet up, and I don't see him anywhere." The lie rolled off my tongue. Weird. Perhaps it was because I was getting used to the job. Maybe people, like Carson, who spent their life having to stretch the truth for their work couldn't stop themselves from doing it in their personal lives as well.

"I can have him paged."

I grimaced. "He'd hate that." I shuffled through the backpack for my phone. "He comes here a lot. Maybe you know him." I flashed his picture.

She nodded. "Sean? Yeah, we know him. Especially since he's a big winner."

"A big winner?"

"He didn't tell you? He won a jackpot three weeks ago. Over two million." She walked me to a large electronic board a few feet away. A variety of messages slid across the screen.

One read: *Congrats Big Winner Sean K!*

Note to self. Work on observation skills.

In my defense, the sign was vague enough, and lots of people from all over came to the casino. Though, I was surprised the rumor mill hadn't started in Wind River.

"That turkey," I said with mock frustration. "He never said anything about winning. Just said he'd teach me the game." I shook my head.

"He hasn't been in here for at least a week or two. We sit on the info for six weeks so winners can get things in order, then we put out a press release. My guess, that's what he's doing," she offered.

"How often did he come here before the big win?"

Shannon hadn't mentioned Sean winning a few million either.

"Easy three times a week. Sometimes more. Truthfully, he probably won back what he's spent over time."

"Broke even," I mumbled.

"That would be my guess." Her radio squawked.

"If he comes in..." I waved a hand dismissively. "Never mind, I'll try him at his house. Thanks for your help, Lisa."

"Anytime," she said before turning and speaking into the walkie-talkie as she moved away.

Dead end for now. Best thing for me would be to head home, watch some more How To Be a PI videos and map out some ideas. Shannon hadn't sounded like Sean was in the wind with his winnings. But her not knowing bothered me, too.

Struck by an idea, I caught up with Lisa who was fast-footing it across the casino. "Quick question. Does Sean have a favorite dealer or table?" By nature, people were creatures of habit and many superstitious. Maybe the dealer would know something.

Lisa stopped and pointed over my shoulder. "That's the roulette section. He didn't have a favorite table, only a favorite blonde. Currently, that's Jessica. She's the shorter one in the middle." Lisa handed me a chip. "You'll need to play to chat. Compliments of the casino." She winked.

The chip was a one-dollar marker. "Thanks. Sadly, I'll likely lose it in the first play but..." I shrugged as if to say nothing ventured, nothing gained.

Jessica wasn't hard to locate. In a sea of dark-haired

women with Native American heritage, Jessica stood out like a giant zit on a pretty face. Her table was first in line for roulette and across from the slot machines. Two guys stood at her table. I moved to fill the gap between them, feeling uncomfortable and awkward and unsure of what to do next.

"Place your bets," Jessica said in a nasally voice. Sean had a type, alright. She was young, reminded me of cheerleader Shannon, only less perky and had an infinity for piercings. Two small hoops in each brow, one diamond in her nose, another diamond, possibly a fake, in her lip, and hands adorned with rings. Most were of the artsy type, twisted metal of dark colors contrasting with silver. Only one, two entwined hearts, sported sparkles.

The roulette table had a green background with several numbers in red and black. At the far end where Jessica stood was a wheel. The men placed their chips, the denomination much higher than mine, on numbers in the black and red area.

I hesitated. "Put my chip anywhere? I've never done this before."

"You can place your bet on any of the black or red but also on the single-oh or the double-ohs," Jessica said in a bored voice.

Double zero? Like me, bad job, bad man. What were the odds?

Logically, I knew I wasn't a two-time loser, but over the past twenty-four hours, I'd experienced pangs of being precisely that. Married a married man and stayed in an unfulfilling job only to finally quit, believing I had support but finding out I had none.

I placed the one-dollar chip on the double-ohs. "My friend Sean swears by this game."

Jessica stared at me, eyes narrowed, probably wondering if I was talking about her Sean.

"He did win pretty big here recently." I scanned the crowd. "He was supposed to be here tonight." I pretended to be slightly confused as I looked around before bringing my attention back to Jessica. I did a half shrug.

She gave the wheel a spin then dropped the ball.

The clicking sound of the wheel moving around and around was exciting. Everyone at the table leaned closer.

When the wheel stopped, Jessica called out, "Double-ohs."

The men huffed. "Beginners luck," one said. He was a portly man, shorter than me with a bushy mustache that matched his bushy eyebrows. When he spoke, his jowls shook slightly.

"Maybe I have Sean's luck," I said, attempting to get Jessica to open up.

Bushy-brow man snorted. "Maybe you don't want his luck. Haven't seen him here since he won. Besides, he won on the slot machine behind you. Would pull the handle when we were between dealers. He did it religiously." He pointed to Jessica, "He wasn't supposed to do that but some of the dealers were more lenient with him than with others."

The unspoken words hung there. Jessica snarled at Bushy, who chuckled in response.

Bushy continued, "What do you think? Someone off him for the cash?" He laughed as if his last remark was a joke. One I didn't find funny. If he were missing, clearly Shannon would have said that, right?

Behind me was the GO BIG or GO HOME slot. Each pull of the handle cost five dollars. Too rich for my blood.

"He played both?" Sean's business was successful, but I didn't think he was the sort of high roller to play a slot several times in one night at five bucks a pop. Maybe I was naive.

Jessica slid a handful of chips toward me with a long stick. My winning amounted to $36.00. Not bad for a free chip to begin with. I could buy groceries.

I continued my probing. "You both know Sean?"

"Her better than me," Bushy said and chuckled.

Jessica's cheeks pinked. "We dated for a bit."

"But not anymore?" Did she not know he had a wife and kids?

"He got boring," she said with a flat expression.

"Sure, he did," Bushy laughed. "Two things about Sean. He likes his risks. Gambling and chasing skirts. So long as the skirt isn't his wife." To Jessica, he said, "You sure you got bored with him and not the other way around? I noticed the new dealer, what's her name?" He snapped his fingers. "Kimmie isn't here. If there were a table where I could bet on him being with her, I'd do it in a heartbeat."

Jessica's lip curled up. "Well, there isn't such a table, Bob. You're at this one, and you need to place your bet now or move on."

Clearly, Jessica was no longer the flavor of the month. Kimmie was whom I needed to talk to.

"Thank you," said the other man. "If I wanted to hear chatter about other people's business and love life, I'd stay at home and listen to my wife talk about the characters on *The Bachelor*." He slammed some chips on black thirteen then faced me. "Beginners luck only lasts so long. You staying or running away with your winnings?" He was tall, thin, and lanky. Bald head, a day's worth of grayish growth on his face, and paint splattered on his arms. His jeans and T-shirt were clean but worn in places. People-watching was a skill I'd honed as a kid. Because dyslexics struggled with language in a variety of forms, learning to read the room became essential. For this guy, I'd say painter by trade, and the way he spoke about his wife told me he likely dressed down just to get on her nerves.

Bushy-brow Bob on the other hand was in a light blue button-down that had been freshly pressed today, likely in the morning. His slacks were dark, his shoes polished. He worked in management.

Lanky man tapped his finger against the table rim impatiently.

"Let's see if this beginner's luck will continue," I said and slid my chips onto the double-ohs.

Bushy-brow Bob chuckled and placed his bet. Jessica spun the wheel, dropped the ball, and I forgot to breathe.

I closed my eyes and waited for the clicking sound to stop. When it did, the table remained quiet. Cracking an eye open, they were watching me.

"Double zero wins," Jessica declared.

"Are you kidding me?" A crazy smile of glee spread across my face.

Lanky man rolled his eyes. "You gonna keep playing?"

I used my forearm to sweep the chips toward me. "Nope. I'll stop here. I'm not sure how much this is, but it's more than I started with, and I like to end on a good note."

"You've got over a grand there," Bob said with a smile.

I sucked in a breath. "Seriously?" My mouth fell open. He nodded.

Lanky pointed a thin finger across the room. "Go there and cash out," he said, clearly annoyed.

I scooped up the chips and left. They paid me in cash, which I was uncomfortable with stuffing into my backpack. I glanced around nervously, expecting to find someone following me.

"There's security throughout the casino, hon, plus in the parking lot. You're safe," the banker woman said.

"Thanks," I said. Nevertheless, I reorganized in a woman's restroom stall by hiding the money in maxi-pad wrappers. Gently, I peeled the adhesive on the outside so I could remove the pad. I distributed the money evenly between the four, aligning the bills with the pad and refolding. Then I tucked them each back into their wrapper. Now, they could be mistaken for heavy flow pads and no one would be the wiser.

Instead of wearing the backpack over one shoulder, I put it over both and even buckled the waist strap, more out of habit from hiking than fear of having my money taken, but it would help should the latter happen. These winnings would give me a cushion I needed, albeit a small one. I could see how people became addicted. Even now I was considering returning to try again until my funds got short.

Outside, the night air was cold, a wind coming in off the river. Keys in hand, I dashed to LC, weaving between the other cars.

Though the lanes had streetlights, there were dark pockets. A casino security car and another cop car patrolled the area. I was a handful of yards from my car when a dark figure popped up out of nowhere. Cloaked in a hoody, he came from the side and grabbed me by my backpack.

"Give it to me," he snarled.

I screamed, twisting and turning in an attempt to wrench myself free of him. He jerked me back by the pack, the movement startling. My keys dropped from my hand, and the pack slipped down my shoulder to my upper arms. I raised my arms over my head and flailed them in the air. Unable to gain purchase to move forward, I changed tactics, another strategy Carson had taught me, and ran backward, crashing into the man behind me.

We went down like a felled tree, stiff and bouncing on the ground, me on top. My attacker *oomphed* when he hit the ground. I'd knock the wind out of him and guessed I had seconds before he would regroup.

I rolled off him and, driven by instinct to survive, kicked him in the man business.

He groaned, covering his groin, and rolled to his side. I'd only caught a glimpse of his face and didn't care to stick around for a further look.

I scrambled along the asphalt to my keys and scooped them up while trying to catch my balance so I could run. In front of me, the security truck was barreling down toward me. The cop SUV had stopped a few feet behind it. I ran full speed toward them.

Leo Stillman jumped from the SUV and drew his gun. "Freeze, police," he yelled.

I skidded to a stop and put my hands in the air.

He grunted. "Not you, Sam,"

I ran past the security truck and took refuge at his side, then pointed to the man who'd attacked me. Only the security cart was blocking the way. The security officer came around to the side of his vehicle where we could see him, arms in the air.

"He got away," said the young guy in a casino uniform. "Like a ghost."

Leo said something under his breath—I'm guessing he swore—then holstered his gun. "You okay?" He scanned me from head to foot.

I nodded. "Shaken up a bit."

"You've had a heck of a day." He pulled a flashlight from his belt.

I shook my head in amazement. "Was the office break-in today? It feels like that happened weeks ago." Today was stretching into a thin band of endless time that showed no signs of ending. I was going to need ice cream or something else of quality goodness to steady my nerves and cap off the day.

Leo clicked on the light and shone it over me as if he didn't believe I was okay. "Did you know him?"

"Why would you think that?" Surprise was evident in my tone.

"Standard question. Ruling out domestic dispute."

I gave him my you've-got-to-be-kidding face.

In typical Leo fashion, he shrugged off my reaction. "What do you think he wanted?"

"My money, I guess. He was trying to take my backpack." I ran my hands over the straps. Carson's pack had held up like a champ.

"Why your backpack? Anything good in it?" Leo stuck his thumbs over his utility belt.

"Over a grand I just won at roulette," I said matter of fact.

The security guard joined us.

Leo said, "You know, no one has ever been attacked or robbed at this casino."

"Until you," the guard said. "Let's go to the security shack. I'm gonna need a full statement."

There went my ice cream. "Since I'm the first, is there some sort of prize that comes with that?" I was ever hopeful.

"Yeah, you're walking away alive with your money. Congrats," Leo said. "I don't like this, Samantha. This is the second time I'm saying this to you today. Trouble is dogging you and I think it's only going to get worse."

Sometimes, he was super annoying. Especially when he was right. I brushed away the goosebumps crawling up my arms. Because after dogging came stalking.

12

MONDAY

I spent Sunday going through the townhouse and tossing more of Carson's stuff into spare Rubbermaid bins we had in the garage. I was so angry with Carson, or whatever his real name was, that I planned to use the ash from his torched stuff to fill his fake urn. I tried to get lost in TV, but the news was stuck on a story about some senator's son being killed in a freak fire, and no shows held my attention.

On Monday, I got back to the business of earning money. Today, the plan was to work more on the client list, clean up the mess the liar had left and, move on, putting him in the rearview mirror. The sooner the better.

Two more on the list decided to cancel before I'd called Marni Edgar, client number seven. Thankfully, she was interested in continuing with my service. She agreed to meet with me and Precious, who I'd sold as my assistant, at

Marni's office. I figured it wouldn't hurt to have Precious alongside. Her professional air would help sell me. Besides, she was ticked she'd missed the action at the casino. I drove LC through How Ya Bean coffee drive-thru for lattes and muffin tops before arriving at Marni's office, and we sat in LC eating and drinking and talking about the past events since we had a few minutes to kill before the meeting.

Marni, a land broker, was a statuesque redhead with curly hair and stunning blue eyes. She met us in the lobby. She wore a pale blue linen skirt and silk shirt with a peter pan collar. Not a wrinkle to be had. I, on the other hand, had dressed as if I was on loan from the local parish with my plain black skirt, gray button-down, and slide-on Klogs that could be worn for day hiking. Functionality was my middle name. Fashion was not. To top it off, I had a white chocolate smudge on my hip from where my muffin top had broken off and landed. Further smearing had occurred when I tried to lick it off.

Marni and Precious were cut from the same cloth. They sized each other up like top-of-the-food-chain animals do.

Precious nodded to the skirt. "Retro Chanel?"

"Top is as well," Marni said. "Pulitzer?" she asked, pointing to Precious's pants.

"Of course," Precious said.

They murmured compliments in appreciation. Apparently, they'd found each other acceptable.

"I'm Samantha True," I said, hoping nothing about me screamed amateur. I cleared my throat, a premeditated lie sticking before I forced it out. "I'm one of the PI's with Holmes Securities."

"You're Carson's wife," she said matter-of-factly and pointed to a cluster of chairs in the corner of the lobby. "Let's take this over there."

"Ah, yes, I am." Lie number two. We settled into the chairs.

Marni crossed her legs and leaned back into the chair, relaxing. "He talked about you. Said he knew if he couldn't get the information, you could."

Precious and I exchanged a quick, confused look.

"What else did he say?" Trouble with this Carson situation was reconciling his deception with his kindness. He'd never been mean to me. I'd had no reason to think he was anything but devoted and loyal. Which made his butthead actions that much harder to accept.

She gave a delicate one-shoulder shrug. "Not much. We talked about the dating scene, and he said he was glad he didn't have to do it. He had you. Said meeting you was the luckiest day of his life."

Lucky? Because I was an easy mark?

My temper flared. A subject change was the only solution if this meeting was going to go well. I didn't want to point out that Carson had been likely feeding her a line of BS.

"I've reviewed your case notes." Sadly, I hadn't really retained much of what I read except she wanted some dude screened. "Character check" was the term. "But why don't you start from the beginning and tell me what you're looking for?"

Marni waved a dismissive hand, her eyes not focusing on me. "It's silly, really. Kinda embarrassing."

Precious chuckled. "Embarrassing is Sam's middle name. Trust me, she's had a heck of a week these last three days, so nothing you're going to say will surprise her."

Marni folded her hands in her lap and picked at her thumbnail.

"I'm really not good at love. Unlucky."

I snorted in agreement, then waved it off when she gave me a puzzled look. "I've been there," I said.

"I met this really nice guy at a friend's party a few weeks ago. We've talked, texted, and gone on two dates." She held up two fingers. "He wants more. I want more. But what if he's an asshat of the highest form? I'd rather not have to go through all that. I asked your husband to check him out for me. See if the skeletons in his closet are manageable. I don't want to find out he's got a wife and girlfriend. Know what I mean?"

I cut my eyes to Precious. Boy, did I ever know what she meant. I checked my phone screen. "His name is Lason Dell. He works as an assistant manager at Ralphs?" I glanced at her.

She nodded. "The northern Vancouver store."

Ralph's was one of the bigger grocery stores on the west coast. You needed anything, Ralph's carried it. New couch? Got it. Shelf liner? Aisle forty-two. An assortment of candles to take the stink out of an Airbnb? Household Goods section. They had rows of wine, organic food, and their bakery had éclairs and lemon bars that could make a person weep with pleasure.

"Okay," I said, "I'll dig around in his closets and see what I can find. Give me a week."

Marni's brow knitted, and I couldn't read what her concern was.

"Maybe two," Precious said. "With the funeral prep and all."

"Oh, right, the funeral," I said. Guessing Marni's look was curiosity, wondering why I was working and not grieving. We humans had a funny way of expecting people to react like we would in a certain situation. Like with the death of a spouse. Only I was afraid that by giving in to my emotions, a mixed bag of disbelief, anger, fear, and raw sadness, I might behave in such a way I could get arrested. I didn't want this experience with Carson to shape my life forever.

"Denial," I said. "It's way easier to cope with this." I tapped the space above my heart.

"Understandable." Marni nodded. "I think I can put Lason off for a week or so. Especially if you find out he's playing me. I'm not interested in becoming the other woman. What's broken inside a woman who takes that role?" She stood and ran a hand down her smooth skirt.

No words. Not one. Just a mouth hanging open like some mouth breather unable to make cohesive thoughts.

"C'mon," Precious said and took me by the arm. She said to Marni, "We'll be in touch."

Outside in my car, I let my head fall back against the seat. "What will she say when she learns about Carson?

"Why does she ever have to know? Why does anyone

have to know? We stuff that urn, and when the ceremony is over, we put this behind us."

"Leo knows. And that lawyer Lockett. And I know."

"Want me to pick up some scarlet letters for you to put on your clothes?" Precious rolled her eyes. She didn't tolerate self-pity well.

"Yes, we can make it modern and do O.W. Other wife." I crossed my arms, and stared out the window, not looking at anything. "I know zilch about surveillance or digging through people's backgrounds. I mean, I married a married man. That pretty much guarantees I'm too dumb for this job."

Precious grunted her frustration. "I need to get to the office."

Frustrated, I turned over the engine then punched the gas, and we shot out of the parking lot. When we merged into traffic, she popped me upside the head.

"Ow," I said rubbing the left side. "What was that for?"

"You said the pity party was over? Suck it up time. You have to compartmentalize. What Carson did is on him. What you do from here is on you. You're a ginormous dumb-dumb *if* you continue to take responsibility for his actions. You were played. Simple as that. Marni Edgar is a smart woman who knows that being played could happen to her."

She had a point. I pointed to her purse. "Pull out your phone and pull up those YouTube videos. I know nothing about surveillance." I pictured the space over Carson's office and all that superspy cool equipment. Maybe this job wasn't so bad after all.

13

MONDAY

Three videos later, I had a plan. Goal, to find out if Lason Dell was a dirtbag. Objective, see the man in his natural habitat.

I was going undercover, sorta.

My first act was to stalk Lason on social media, but he had his accounts locked down tight. Only things I could see were a variety of memes. No Instagram or Twitter.

I drove to Ralph's. According to Carson's notes, Lason Dell was the assistant manager of the online shopping department known as *Click and Go*. I'd called ahead, asked for that department, and he'd answered the phone.

A stroke of luck finally. He was working.

I made up some bogus question then quickly got off the phone and entered the store. Once inside, I wasn't sure how I could draw him out. The *Click and Go* wasn't like the deli or bakery with a "storefront." The entrance was a single door painted to blend into the wall with an *employees only* sign. I couldn't walk up to the front desk and ask to speak to Lason.

I strolled through the aisles of the store, contemplating my options, when I struck gold in produce.

A woman, easily no more than twenty, stood before the beets with a handheld scanner in one hand and a clear produce plastic bag in the other. Her lips were moving as she read off the scanner. Another person who wasn't a swell reader. #MyPeople. She sported a pixie cut of blond hair dyed a light pink, her brows were pierced three on each side, and she wore skinny jeans and a Beatles T-shirt under her mustard-yellow Ralph's vest. Next to her was a push-cart, the kind you see at lumberyards, stacked with four plastic crates, each loaded with a variety of foods. A *Click and Go* sign hung from one of the crates.

"Hey," I said and picked up a beet.

"Hi," she said and raised one pierced brow. "Do I know you?"

I shook my head. "I was wondering about *Click and Go.*" I wasn't sure where I was going with this, but I hoped I could bring the conversation around to Lason at some point or another.

She scrunched up her nose, looking puzzled. "Wondering how it works or about the job opening?"

Shazam! Sparks of joy burst inside my head. "Yeah," I said. "Curious about the job. What's it like?"

She gave a one-shoulder half-shrug, her spine straightening with what I assumed was a coolness factor.

She believed she instantly had it over me. She had the job she thought I was interested in.

She leaned toward me and said softly, "It's easy. Takes no brain power."

"Sweet," I said, putting the beet back. I pointed to her handheld. "So you get a grocery list or something on that and go out and shop?"

"Yeah, totally. That's basically it. Sometimes we don't have what the customer wants, so we have to make substitutions. I just go with the more expensive product. That makes everyone happy." She smiled. "Customer service is key."

Why hadn't I ever used this service? I hated grocery shopping, and the idea of someone else doing it for me sounded like nirvana.

"Really cool," I said.

Her attention was on something over my shoulder, then she pointed with her chin. "Here's the guy you need to talk with." She called out, "Hey, Lason, come here a sec."

Lason Dell stood slightly over six feet with broad shoulders like a swimmer. He had dark brown hair and light brown eyes and was the sort of guy who always had a smile. He said hi to several customers on his way to us and even stopped to help an older lady reach an item on the top shelf. I was instantly suspicious. Lason Dell was one of *those guys*. A nice one. And it was my job to find out if his Mr. Boy Scout persona was an act.

Like my new friend, Lason was dressed in jeans and a T-shirt. Only his jeans were dark-washed, a more professional look, and his T-shirt was a plain light blue that actually complimented the hideous yellow vest color.

I liked the look of him and understood why Marni was scared she might fall for him. Lason Dell was the boy next door, jovial and easygoing. How could he possibly break a girl's heart? But then, I never expected Carson to have another family, so my judgment and first impression skills weren't to be relied upon.

"What's up, Kylie?" Lason asked my new friend. Kylie. It suited her.

"This woman here was asking about the job opening." She nodded to me. The way she said woman told me she thought I was old. I was guessing the dark circles under my eyes were making me appear older than my youthful thirty.

Lason stuck out his hand. "Awesome, you have time to fill out an application now? We're only looking for twenty hours of help at this time. That could go up. Unfortunately, twenty hours doesn't give you benefits if that's what you're looking for."

Well, I hadn't been until that moment. Crapola. I'd forgotten about benefits. I'd had benefits with the photography studio but Carson had said if I left, we could get a family plan. He was...had been...self-insured.

We shook hands. His grip was firm but not overpowering. "I don't need benefits," I lied and silently prayed I wouldn't need a doctor visit until I got this issue sorted out.

He waved for me to walk with him. "So you're good to do everything now?"

Falling into step with him, I shrugged and said, "Why not?"

"Great, let's go back to my office. You can fill out the application while we talk. That'll be the interview. What's your name?"

"Samantha," I said.

"Samantha. Awesome." He held open the *Click and Go* door for me and gestured for me to precede him.

Behind the door was a short hallway that opened into a larger room. On the right, two registers were against one wall. Several carts like the one Kylie had been using were lined up in rows in the center of the room and stacked high with groceries. Some had large signs hanging from them, reminding workers there were items in the freezer. On the left, and across from the registers, were the steel double doors to a freezer. Directly across the hallway were glass floor-to-ceiling windows and a large sliding door. Covering the windows were graphic decals. I could see out of them, but those on the other side couldn't see in. On the other side of the windows and doors was the parking lot.

"This is where customers pick up their order. They call in when they arrive, tell us their spot, and we bring it out to them. Because it's done online, the order is already paid for. If they have coupons, we come back in and adjust the price. Easy peasy." He pointed to an opening along one of the walls opposite the glass doors. "Let's go in there."

The room was a small office with a desk and two chairs. Inspirational sayings and promotional sales flyers were tacked to a large bulletin board. Lason sat behind the desk, made some clicks on his computer, then swung the screen to face me. He handed me the keyboard.

"Typically, you can fill out an application at home or up at the customer service desk, but I figure if I have a fish on the hook, which is awesome, I should strike while the iron is hot." He gestured for me to start typing.

So far there were two things I would tell Marni. Lason used mixed metaphors and "awesome" a lot. His desk was devoid of pictures of any kind. No signs of kids or a woman.

"Is this your office?" I kept my attention on the online form and answered the personal questions.

"The company intended it to be, but I share it with everyone. Sometimes the staff needs to make calls and have a place to work. Why should I hog the desk, know what I mean?"

I nodded like I did, assuming he was either super nice and thoughtful or really crafty.

"I'm going to step out and check on a few things, give you some peace to complete the application. If you have your driver's license and social security, I can copy those now and make this move along faster." He stood.

I dug into Carson's backpack and pulled out the cards he wanted, then continued to type in the pertinent info like my birthday and home address.

"I'll give you a few," he said and stepped out of the room.

The location of the room and the way the desk was positioned, no one could see in unless they were by the freezer. I finished the application as I listened for the sound of his footsteps to fade. I contemplated my next move. The room was sparse on places to look for anything that might incriminate Lason. No filing cabinet. No shelves or credenza. Just the desk and bulletin board. I quickly shifted through the papers on the board. Nothing. Only a picture of what I assumed was an employee, their new baby, and their spouse, who was not Lason.

Out in the large room, employees were chatting. I stuck my head out and scanned the area. No sign of Lason. No sign of a copier either. Best guess was he went to customer service to copy my stuff. This gave me a few minutes to snoop. I scuttled to the desk, one of those metal and faux wood-top jobs with two drawers to the side and one center. The bottom side drawer might hold files, so I tried there first. Nothing. Mostly blank manila file folders and a couple marked *schedule* and *emergency contacts*. I pulled the latter out and flipped through the pages. Lason's emergency contact listed a woman and supplied an address and number. I used my phone's camera to take a picture, then stuffed the file back into the drawer.

Frustrated at how technology now made snooping super hard, or possibly easier if one were tech-savvy and could do it from their house in their jammies, I was slamming the center pencil drawer closed when Lason entered the room.

Easily I jumped ten feet, springing back from the desk as if it were on fire.

"What are you doing?" His brow furrowed.

"Looking for a pen," I said, going with the first thing that popped into my mind.

"A pen for what?" He crossed his arms.

"To sign the application." I pointed to the screen.

"It's digital."

"Yeah, but don't I print it and sign it? There's a print button on the screen." When in deep water, keep treading.

Lason laughed. His arms dropped to his side. "We don't keep anything paper anymore. You can digitally sign the application now."

To my ears, my laughter sounded false. "It's been a while since I filled out an application." At least that was true.

Lason gestured for me to go back to my chair, which I did, and he took a seat behind the desk. He handed me my license and social security card. Swiveling the screen back to face him, he scanned the screen.

"Wow, nearly ten years at the same place. Why did you leave?" His focus was back on me.

Hm... "Because my boss was the king of all buttheads" was likely not the best answer. "I wanted to start my own business. From my house." Let him think I was talking about photography. Then, inspiration struck like a light-ning bolt. "That's why this job is so appealing. With the part-time hours, I can also work on my own business, and there's no conflict of interest. That's important to me. Being honest."

"Me, too," he said. "If you want time off because your favorite band is coming to Seattle, tell me. We can work something out. I hate when people call in sick and say their Uncle Bob has died, and we all know they don't have an Uncle Bob. Those people don't last long here. We all get along here. We treat each other like family, and family doesn't lie to family."

I snorted with bitterness.

He pointed his index finger at me. "I like you, Samantha. I like that you're chasing your dreams but not so proud to do other stuff while in that fight. I think you'd be a good fit here."

"Have you had a lot of applicants?" This had been too easy.

"Nope, not really. Corporate does a sucky job of getting the word out about our department. Won't even hang a sign from our door, but they'll put signs all over deli or bakery when they need help." Now he was the one with bitterness in his voice.

I smiled and took a leap. "How soon do I start?"

"Three days. Background check takes twenty-four hours. If that goes well, then I'll call you with information about training. After which we'll get you on the schedule."

"Awesome," I said using his term.

"Yeah, for sure." He glanced at my hands. "I noticed you're married."

This was it. This was going to be the payout. Lason was gonna hit on me. My expectations were that he was a dirtbag and had to prove otherwise.

"Is that a problem?" I asked and hid my ring under my other hand.

"Not if it's a problem for your husband. We do have some later hours in the evening, and we've had people quit because their spouses don't like them to work nights or weekends. I try to manage the schedule so you aren't repeatedly getting the non-preferred hours, but we all take our turn."

"That's not going to be a problem," I said.

He raised his brows. "You sure?"

"Positive." No need to go into the whole dead not-husband story.

Lason planted both hands on his desk and rose. "Awesome then." He stuck out a hand.

We shook, and I exited from the sliding glass doors.

From inside my car, I called Precious to give her the rundown and then Toby to run a check on the name and address. I made notes about Lason in my handy journal to help with later recall. Then I plugged the address from Lason's emergency contact into my GPS and headed out.

Samantha True was on the case.

14

MONDAY

V ia an all-caps text message from my mom, I was told to join my parents for dinner in downtown Wind River. It was the last Monday of the month, which meant my mom had held a town hall meeting, and she and Dad were following it up with dinner at the Frontiersman. My mom always good stories of townfolks after a meeting. Bonus, she'd be pleased that my hair was washed and brushed and I wore a skirt. I arrived at the Frontiersman five minutes late. My parents were at the table when I slid into my seat.

"How'd the town hall go?" I asked Mom. This was a topic she could lament on for hours. My mom was a mayor that most people liked, but those who didn't like her showed up to the meetings with long lists of complaints. She handled these meetings with swift precision and didn't drag them out.

"Same. James Janikowski is still upset about sharing parking with the library."

Mr. Janikowski owned the real estate company next door to the Frontiersman. His wife taught ballet.

"Good job this evening, Elizabeth," Mrs. Peterson said as she walked by our table.

"Thanks, Joanna," Mom said with a smile. Mrs. Peterson had been my reading teacher through elementary school. She'd volunteered to learn the new reading program mom had found that was specifically for dyslexics and taught it to me, Hue, and others over the years. She'd also been a key staff member who partook in the annual fifth-grade week-long pilgrimage called Cispus, also known as outdoor school. A rite of passage for all fifth graders in the Wind River school district and an event that fueled my love for being outdoors. To this day, I had nothing but warm fuzzy thoughts about Mrs. Peterson.

She stopped next to me. "I was sorry to hear about your husband, Samantha." She squeezed my shoulder.

Her condolences caught me off guard. Then I remembered Dad had put in an obituary in the paper. Was I supposed to be a grieving widow? I blew out a deep sigh. "Thanks, Mrs. Peterson. It's been quite a shock." Truth.

She leaned in closer and said in a whisper, "Mr. Linn said he left you with some debt issues. My Earl did the same. I got back at him, though. Buried his butt in a cheap oak box instead of the fancy mahogany casket he'd picked out. The inconsiderate boob. Don't be ashamed to do the same." She gave my shoulder another squeeze.

"Thanks," I said. I suppose there was some good to the lie I'd told Mr. Linn. If word got around about the debt, then at least that might explain my reaction, or lack thereof. "From what I understand, Carson's car hit a tree and the tree fell onto his car and caused the gas to spill out. Boom. Explosion. So, casket isn't really an issue."

Her mouth made a tiny O. Then, her brows shot up as I presume she had a thought. "Even better. Some of the local discount stores sell those vases that can be used as urns for ten dollars."

"Good to know." I worried my wedding band around and around my finger.

"You hang in there," she said. Mrs. Peterson waved goodbye to my folks and was gone.

"Are you doing okay?" Mom patted my hand, forcing it to be still.

"Yep," I said. I'd ordered a beer, a local IPA. The moment the waitress sat the bottle before me, I raised it in a silent toast then chugged half of it down.

"Samantha, are you really okay? You seem fragile." Mom moved my beer slightly out of reach.

She did this to have my full attention. I gave it to her. "I really am," I said.

"Do you need money?" Mom shot a look of worry to my dad. "Are you okay being alone? Do you need to move home?"

"What? No," I said. "I'm fine. I got a job at Ralph's today."

My parents shared another look that I couldn't interpret. "I bet Mr. Toomey would take you back," Dad said.

"I bet I'd rather run naked through town on a wintery day than go back to work for him." I gestured for my beer. My mom pushed it back toward me, and I raised it for another chug. "Seriously, I've got this. It's all good."

Dad said, "Rachel called today. She's going to be deploying at the end of summer."

I put my beer down. Having to leave her daughter was one of my sister's greatest fears. "What's the plan? What about Cora?"

"She's going to come live with us until Rachel's deployment is over," Dad said.

"She's heartbroken to leave Cora," my mom added.

"You don't have to worry about me moving in, too," I said.

"What a relief," my mom said and took her own healthy sip of her cocktail.

Dad waved a frantic hand. "It's not that we don't want you home, Sammy. It's that research shows when adult children move home, they sometimes never move out. I think there's even a movie about it. Something about failing to launch. We only want—" He fumbled the last few words, making unintelligible sounds instead.

"Stop while you're ahead," I said. "Besides, I'd move back to the apartment before I move home."

Dad said, "We make a good wage from the tourists. Renting it will cost you more than you expect, and with the debt issue..." He took a drink.

"I'm not moving home," I said and put my bottle down with a bang.

"Evening Mayor, Russ, Samantha," said Chuck Elm,

owner of the market and tech shop, as he approached the table. "Pardon me for interrupting your family time." He turned to me. "I just wanted to say to you, Samantha, that I was sorry to hear about Carson." Chuck was a hippie of the highest form. He had a long scraggly beard, and his hair was pulled back into a graying ponytail. He wore Birkenstocks in summer and Birkenstocks with socks in the winter. He apparently had an endless supply of Beatles T-shirts since he rarely wore the same one twice.

"Thanks," I said.

"He did some work for me that I'm very appreciative of." Chuck shifted, looking uncomfortable. He cleared his throat. "If there's anything I can do to help with these debtors..."

Wow. Rumors did travel at the speed of sound.

I shook my head. "It's fine, Chuck. It'll work out." Wanting to change the subject, I said, "He put in a security system for you, right?" I briefly remember something of this nature happening.

He cleared his throat a second time and looked over his shoulder. He took the empty seat next to me, spun it backward so the back faced the table and sat. He lowered his voice, leaned toward me, and said, "Yeah, at first. But he helped me find my kid brother. He took off two decades ago. Served time in the armed forces and was never right after a few combat situations. I'd been looking for him for a while, but Carson managed to find him in no time." He nodded, his smile sad. "My brother died a few months back, and I got to be there with him for his last days. Thanks to Carson."

Wow. I guess there was some good in Carson after all. Yet, something Chuck said didn't fit. Maybe it was because I'd been totally clueless about the PI aspect of Carson's company or maybe I didn't make the leap like everyone else and equate a security systems guy to PI.

I was curious. "So how did Carson know you needed help finding your brother?" Like how did he know to approach Shannon about Sean? Was it something simple like, "Oh, by the way, I'm also a PI, so if you need anything..."

Chuck shrugged. "We got to talking after he finished installing the security system, and he told me he did PI work as well. He did some stuff for Graycloud, too."

Graycloud was a leader on the Cowlitz tribal council and a long-time businessman. He had a motel and diner on the outskirts of Wind River that abutted Cowlitz land.

"What sort of stuff?" I glanced at my dad. He played poker with Graycloud. Chuck, too.

"Nothing." Chuck waved his hand dismissively.

"Nothing sounds big if it required him hiring a PI," I said matter of fact.

Chuck laughed. "Not too much. More security. He'd been having problems with harassment."

I must have looked as confused as I felt. No one in their right mind would harass Graycloud. He was formidable, a strong advocate and community voice.

Chuck said, "Someone was sabotaging his business. Trouble with the health department, break-ins, that sort of thing."

I put the pieces together. "And Carson set up security

to help catch whoever it was." That made more sense. Unanswered questions nagged at me.

"Yes, that's what Carson did," Dad said. "He was very helpful."

Why did a man move to another town, take a false identity, and start over? What was he running from? I couldn't imagine Carson running from anything. So, I had to wonder, why here? What brought Carson to Wind River? And why hide the PI portion of his job from just me?

I scoffed, briefly forgetting that Carson hid pretty much all kinds of truths from me. My parents looked at me in question.

"Was it something I said?" my dad asked.

"You're right. Carson was very helpful *in that situation*." Implying that currently the situation Carson had left me in wasn't very helpful. It was nice to share the sentiment, even if they were thinking of the money lie I told.

"We're sorry, sweetheart," my mom said, putting her hand over mine.

I turned to Chuck. "I hope things with Graycloud are better."

Chuck pulled at his beard. "Hard to say. This has been going on for so long." He looked at my dad. "What would you say, Russ? Ever since we got those offers for the land, things have been off. Each of us having a bit of trouble."

I studied my father. There had been no mention of trouble.

"Just a break-in," he said to me then turned to Chuck. "We all run businesses. Break-ins are bound to happen.

There's a meth problem in this country, and Wind River is no exception."

"When was this?" I asked.

"Before Christmas," my mom said. "Stole a few computers but your father has so much paper, books, and boxes in that building, the burglars probably gave up looking for anything of value." She chuckled.

"What land?" I had a million questions.

My father sighed. "A long time ago, your mother and I bought land out by Graycloud's diner."

My mom jumped in. "It was before the tribe was given designated land by the government. Graycloud's idea was that if locals bought land near where the tribe had settled, then maybe we could use it to help the tribe get established. There was always the chance the government would take the land into trust and we'd break even." It was Mom's turn to scoff. Native American rights were high on her list of priorities. "But we know the government is slow to move and doesn't always do the right thing, so we decided to take matters into our own hands."

She continued, "Our goal with the land is to sell to builders who will create jobs for locals, specifically tribe members. Or better yet, sell to a tribal member and help them build something. Start a business. Anything."

"My mom was part Cowlitz," Chuck said.

I looked between my parents. "Did the land get put into a trust to the tribe? Isn't it now protected land?"

"Nope," Dad said. "It's prime real estate so the government didn't touch it when it gave the tribe their land. But it butts up to tribal land so lots of people assume the same."

"So, you"—I pointed to my parents—"Chuck, Gray-cloud, and who else own land there?"

"The Stillmans, Jimmy Linn, the Wagenknechts, and the Kleppners."

"Sean and Shannon?" I was surprised.

"No, Sean's parents," Dad said. "You know how adamant Sean senior is about keeping outsiders out of Wind River." Dad rolled his eyes and shook his head.

Pride flowed through me. My parents were good people. And they were good citizens in their community. "And no one has tried to buy and develop the land?"

"Sure," Chuck said. "It's value has soared. Million-dollar views. But it backs up to the reservation, so there are some limitations."

Dad said, "We've had several offers, but we never felt like the projects were beneficial to the community. Or they only wanted certain parcels."

"Last year some big company tried to buy the land for a fancy resort. Showed us some impressive numbers on paper about how many Native Americans they would employ and how it would help the community," Chuck said. He patted my dad on the back and smiled. "But your dad did some digging and didn't like what he found."

I raised my brows.

Dad smirked. "I found nothing."

"Nothing bad?" I was confused.

"Nothing, nothing. A shell company, it looked like to me. Had another resort like the one they proposed up and running in New York and one being built outside Houston. All somewhat near reservations. I didn't like it. Another similarity to these resorts is the quick access to main interstates. I once did a story on drug trafficking, and these resorts would be good gateways for drug trafficking and money laundering." Dad raised his brows and wiggled them.

"You watch too much crime TV, Russ," my mom said. "Money laundering isn't done through high-end resorts. It's done through car washes and strip clubs."

I teased, "That sounds a lot like stereotyping. And now you sound like you watch too much crime TV."

Everyone chuckled.

Dad continued, "This company talked about how it would help the community but, personally, how can one be invested in our community if they don't live here? Raise kids here? That was the heart of this matter."

"They can't," my mother said as she took my dad's hand. "So we all agreed not to sell."

I nodded in understanding. "At those poker meetings, are you guys really playing poker?" I teased. It sounded like much more was happening.

Chuck and my dad laughed.

"Yeah," Chuck said. "Mostly, though, we pick your dad's brain about fantasy leagues."

Everyone laughed. Dad was reigning champ in his fantasy league three years running. I'd been trying to get into the league for the last two years but had been told that, as long as he was winning, another True wasn't allowed to play for fear that we'd sweep.

We spent the rest of dinner in pleasant conversation, though my mind continued to drift to all my unanswered questions. And more kept piling up.

Afterward, I decided to sit in the park for a bit to think. The deck of the Frontiersman overlooked the dark blue of Windy River. Between the river and the Frontiersman was a portion of the park.

I found an empty bench and stared out at the water. Bits and pieces of the last few days weren't adding up. Nothing I'd learned about Carson since discovering his betrayal should have been kept a secret from me. Okay, maybe the wife thing might have been hard to tell me. But why not tell me he was also a PI? Why make me one, too? I got not being able to tell me confidential information about Chuck and such, but the secrecy felt over-the-top. Was the term private investigator viewed negatively? Enough to keep it on the down-low?

I had to admit, Carson using the security system business as the main way to become established was clever. Who wouldn't trust the man who set you up to be safe? Of course, the BTK killer (bind, torture, kill) worked at ADT Security Systems, so there was that.

And what was with the backpack? Why make sure I get the PI business? A business I was wholly unskilled for. Signs and clues were around me, but I was missing them. I was afraid my anger was blinding me to what I should be seeing, and I didn't know how to get over it.

"Mrs. Holmes?" a male voice said from behind me.

"Not it!" I said and raised my hand like Precious and I had always done when someone had to do the grunt job. I chuckled. Cracking myself up with my own joke. Precious would be proud.

"Excuse me?" the man said. He stepped into my periphery.

He was just shy of six feet, dark hair with a former receding hairline that now sported new growth. He wore flip-flops and long cargo shorts, much like Carson had preferred to wear. They seemed to be around the same age. Carson's pockets had always held the most interesting gadgets. Hey, maybe that should have been a clue.

I faced him and said deadpanned, "I said I wasn't Mrs. Holmes. I don't know a Mrs. Holmes."

"Oh, I thought you were married to Carson Holmes."

I waved away his words. "Married might not be the right word. Regardless, that didn't make me Mrs. Holmes."

His brow furrowed. "I'm afraid I don't understand."

"Me, either," I said.

"Do you mind if I sit?" He moved toward the bench, a small smile on his face.

If I said no, would he just stand there? Go away? The idea was tempting. I slid to the end, giving him room.

"I knew your husband." Sitting next to me, he nodded solemnly.

"I figured." Carson's pack was between us, my phone sticking out of the front pocket. Needing to fidget, I took it out and rolled the phone over and over in my hands.

"He was a good guy. A funny guy. Quick wit." He leaned against the bench and laid an arm across the back, his hand by my shoulder. The urge to move away was strong.

"If you say so. How did you know him?" I prepared for another curveball.

"We did some work together." His attention was on the water, and there was a sadness in his voice.

"What kind of work?" I couldn't wait to hear this.

He glanced at me. "All kinds of stuff. Mostly we consulted. I'm sorta in the same business as him." He studied his fingernails and continued, "I gave him my overflow accounts, and he'd help me out with more diffi-cult cases." He held out a hand, ready for a shake. "Joe Cooper."

His hand was strong but damp, and it took a lot for me not to wipe my own hand on my skirt when he let go. I said his name over in my head several times trying to remember it, then added a feature for association. Joe, whose hair plugs were raked with a hoe, Joe.

"Samantha True," I said.

Joe didn't look like a PI. Not that Carson had either. But Joe seemed more the sort to stand before a boardroom table, bark out orders, and push other's pressure points. There was a hardness about him, something that made him come off as controlling. Maybe it was the lack of warmth in his narrow eyes. But, I suspected, any PI who experienced the underbelly of life would have a similar look.

"Ah, that's why you don't identify yourself as Holmes. You kept your maiden name."

I nodded. "Where did you say you were from? You mentioned having a PI firm."

"I said I was in security."

"Actually, you said you did the same sort of work, but now I know it was security. And Carson helped with that?"

Cooper chuckled. "Carson had a knack for weaknesses and how to exploit them," he said. Rather pointedly, I thought.

"Did you want something, Joe Cooper?"

"To offer my condolences." He smiled softly, but the sentiment didn't reach his eyes.

"And?" My father was a beat reporter who could sniff out a story buried deep in a pile of poop. I wasn't his child for nothing.

Cooper chuckled. "You have me there. I'm sorry to bother you. I went to the office, but no one was around."

"Did you try calling the numbers on the office window?" Currently, the window was a large board from the local hardware store. Would he bring that up? What did it mean if he didn't?

"No. This is an issue better handled in person."

I sniffed a lie.

He continued, "It's not easy to lose someone and, trust me, I want more than anything to leave you to grieve, but Carson was working with me on something sensitive in nature. Something that could get me in trouble if my client finds out I shared. I was wondering if maybe you came across a file with my name on it?" He ducked his head in embarrassment.

I lied, too. Sorta. "There are no files. I have nothing. Certainly nothing with your name on it." That last part was true.

"Maybe it's in a safe or safe deposit box?" Cooper pressed.

"None of those, either." Truth again. No need to mention the secret IT room or cloud.

Cooper harrumphed. His hand repeatedly balling up into a fist and then releasing. "Is that Carson's backpack?" He eyed the pack between us.

"I wish I could help you, but I can't." I stood and glanced back at the Frontiersman, slipping the backpack over one shoulder. I tucked my phone in my skirt pocket.

Leo was walking toward me, dressed in his uniform. Maybe he had information about the guy who tried to grab my backpack.

Cooper stood as well. "I'm sorry if I'm being pushy, but I could be in real trouble here. Is there a laptop or bag where he could have stored it? Maybe he put the files on a thumb drive? How did you get his pack?" He eyed the pack on my back.

My spidey senses went on high alert. Maybe it was a coincidence to bring up the backpack, but I didn't really believe in coincidences.

"Hey, Leo," I said calling attention to him. Cooper needed to know that a cop was approaching and I was on a first-name basis with him.

"Samantha," Leo said and surveyed Cooper. He came to stand next to me.

"This is Joe Cooper. He says he knew Carson, and Carson did some work for him."

"With me. Not for me." Cooper thrust out his hand.

In my skirt pocket, my phone came alive, buzzing and

honking out the most atrocious noise I'd ever heard. I dug it out, pulling the pocket with it so that it fell like a droopy ear.

I studied the phone. The app Toby had installed was glowing red, so I pressed it. Immediately, a video came up. I recognized my house. A strange man was going through it, tossing cushions off the couch like a trainer tosses fish to seals. He seemed familiar, and it then dawned on me this was the same guy from outside the paper and Lockett's office. Possibly the same guy from the casino.

"Are you kidding me?" I yelled. "Get out of my house!" I screamed at the video. He continued to toss my place. Then the unimaginable happened. Precious stepped through the door. A large urn in her hands.

Leo pressed against me so he could see the screen. He mumbled something into the mic on his shoulder.

"Run, Precious!" I said. I put the phone close to my face and watched as the man charged toward Precious. She flung the urn at him, but it crashed against the wall. He reached Precious and pushed her into the wall. She crumbled into a pile on my floor. He stared down at her for far longer than normal. Not that anything about this moment was relatively close to normal.

"Police are on their way, Samantha," Leo said, then continued to speak cop talk into the mic on his shoulder.

Something inside me snapped. The world around me became hazy with a red-tinged glow. My barely contained anger exploded out. I glanced at Leo, then lunged for his gun. "Gimme your gun. I'm going to shoot this menace."

Leo quickly side-stepped me and batted down my hand. "Are you crazy? You can't have my gun."

"I can't sit here making fake polite conversation with this stranger. I have to *do something!*"

Leo eyed Cooper, then said to me, "I'll take you there myself. Come on." Leo grabbed me by the elbow and hustled me away. "Are you insane? Going for a cop's gun? I could arrest you for that."

"I'm angry," I said and noticed I was outpacing him to the building. "And I'm not going to take it anymore."

15

MONDAY

By the time Leo and I got to my house, which was minutes later, the burglar was long gone. Leo wanted to clear the place before letting me in. But on the ride there, I'd watched from the video monitor on my phone and knew the man was gone. I'd watched him get a text and bolt and then Precious come to and prop herself up against the wall.

While Leo went off to make sure the house was empty, I rushed to Precious. A slow trickle of blood ran down from her temple.

"How you doing?" I asked, crouching next to her. "You want me to call the paramedics?"

"He had the power of Bigfoot but definitely not the manners," she mumbled.

I took her hand away and looked at the large bump and small cut on the side of her head. "I don't think you need stitches. Come on, let's get you to a chair." I helped her up.

My downstairs living room, dining room, and kitchen had been tossed. Drawers opened and emptied, cushions off the couch, food spilled from the pantry. What photos I'd left on the wall and fireplace mantel were broken, smashed to the floor, their backs torn off.

"Do you think it was Bigfoot?" she asked as I lowered her onto the couch.

"Why would Bigfoot be in my house?"

"Why, indeed. Maybe because you live by the wildlife reserve. Maybe he was hungry." She leaned back, resting her head against a cushion.

"I'm going to get you ice," I said and went into the kitchen.

"You know what a crime scene is?" Leo said angrily as he came into the room. "Because you're messing up mine."

I packed a Ziploc bag with ice. "You're just mad because I refused to wait in the car. You and I both know he was wearing gloves."

"That explains why his hands were so soft. I don't imagine Bigfoot has soft hands," Precious mumbled. I put an ice pack to her head and put her hand over it to hold it in place.

Leo assessed for a head injury, asking her to track his finger. "What if he wasn't alone or left a booby trap or something? Did you think of that?"

Nope, I hadn't. But I trusted Carson's system. Had there been a second guy, the video would have picked him up. There was a camera at the top of the stairs, though not in the bedroom. Apparently, Carson did draw the line in some places. Go figure.

Leo rubbed up and down Precious's arm. "You're gonna be okay, Precious. Maybe a slight concussion."

"What a mess," I said, suddenly overcome with exhaustion. I sat in the middle of my living room floor and buried my head in my hands. Seeing Precious get hurt had scared the living daylights out of me.

"I don't know what's going on here, but my guess is you're in over your head," Leo said, coming to stand next to me.

"You think?" I mumbled from between my hands.

He nudged me on the shoulder, and when I looked up, he was offering me a hand. He pulled me up and guided me to the overstuffed chair. After fixing the cushion, he pushed me into the seat.

"What *do you think* is going on?" Leo squatted beside me. Was this probing a part of his investigation or because he knew me? Not that it mattered, but I was scared, and having a cop in the house was nice. Having a cop friend in the house was even better.

"I honestly don't know. Nothing has made sense since I was told Carson was dead."

When the doorbell rang, we exchanged a questioning look, then I rose to get it.

"Bigfoot's back," Precious mumbled.

Standing on my doorstep was a tall, heavily bearded man who appeared to be my age. Clearly from Portland with his thin wire glasses, tight skinny jeans, and a salmon-colored button-down shirt. Attached to his pocket was a name badge. Cam, messenger from The Mountains.

"Good evening, ma'am. I'm Cam. I've come to talk to you about your ignorance. We all have them, so no judgment, but I'd like to help you with yours."

I must have looked as incredulous as I felt.

He put up a hand in an attempt to stop me from speaking and smiled kindly. But he had nothing to worry about from me. My brain couldn't even process what was happening here.

"I know I've shocked you. Maybe even hurt your feelings. But I do it from love. Sister, I want to help you find the truth." He handed me a pamphlet. On it was written Mountain Church. A silhouette of a mountain with a cross and a Sasquatch were under the church name.

"Are you kidding me? Is this a joke?" My mind was still on the break-in. I glanced at Precious and wondered if this guy's appearance on my doorstep might be some sort of poorly timed joke.

Cam gave a slight smile. "I know, weird, right? But at Mountain Church, we can help you find your way. We can help you find the truth and see there is so much more around you. If only you open your eyes and look." He tapped the pamphlet. "We can help wash away your sins. And you do have sins."

My fuse was already frayed and short from the break-in and Precious being hurt. I wasn't in the headspace to be reasonable. His words struck deep, and all I heard was a personal attack on my morals. I hadn't asked to have a man cheat on his wife with me. I hadn't asked to be the other woman. And, yes, ignorance was my defense.

"Sin?" I fairly screamed in his face. "You want sin? I'll commit one right now. Then at least we can be on the same page." Cam stepped back, and I stepped forward. I knocked the pamphlets from his arms like a football player strips a quarterback of the ball. Sudden and hard. Paper scattered everywhere.

"How dare you come to my house and talk to me about my sin?" I screamed, picking up papers and ripping them in two.

"Hey," Cam said, "stop!" He tried to snatch the handful of papers from me. I stopped ripping and began repeatedly whacking him with them. He covered his face.

"What about your sin, Cam?" I screamed.

An arm came around my waist, lifted me from the ground, and spun me to the side. I was wildly beating the air with the pamphlets.

"You've come at a bad time," Leo said to Cam. "And might I see your permit that allows you to go door-to-door?"

I stopped swinging and slumped against Leo, my feet dangling from the ground, tears on my face.

I assumed Cam showed his permit because Leo set me on the ground and faced me. He stared hard at me. "Help pick up these papers and let this guy go on his way."

I nodded mutely. I picked up as many as I could then thrust them at Cam, who was staring oddly at me. When Leo wasn't looking, I kicked Cam in the shin then stormed into my house.

A few seconds later, Leo followed, shutting the door behind him. I'd thrown myself back into the armchair and was wiping tears from my face. Precious was holding a pamphlet.

"He looked like Bigfoot, right?" Precious showed me the image with the Sasquatch under it. "So weird."

"I feel like I'm in bizarro world."

She said, "I think I was supposed to be here tonight so I could find out about this church. I'm going to check it out. You should come with me."

"I think I'm uninvited," I said.

"You two are a mess," Leo said then pointed his finger at me. "You need to get a grip." He'd basically said the same thing to me when I'd vomited all over his crime scene those many years ago.

"Really? Okay, I'll do that right now," I said and showed him my middle finger.

He nodded. "Very mature."

"I'm having a really crappy week, Leo. Try to see things from my perspective, if only for a second. I've been living a lie. I don't know what's real and what's not. My car was repo'ed, I had a guy try to steal my backpack, and a man break into my house. *After* someone broke into my office that I didn't even know I owned. So, *forgive me* if my seams are starting to split." I pointed to the door. "*Forgive me* if I fight back when someone tugs at them." I let my head fall back to rest against the chair. "Are we done here? I have a house to clean up."

The chair dipped slightly as Leo sat on the edge. I eyed him warily.

"Forgive me for being an ass. You have had a helluva week and"—he cleared his throat—"you're holding it together remarkably well. Between this happening to you and someone trying to torch Graycloud's restaurant, I don't know what's going on anymore."

I sat up, astonished. "What? When did this happen?"

"Last week...Thursday, I think." He rubbed a hand down his face, looking as exhausted as I felt.

Thursday was the day after Carson died.

"Is Graycloud okay?" I couldn't imagine anyone messing with the giant.

"He's irate. He thinks someone is trying to get his land." Leo pinched the bridge of his nose and sighed wearily.

"Someone is stupid," I said. "But they must know the land isn't protected."

Leo leaned back, studying me. "How did you know that?"

"I learned about it tonight. I also learned our parents"—I waved a finger between us—"are also landowners up there."

"Yeah, I found out about that a few months ago." Leo looked lost in thought.

"Did you know my dad and Chuck also experienced issues at their place of business? Break-ins. I find that curious." Curious was my preferred word for my interest. It sounded better than nosy.

"Coincidence maybe?" He didn't look convinced.

"I'm not sure I believe in coincidences."

"Me, either," he said.

"My parents' restaurant has had deliveries gone missing," Precious said.

"Not a coincidence," Leo said.

"I pity the fool who rumbles with Graycloud," I said, wishing I had the same awe Graycloud commanded and strength he exhibited.

"Maybe you should get some help. Beyond the police. We're overwhelmed with stuff right now, and you won't be on the priority list. Not that we won't investigate this. It's just that—"

"I know what you're saying." I slumped back. I was on my own.

Leo rubbed his chin. "What about that lawyer guy, the one who told you about Carson?"

"Yeah, funny thing about him. He doesn't exist."

"What? I talked to him." His expression told me he thought I was nuts.

"I went to his office. It was cleaned out. Like he was never there." I blew into my hands and made like I was tossing air into the wind. "Gone, like a ghost."

Leo grunted in frustration. "Irony here is I would tell anyone else in your position to get a PI and try to figure this out. You need a professional to track down that lawyer and Carson's real identity."

"Wait, I'm a PI."

Leo laughed, a real deep belly laugh. "Please, stop joking."

"Show him," Precious said. "He's the sort that needs proof." She laughed at her own joke.

I pulled up the image of my license on my phone and waved the screen in front of his face. "See. I'm legit."

That shut him up. He grabbed my phone. "I'd like to know who signed off on your test. You did take a test, right?"

"Of course, I did," I said with false bravado. I would like to know who signed off on it as well.

"When?"

"When what?"

"When did you take it?"

"A while ago."

"Why?"

"Why what?" I could play this game all day if it meant he would drop the subject.

He sighed heavily. "Why did you take it?"

I scrambled for an answer. I'd always heard to stick as close to the truth as possible when lying. "Well, I'd started studying for it when I was in college. You know, back when I was studying to be a forensic photographer."

His eyebrows shot up. "And that was so successful you figured, why not be a PI, too?"

"I *had the flu!*"

He rolled his eyes. "Continue with the story."

"At first, I thought it might come in handy as a good backup plan." I gave a one-shoulder shrug. "Then I got a wild hair and decided to do it. You know...I'm not good at being a failure, so..."

"So ten years later, you decide to take the PI test. All while your husband is a PI, but you think he installs security systems." He narrowed his gaze, disbelieving.

Yeah, the whole thing sounded lame and unbelievable.

He turned to Precious. "Look at me and tell me she's telling the truth."

"Which one of you? I see two." She gave him a half smile.

He faced me. "My guess?" he said, pointing a finger at me. "Your husband—I'll just call him that—took the test and put your name on it. Question is *why* and who signed the test? They had to be in on it."

"Pfft," I said. "That's a crazy idea." I couldn't meet his gaze.

"Find out who signed that test and start asking questions." He closed his eyes and pinched the bridge of his nose. "I can't believe I just said that." He opened his eyes, his attention back on me. "Hire someone, hire that guy who worked with Carson. Get to the bottom of this. And watch your back."

I said, "Consider it done."

16

FRIDAY

I spent the majority of the week being a good sister to Rachel, helping her through the process of coming to terms with deployment and leaving Cora with us. Correction, with my parents. She stated more than once she feared my influence over my six-year-old niece.

I also helped Precious. I took her to the hospital to have her head looked at then stayed up with her watching *Harry and the Hendersons*. I even helped in her office with filing while she logged data and information from her weekend out in the Hoh National Rainforest with her Bigfoot buddies a few weeks back. The entire group was very secretive. She wouldn't even let me peek at what they'd discovered, but I could tell she was excited about it.

On Tuesday, I did a second drive-by the address on Lason's contact form. I struck gold as a woman my mom's age (I'm guessing, she wore a large brimmed hat) was out in the yard gardening. On Wednesday, Toby's search told us the woman at the address was Molly Smith. Further digging indicated she was probably his mother. Unless Lason was into cougars, I was pretty sure Toby's findings were right. Toby hacked into Lason's social media, and there was nothing remotely scandalous there either.

Wednesday, I spent following Sean Kleppner who appeared to lead a very boring life for a man who'd won two million dollars. He went to work. He went to lunch. He went home. A quick call to Shannon led me to believe this was his M.O., and I simply needed to wait him out in order to get the money shot. This PI thing was dullsville.

Finally, Ralph's called. Training to grocery shop for others spanned two days. Ralph's spent an entire day telling us how to talk positively to customers, assuring us we'd get stopped a lot and asked to solve problems. Apparently, the small handheld walkie-talkie assigned to me each day was my lifeline to a manager should I ever have a "rabid customer run-in."

Once, Carson bought me a can of bear spray. I made a mental note to pack it when I worked at Ralph's. I'd shopped at Ralph's on triple coupon day; the scene was something out of a horror movie, weapon wielding, name calling, and all. And that was customer to customer.

On Friday, my last day of training, I follow another *Click and Go* employee named Natalie as she filled an order. Natalie was in the restroom while I waited in the main *Click and Go* space, watching others process orders. A woman my age came in and plopped down on one of the flat-bed carts and tucked her head in her hands. She was pretty in that overdone way. Her dark hair was dyed pink at the tips, her clothes were form-fitting, and she made the tacky, rubbery, neon-yellow vest we wore look like a fashion accessory. I made it look like a gunnysack.

"Lason Dell has done it again," she told the room, looking between her fingers to see who was paying attention. Our eyes met, and I shrugged. I had nothing to contribute.

But my ears perked up. A few of the guys made faces at each other then went back to work.

"When are you going to learn, Tara? You have to ignore Lason." This from an older woman ringing up groceries at the register and bagging them. As much as Tara was put together, this woman was frumpy. Baggy T-shirt, baggy jeans on a pear-shaped figure, and Ugg slip-on boots that looked like slippers. Her gray hair was cut in a short bob, and she sported a no-nonsense expression.

Oh, no. Was Lason a douche bag? I dreaded having to tell Marni that. Of course, who would be surprised? Not the girl who married a married man. Nothing could surprise her anymore.

"You know how hard it is for me to do that, Jean? You know how I feel about him." Tara shook her head. "I can't even focus on what I'm supposed to be doing. Maybe I need to go home."

Someone in the room groaned. My guess it was one of the guys.

Were Lason and Tara fooling around? Was Lason a woman hopper? Only left one when he was comfortably in with another? I was beginning to think so.

Tara huffed. "It's not like I'm leaving you short-staffed. The new girl can do some orders."

Everyone in the room stared at me.

Jean said, "She looks smart enough to pick it up quick."

"Thanks," I mumbled.

Natalie came out and stood next to me. "What's going on," she asked under her breath.

"Something about Tara and Lason Dell. She thinks she needs to go home."

Natalie rolled her eyes. "Of course, she does. Lason is such a dufus when it comes to her. We're so tired of it. Their stupid drama."

I had more questions, but thought that when we were on the floor might be a better time. Less listening ears.

Jean said, looking at Natalie, "You think you and the new girl can do two at a time. We're swamped today."

Natalie shot Tara a look of contempt before answering Jean, "Yeah." To me she said, "Get a cart and four baskets." She nodded her head to the supply area. The baskets were large black industrial and double-the-size of milk carton crates. They folded down nicely and, when open, stacked one onto the other. Managing the cart wasn't rocket science. There were two levers, one red, one green, and a u-shaped handle that made steering awkward but doable.

Jean snatched some papers from one of the boxes on the wall. The boxes were four down and four wide. They resembled employee mailboxes, but there were no names to indicate a box belonged to anyone. Almost every box had paper in it. Jean handed the papers she took to me. It was an order. The time was highlighted. I had four hours to get it done before the customer came to pick it up.

Natalie pointed to boxes. "That's how you'll know it's a busy day. The red marker over the box says that's where we are in the orders. You'll come in, grab the order with the red marker, move the marker to the next box, then scan your printout with your handheld." She tapped a bar code on the corner of the printout. "Others toss the printout, but I keep mine so I can refer to it. It's up to you." They'd gone over this in training, but the review was helpful. I kept the printout in my vest pocket.

I glanced at the paper-lined mailboxes. "Busy is an understatement," I said, noting all but three boxes had an order. Jean had taken my papers from the first box. There was a lot of work that needed to be done.

"Payday," one of the guys said. "Always swamped."

Tara was gathering her purse and a raincoat from a locker across the room. "If Lason calls and asks about me, you tell him he did this. That he's responsible. Tell him I complained of feeling nauseous. That should give him a good scare." She stalked out of the room, the door swinging closed slowly behind her.

My impression of Lason from Tara wasn't stacking up to be good. I made a mental note of my observation, fearing I might forget something, wishing I could jot everything down. I made a second mental note to record this in my notebook first chance I could break free from Natalie. Particularly the part about feeling nauseous.

"Come on," Natalie said. "It's going to be a long day."

I followed her out into the store, our carts between us.

"Let's try to stick together in case you have questions." She reviewed the order with me, reminding me that it was broken up in sections, how the items were placed in the store. She showed me how she noted any substitutions. Apparently, substitutions increased the closer the order was to payday.

"Always go high with subs," Natalie said, pushing her cart toward the produce. "Higher value, better brand. You know."

I nodded. We worked in silence and quickly. After the third item, I found a system and didn't need the printout. Read item, scan it with handheld, bag it. Not a lot of brain power, but I enjoyed it. I was able to think a lot while I worked. I could move at my pace. No one was hovering. And bonus was this job put money in my pocket. Until I figured out the PI business, I was going to hang onto this job. A crash mat wasn't bad. I needed a safety net the way my luck was going.

Natalie came over and read my list. "Looks like I have a vegetarian and you a meat eater. I'm going to head toward the dairy section. You do the meat and meet me there. Sound good?"

"Sure," I said. We separated at the bakery. Once out of her sight, I dictated my observation and the incident with Tara in an email to myself, afraid my notebook would draw unnecessary attention.

The meat section took up a corner of the store. The meat counter was the point of the corner and jutted out with long rows of coffin coolers to each side. Regular meat on one side. Organic, free-range, grass-fed, and hormone-free on the other. Next to the organics was the deli counter.

I was loading five packs of organic ninety-six percent fat-free ground beef into a carton when I glanced at the meat counter and froze.

Tyson Lockett.

He was standing there big as he pleased, not looking over his shoulder but studying the meat in the display. He wasn't dressed in his gray suit, but a karate uniform—a gi —with a black belt around his waist.

I acted on instinct. I rolled my cart behind him, blocking him in, and waited.

He completed his order and made to leave, not looking at me. "Excuse me," he mumbled and tried to go around me. I rolled forward playing the blocking game.

That's when I got his attention. He glanced my way and rolled his eyes. Not in the least bit surprised to see me.

"What's your game?" I bit out.

"What? I don't know what you're talking about." He met my stare with a steady look of his own.

"Are you even a lawyer? Am I going to find out that you and my husband"—I did air quotes—"are conning me or something? I went to your office." More air quotes around office. "Was that even real?"

Tyson shook his head. "No, that wasn't my office, but I am a lawyer."

I wagged my finger at him. "And I'm not the only one looking for you. Some tall dark Neanderthal is, too."

Tyson shrugged. "I told you to just walk away from this."

I suppose with that black belt around his waist he wasn't too worried about the other man. I made a mental note to take self-defense classes.

"Yeah, because walking away from a relationship and marriage is something people do with ease." I repressed the urge to smack the meat packages out of his hands.

"I know this can't be easy, but it's for your own good," Tyson said and tried to step past me. I blocked him again. He juked to the other side, but I backed up and cut him off with the cart. We did this back and forth game a few seconds before I snapped. I stomped on the brake and moved to stand in front of him. I poked my finger in his chest. He backed up a step.

"You owe me an explanation. Or something. Since that day in your office, I've been almost kicked out of my house, my car taken, my business was broken into, my house was broken into, I've been followed, and...*and*"— my voice rose several octaves as I got into his face —"someone tried to steal my backpack. Then this guy tells me Carson took off with some confidential work—"

"What guy?" Tyson said, his voice low.

"Another PI, Cooper was his last name. Asked if Carson left me a thumb drive or something."

Lockett surveyed the store before returning his attention to me. "Stay away from him. Trust no one."

My anger flared. Warnings without explanation were just words. "Stay away? Ever since you told me Carson was dead, I've been in the dark. I'm two steps behind whatever the heck is going on in my life and *you*"—I poked this chest so hard my finger bent back—"*you* put me there. Maybe you should think about enlightening me a little. Because if I die, it'll be on your head." A shiver of fear ran through me. I'd said the last part as a threat in hopes to make him react. Instead, I scared myself.

"Help me," I pleaded.

Lockett sighed and narrowed his eyes. "Cooper is bad news. Carson knew that at the end. Cooper's probably making sure Carson didn't leave you anything from the grave. He didn't, did he?"

"You mean other than a bunch of lies and a PI business I don't know how to run? No." I purposely skipped over the backpack.

"Good. If he did, get rid of it. Don't tell anyone. Once they realize you know nothing, they'll leave you alone." Lockett came off confident with his assessment.

I recalled the conversation Cooper and I had. If what Lockett was saying was true, then Cooper knew I had nothing. The person who broke into my house had found nothing because nothing was stolen. Only time would tell if this stranger was telling me the truth.

"I hope you're right," I said. "But why should I believe anything you say? Is your name even Lockett?"

Lockett rolled his eyes. "It is, and I'm really a lawyer. My advice to you is to butt out of everything. Go away. Go on vacation. Get out of town."

I scoffed then pointed to my vest. "Remember the part about my account being cleaned out?"

He took me by the upper arm and leaned in close. He

appeared frustrated, though his attention was everywhere before briefly fixing on me. He seemed slightly...alarmed? "Trust me, Samantha. These guys are not good guys," he insisted.

Was he a good guy? I wasn't sure.

"Are you sure Carson didn't leave anything behind?" He stared hard at me, watching my expression.

I nodded, mute.

"Then you're going to be okay. Do you understand?"

I nodded again. Not sure that I did understand, except to know that the backpack was significant. "Why did he involve me in this?" I mumbled more to myself.

Lockett gripped my arm tighter. "If you should find something, something unusual, just get rid of it, or give it to me and I'll get rid of it."

"There's nothing," I said and pulled from his grip.

"Take care of yourself," he said and stepped around my cart. He arched a brow, waiting for me to nod, then took off, walking briskly away. It was then I noticed he was barefoot.

Weird.

Locket left me with one hope. That the players looking for whatever Carson left behind might believe I didn't have anything. Maybe life would settle down, and I could catch my breath.

Admittedly, I was curious to know more about the real Carson and why he'd picked me. As angry as I was with him, as disgusted as I was by his actions, I was also just as curious.

17

FRIDAY

After my shift, I found myself sitting in my car, thinking over everything Lockett said. Particularly his warnings. What I needed to know was, could I walk away from this without any answers? I didn't have to search inside myself for long to know the answer. No, I couldn't. Everything I'd done over the past few days told me that.

I could have easily shut down the PI business and never taken one step into that world. I didn't have to go back to Lockett's office or taunt the stranger in the car. Why did this happen to me? I didn't know. But I was going to find out. I refused to be the stereotypical victim.

I dunno, Officer. He just did these things that seemed odd, but I preferred to be blissfully ignorant. Are you sure that's a body in our septic tank? Or backyard? Or closet?

A glance at my watch told me Toby was not in *high time* so I gave him a call.

"Dudette," he said after answering on the second ring.

"Dude." I smiled. "I have a question for you."

"Hit me." He made a suck-in sound, likely taking a hit off his vape pen.

"Can you keep a secret?" Toby needed to know the truth about Carson, and I needed his help.

"Is it about aliens or Bigfoot? Because I might have a hard time keeping that kind of secret."

"It's about Carson. And it's not good."

"Frack, that sounds ominous." He took another puff. "Do I want to know this secret? Because I don't know if I do."

I let the silence sit between us. Another person knowing my secret shame was not high on my must-share list. But I needed his help, and he needed to know the stakes.

"Toby, Carson was involved in something bad. The office has been broken into. My house has been broken into. Someone is looking for something. I need to know how deep this goes."

He blew out a puff. "Well, I suppose it's serendipitous I picked a mint and vanilla flavored juice. Hit me with the truth."

Like ripping off a Band-Aid I said, "Carson was legally married to another woman, and Carson Holmes wasn't his real name. We were his pretend life."

A low, slow curse came out of Toby's mouth. "For reals?"

"Yep." I stared out the window and scanned the cars around me. Once again, I couldn't shake the feeling of being watched. "But listen, no one knows. Well, Precious knows. You know. Leo Stillman and this guy Tyson Lockett."

"Your dad said there's a funeral for Carson. What? How?"

"I'll bring an urn with fireplace ash in it." Maybe I'll put a bag of dog poo in it instead. That felt fitting.

"Jeez." He took three quick puffs and one slow blow. "I don't know what to think. He completely fooled me."

Ready to move on from this conversation, I said, "Fooled everyone. I need you to get your head in the game. I need your help."

"Totally. Send it."

"Can you try and get me the specifics on someone? I want to know where they're from. Where they live now. Everything you can find. See if you can find a connection between him and Carson. See if you can find the real Carson."

"I can do my best. What's the name?"

I gave Toby everything I could think of about Lockett, told him to look for his law degree. Something about the way Lockett had spoken about Carson today made me think the two had history that extended beyond Carson committing polygamy and setting me up to be a PI. There had been a familiarity there. Toby said he'd get back to me as soon as he had something of value.

"And Toby," I cautioned, "be careful poking around. We're being watched. Maybe do this before you get high."

He laughed. "Wrong. Do it *when* I'm high. I can be *super* paranoid. Make it work to my advantage."

I didn't want to disagree and start a debate. I'd have better luck crossing my fingers.

"Also," he said, "did you call Mrs. Wright? She's been lighting up my phone. Says no one has been out to work on her case since Carson did the initial."

Wright? I closed my eyes and tried to see the case files. Wright! She was the last one on my list to contact.

"I'll call her right now," I said.

"Awesomesauce. Now, I can get some peace," he said before disconnecting.

I reached for my backpack to get the notebook where I'd written Wright's phone number and case info.

I held the backpack in my hands. Everyone was looking for something. The pack wasn't a thumb drive like Cooper was looking for, but I still padded down the pack, searched through the pockets. Nothing.

I glanced over my shoulders to see if anyone was nearby. Sitting in the parking lot suddenly didn't feel so safe. Not that going home would be any safer. After the home invasion, I was spooked staying there. Found myself sleeping on the couch with my old high school baton beside me. I'd done another sweep for bugs or cameras that weren't placed there by Carson and found nothing. Toby reassured me several times that no one could tap into our video.

But this *no one* was scary. This *no one* seemed to show up where I was. This *no one* was a step or two ahead of me.

Because I was paranoid and afraid I was being followed, I moved my car from around the side of Ralph's where the employees park to the front. I found a spot under a light near the front and sat idling there.

No other cars moved. I wasn't sure if I found that comforting or not. I was a complete dumb-dumb when it came to technology. Maybe no one had to follow me because there was a GPS tracker on my car. If the gadgets from Mission Impossible were to be believed...well, I wasn't going to go there.

I sat with the backpack on my lap, my notebook open and resting on top. I gave Mrs. Wright a call. Carson's note on the case read *Possible infidelity. Maurice is not coming home when called. Goodwill case.*

My two other cases were about the character of two men. I wasn't surprised this one was any different. This work didn't leave me feeling warm and fuzzy toward the male species. I wasn't sure what "goodwill case" meant and made a note to ask Toby.

Mrs. Wright answered on the second ring. I introduced myself and reminded her that she had sought services from Holmes Security.

"It's about time someone from your business called," she said with a clipped New Jersey tone. Mrs. Wright sounded older, my guess maybe in her sixties.

"I apologize for the delay. There have been some private issues—"

"Yeah, yeah, I heard about Mr. Holmes. I'm sorry he died. He was a nice man."

I winced. "I'm not sure if you're still interested in retaining our services or not," I said.

She paused. The only sound coming through was the

tinny click of aluminum blinds being bent down and her huffy breathing.

"You think *you* can prove my Maurice is being unfaithful?" The tinny click came again, and I assumed she was no longer looking out the window.

"I can do my best. Yours wouldn't be the first case of infidelity I've worked on." So, I stretched the truth a little. Seems like people everywhere were doing it, so I figured it couldn't hurt.

"All I want is proof that he's going over to that woman's house. She's probably feeding him and cuddling him. Vindictive, that woman is."

I arched a brow, even though she couldn't see me. Did Mrs. Wright not feed Maurice to the extent he set out to find another woman who would? Of course, if that was the case, Maurice should just leave. Not play both women.

"You don't want a shot of them together?" A money shot would be the clincher.

"Nope, don't need it. If you see Maurice going into her house, that's enough for me. She has been warned to stay away from him. He has been warned as well."

I sighed. It wasn't my place to make judgments. "Okay, what's the address?"

She rolled off the information. "Lazy, that's what he is. She only lives two blocks away. I tried following him once, but he jumped a fence and gave me the slip."

Maybe I was wrong about Mrs. Wright's age. Or maybe she was a cougar.

She continued, "I changed my mind. I want a picture. And when you get that shot of Maurice slinking into her house, I'm going to march up to Mrs. Wong's door and 'a-ha' her so loud the entire neighborhood will hear. It'll get Jersey over there real fast." She dropped her voice to a hushed tone. "You might want to stick around for that. You might have to break up a fight."

"Oh, okay," I said. I'd never broken up a fight before, much less a catfight. Never even been in one. "Can you describe Maurice?"

"Sure, I have a picture if you want to come by and get it. Your husband asked me to get one. I'm surprised he didn't leave notes or something so I didn't have to repeat all this. Embarrassing, it is."

"I apologize for that. He left me a bit of a mess." The words tumbled out before I could think about what I was saying, and I cringed at my lapse in professionalism. Precious would be horrified.

"Oh, honey, they all do," she said. "Now, Maurice is a ginger. His throat, ears, and underbelly are white. He's got the prettiest blue eyes I've ever seen."

I tried to picture a man with that description and couldn't. I scratched my head as I tried to figure out how to ask my next question and not sound stupid. But I had nothing. So I skipped it.

"Okay, how about I come over tomorrow at ten and get that picture? Then I'll stake out Mrs. Wong's for a bit. Is there a specific time you notice Maurice slipping away each day?"

"Nope, sometimes he'll leave at night and not come home until the next morning. I think that woman locks him in her house. But other times, he'll leave in the morning and will come home around dinnertime. I always make sure he has a good dinner."

I had a sneaky suspicion we were talking about a cat or a dog and not a man. "Is Maurice there now?"

"Oh, yes, I've locked him in his room. He is *not* happy with me."

Either that or I had my first hostage situation. Confident that wasn't the case, I confirmed that ten would work for tomorrow and ended the call. A straying cat I could handle. In fact, the case came with some relief. Hearing others' problems wasn't easy.

Particularly when my problems seemed insurmountable. I stared at Carson's backpack in my lap.

This backpack was likely the key to getting answers, and tonight I was going to find out why.

18

FRIDAY NIGHT

But first, I needed to get the money shot on Sean Kleppner. Not that I was looking forward to telling Shannon her suspicions were true. Easily, it was my least favorite part of the job, and I hadn't had to do it yet.

I swung by the casino, hoping to meet this Kimmie person. What I found were the same players at Jessica's table that were there Saturday.

"Fellas," I said, sliding onto the chair between them, flipping a chip between my fingers. "How's it going?"

Lanky grunted his annoyance.

Bushy Bob smiled. "Back to try your luck?"

I shrugged. "It's only a dollar. What are the odds?"

"Are you going to play or are you two going to chat?" Jessica asked with a faux smile. Her tone was definitely not one of a happy person.

I raised my brows at Bushy Bob and grimaced. "Yikes, bad mood?" I whispered.

He nodded toward the table next to us. "Kimmie's out again."

"It's not her night off?" I asked Jessica.

Her lip curled up ever so slightly. "Place your bets."

I did the same as last time. Double-ohs. "Big money!" I said, rubbing my hands together.

Jessica rolled her eyes. "The most you'll get is thirty-six dollars."

"I know," I said excitedly. "That's a lot for me these days. I'll take it."

Bushy Bob chuckled. I think even Lanky had a laugh. Jessica spun the wheel.

"I sure wish I could find Sean," I said, watching the wheel go around. "I'm getting worried about him. I told my dad about Sean winning—Dad owns the paper in Wind River—and he can't get a hold of him either."

No one said anything. The wheel stopped on double-ohs, and my mouth dropped open.

"You have *got* to be kidding," Lanky said and sat back in his chair. Bushy Bob clapped me on the back in congratulations.

"I think it's because you're next to me," I told Lanky. "Like a good-luck charm."

He rolled his eyes.

Jessica pushed my chips to me. "Are you done now?"

Hm, was I? The lure to place another bet and win was powerful. I could see how quickly this could become a fun hobby. I didn't have any information about Sean so I used that as my reason to stay.

"One more, for old time's sake." I placed my bet.

The others did the same.

"You know, if my dad finds Sean before I do and Sean is in a compromising position, I don't think he'll write an article solely about Sean being a big winner. Nope. I bet the story angle will be about the fall of instant big money winners. Dad'll want to interview people here. He'll find out about Sean's extracurricular activities. Sean's wife will read the article. The whole thing will become a bad scene," I said. I was confident Dad *wouldn't* write such an article. Dad wasn't a clickbait kinda guy, but I took a gamble Jessica didn't know that. She didn't strike me as the newspaper-reading type.

Jessica surveyed me, then turned back to the wheel and gave it a spin. Not looking at me, she said, "You know that older hotel off the interstate between Wind River and Woodhaven? They have a card room. Who knew? I guess because they're on the tip of the reservation and owned by the local tribe, they're allowed." She gave me a pointed look. "Maybe you should take your gambling to that establishment." She was talking about Graycloud's place.

"Card rooms are allowed off reservations." Working in a casino, shouldn't she know that?

"Hey, hey," Bushy Bob said to Jessica in a jovial, cautionary voice. "We can't be mean to the winners. Because one day they'll be the losers and spending their hard-earned cash at your table. I'm a prime example."

Jessica cut her eyes to me. My gut said she was telling me something more than to take a hike.

I nodded slightly. The wheel stopped.

"Double-ohs," Jessica said with surprise.

Bushy Bob clapped his hands with glee. "Good for you." He patted his beefy hands against my back. "You should keep going."

I sat in stunned silence.

"Do you plan on coming back on certain days? Let me know so I can avoid them," Lanky said.

Jessica pushed my chips to me. I collected them and stood.

"Thanks everyone," I said, "but I'll quit while I'm ahead."

"You should come back at least one more time," Bushy Bob said. "Thirds a charm and all that."

I glanced toward the exit. I sure hoped today wouldn't be a repeat of last time. I thanked them again, cashed out, and requested a guard to walk me to my car.

Even as I drove away, I waited for the boom to drop. At any moment, I expected to be T-boned by another car or someone to jump up from my back seat (No one was there. I'd checked when I got in.).

Nothing happened, but I sat on the edge of my seat anyway, constantly checking my mirrors.

The Soaring Eagle was an older two-story motel with ten rooms that faced the interstate with a handful of cottages behind it. The cottages were the moneymakers because they looked at the river, and the views were amazing. At night, with timberland in the background and a full moon, the Windy River looked like a black silk ribbon strung through the trees.

Though the buildings were old, they were well cared for. Also on the property was a diner called The Chief, a popular hangout for older locals. The large backlit sign of the diner depicted a Native American in full headdress with a scornful expression. In fact, the cook and owner of The Chief, Graycloud, resembled the dude on the sign. Intimidating, even if he did make the best cinnamon buns in the entire world.

I drove through the parking lot, looking for Sean's work truck. Truthfully, I'd have been surprised if he parked where anyone driving by could see it. The parking lot could be seen from the interstate. I pulled around the back to the cabins and drove slowly down the gravel drive that divided the cabins from the back of the motel. Alongside the third cabin was Sean's work truck.

Bingo!

Parked next to it was a small beat-up Corolla. I rolled to the next cabin that was empty and pulled into its parking spot, removing me from Sean's cabin's sight line. I texted the Corolla's plate number to Toby for owner confirmation. He got back to me minutes later. Kimberly Mugg. He even sent her driver's license photo. She looked remarkably like Shannon, and I was a struck by how predictable Sean was by sticking to his "type." Did I resemble Carson's wife? Was I his type? Had that been my appeal? Was she, the real wife, older and I was the cliché "newer model"? Thinking about all the what-if's gave me a stomachache.

I tucked Carson's pack under my seat and pulled my camera from the bag stowed on the passenger floorboard where I had prepared it for nighttime photography. Like all true PNWer's, I kept a Seahawks fleece pullover in my back seat, so I pulled that on then quietly exited the car, making sure to lock it and tuck my keys in my pocket.

The evening was eerily quiet, even with the trucks and cars speeding down the highway. The space where the cabins were located seemed in a bubble of their own. The quiet river to my right was a murky, winding swath and made me think of the phrase "the tangled webs we weave."

Chills in the form of goosebumps ran up my arms. I hung my camera from around my neck and wished I had something other than my key to use as a tool for defense. Worse case? I was prepared to bean someone upside the head with my camera.

Using the cabin as cover, I crept around the backside, avoiding slashes of light. Not that there were many. Sean had pulled closed the curtains in every room. Only peeks of light crept through minuscule cracks. I crouched low and penguin-walked to the cars and felt their engines. They were cold; Sean and Kimmie had been here for a while. I moved out of sight of the door, placing myself around the corner where I could hear if they came out. I crouched against the cabin, leaning my back onto it for support.

The chances of getting a money shot were slim unless Sean and Kimmie came out the door and offered it up to me. Perhaps I could catch them in an embrace when they separated for the night?

I texted Shannon to see if she had an idea of when Sean typically came home.

She replied: *Tomorrow. He's on a camping trip with friends.*

Me: *U know w/who?*

Shannon: *Orville and someone called Mug*

I groaned. Cael Orville and Sean had been friends since grade school. I had no doubt Orville knew everything Sean was up to and was the keeper of secrets. The fact that he would lie for Sean didn't surprise me. The audacity to tell Shannon he was camping with someone named Mug infuriated me. I bet he sold it to himself that this way he wasn't really lying. I was of a good mind to rap on the door and use my camera to brain him, strictly on principle alone.

I replied: *Is this normal for him? This trip?*

Carson had taken lots of trips, but he'd done that from the beginning, so it was my normal.

Shannon: *No, says he stressed* (eye roll emoji)

Asking her if she knew about the millions he'd won would require a delicate hand. I waved my thumbs over the keyboard unsure of how to broach the subject. If Precious were here, she'd tell me to just ask. She was a rip-the-Band-Aid-off type person. But this didn't seem like a situation that would benefit from ripping, so I went with the middle line.

Me: *He gambled enough. Any chance he won?*

Shannon: *He always won and then he'd lose it the next time. Up and down.*

Me: *Word on the street is he won big*

There was a long pause.

Finally, Shannon: *How big?*

Me: *Let me find out the facts and get back to you.*
Shannon: *Okay.*

So she didn't know. Darn that Sean Kleppner. He needed his butt kicked. I hated lying to her, but I didn't want to bring her any more pain until I had the money shot and she could make good on it. I really wanted to nail Sean's heiney to the wall.

When a breeze from the river swept across me, I shivered. Then my stomach growled. There began my long debate whether I should go get food or wait. In hindsight, I was woefully unprepared and made a note in my phone to stock stakeout food in my car.

My end game was to get the shot, and I would stay as long as I needed. Food would be essential. I scampered to my car to get some cash. Then, staying in the shadows, I jogged to the diner. Scorch marks stained the earth, and dark soot spots were along the concrete side of the diner. Graycloud was lucky he'd caught the fire in time. He could have lost the diner and the motel.

Walter Graycloud was behind the counter reading a paperback. Two truckers were in a booth.

He eyed me when I stepped up to the counter, his gaze lingering on my camera.

"Hi," I said. I was hoping his friendship with my dad would be to my benefit. "Can I get a few things to go?"

"To go where? Back to cabin four that you haven't paid for?"

"I...ah..." I scratched my head and glanced at the truckers to see if I recognized them. I didn't. "Did you happen to hear about my husband dying?" I said quietly.

He nodded once.

"And that I inherited his security firm, which also offers PI services? I mean, not that I knew he was a PI... Apparently, some others did, but besides that."

He nodded again.

I whispered, "I'm on a case and need some food and coffee, please."

He lowered his book to the counter and picked up a Styrofoam cup. He filled it with coffee. "Do you know, Samantha, that the views from the cabins are stunning? Except the bedrooms. Those are on the side of the cabin and only observe another cabin's bedroom." He stuck a lid on the cup.

His message was loud and clear. My money shot was going to cost me.

"Do you have any more cinnamon rolls?" Chances were slim considering the late hour.

"I have two."

"I'll take them." I beamed at him. At least there was this perk.

"Your father says that you don't sleep well in your home," Graycloud said.

I shrugged, trying not to commit either way. I hated that Dad was worrying.

Graycloud put my rolls in a container and set them on the counter, the coffee and a cabin key next to it. "Typically, when the sun comes up, the people in the cabin next to you leave. Not anytime sooner. So you might want to make sure you draw your curtains so they won't disturb you."

I put my wad of cash on the counter. "Is this enough?" He let me keep a few bills.

"Samantha," he said as I was about to push open the door. "An eagle cannot hunt or stalk its prey if it is tired. That's when the eagle becomes prey."

I nodded once and escaped to the cabin where I caught a good night's sleep after eating both buns. The coffee had no effect, which spoke to how tired I really was. I set my alarm for fifteen minutes before sunrise and, through the dusty window of my cabin, caught the last moment of Sean and Kimmie embracing by their cars. With sleep still in my eyes and not fully awake, I fumbled my camera and missed the money shot by seconds. The rat bastard.

19

SATURDAY

L ater that morning, after parking in the garage, I checked my app to make sure no alarms had been triggered and the boogeyman wasn't hiding in my house. One day, those cameras were coming out. Having them was creepy. Even when using them to look for an intruder. For now, though, they were a tool I'd use. I had a few hours before I had to be at Mrs. Wright's.

I entered the house, going straight to the kitchen. From the fridge, I took out a bottled water and a wedge of cheese. From the pantry, I took a bag of crackers and then headed upstairs, making sure the locks were engaged on the doors beforehand.

In my room, I shut and locked the door and dumped everything on my bed. I used a bug sweeping device Toby gave me from Carson's secret room above the office. This device was high tech enough to look for cameras, too. My teeth were clenched tight as I pondered what I would do if

I found something. I already felt violated as it was. Was it possible to feel even more violated? I supposed so. Or maybe angrier.

Once I was sure everything was clear, I devoured a portion of the cheese and crackers while I stared at the backpack I'd laid out on my bed. There was a clue here somewhere. Had to be.

Was this what everyone was looking for? Had the mugger at the casino really wanted this and not my winnings? But what about this pack was the clue?

After wiping my hands on my pants, I dumped my stuff out of the pack and pushed it aside. The pack was my focus. It was your average-everyday North Face pack, not for hiking, but for carrying work stuff. It sported two sleeves for devices, a mesh pocket for a water bottle, and an outer pocket for little things like pens and lipstick. I ran my hands over the outside, not really knowing what I was doing or looking for. This pack might be a dead-end for all I knew. It's not like Carson had set me up for success here.

I dug my fingers deep into the pockets, feeling for nooks and crevices. I checked seams to see if any might have been resewn or come undone, hoping that when the guy at the casino grabbed the pack, something might have torn.

But...nothing. I had nothing. The waist and cinch straps weren't out of the ordinary either. I tossed the bag down in frustration and ate half the bag of crackers and the rest of the cheese while I considered my options.

Maybe this wasn't what everyone was looking for. Maybe the casino hood was actually after my money.

This time I used the top part of my socks to clean my fingers before I picked the pack back up. I slowly pressed my fingers over every inch of the shoulder straps, but no a-ha moment. The back of the pack, the part that rested against my back when I wore it, had three metal strips surrounded by padding. I ran my fingers over the outside of the steel bars, pressing through the padding to feel them. The middle bar appeared to be double in thickness compared to the others. I wasn't sure this meant anything, but I had nothing else, so I decided to play it out. I checked the seams again around that bar and found a slight overlap of thread and the tail end sticking out. Backstitching, done too close to the thread ends. If my gut hadn't been telling me to keep going, I would have stopped and missed this. If sloppy backstitching was anything at all.

On the top shelf in my closet, I had a small sewing kit for emergencies that I checked for a seam ripper. Coming away victorious, I removed two inches of the seam and stuck my fingers into the hole, trying to pull out the metal bar. I wasn't about to ruin a perfectly good, expensive backpack if this endeavor turned out to be nothing. The bar appeared to be two inches wide, a foot in length, and flat like a tongue depressor. Only metal and double thick. Starting from the top, I worked the bar down toward the opening, and from there I was able to grab it.

The bar was actually two bars taped together with two

bands of duct tape at the top and bottom. On the top bar, two sets of numbers were crudely etched into the metal.

I blew out a breath and plopped to the floor.

I had no idea what this meant.

Suddenly, I was scared. This...these numbers were what people were looking for. Right now, I had the upper hand.

But for how long?

With shaking hands, I separated the bars, the second being a plain metal bar that I guessed was what the company always put in their packs. I slid that one back into the spot where it had come from. Using a dime as a thimble and dark thread from my kit, I sewed the pack closed, trying to make it look like it was done at the manufacturer, silently thanking my mom who taught Rachel and I the basics of sewing.

The job was decent. I would need a machine to do a better one. Afterward, I stood, the bar with the numbers in my hand, and wondered where I could hide it. I came up blank; my house wasn't a safe option. The office could easily be tossed again. Would they stop there or go to my dad's newspaper? What if I mailed it to my sister? She could keep it at the Naval hospital, but I didn't want to involve her in any way, shape, or fashion. She was a single mom and had enough on her plate.

In a memo app on my phone that required a password, I made my own encrypted message using the numbers. Then I stared at the object some more, the metal feeling hot in my hand. My biggest fear was that wherever I stashed it would put that person at risk, and there wasn't anyone I hated enough to do that to. No doubt I needed to get rid of it, but the trouble was figuring out where and how.

Also, I half expected someone to break into my house at any moment. I didn't trust that *the others* weren't watching me, no matter that the bug sweeper didn't find anything. Even fully clothed, I felt naked and vulnerable. If someone burst into my house right now, I wouldn't be able to protect myself. Beside me was mace, and I might be able to spray one guy if he came alone, but I'd be screwed if more than one showed up. Trouble was I was a lightweight in situations like this. Manufactured adrenaline from action movies and thrillers made my knees physically knock. How would they be in real life? The other day, when the guy broke into my house, I shook uncontrollably from the fear and anger. And I'd watched it unfold on a screen with Leo next to me. My previous reactions didn't give me the confidence I needed to protect myself.

Leo.

I found my phone and scrolled through my contacts to the Ls. Under his name, he'd put *voice of reason*.

I pressed call.

"Samantha?" he said after the first ring.

"Yeah, you got a minute?" I let out my shaky breath. Calling Leo was an action plan. I liked having an action plan.

"What's happened now? You dead?" He sounded his typically terse self. Only people were talking in the background, so maybe I had interrupted something.

"If I were dead, would I be calling you?" I snorted to show my sarcasm.

"With you? One never knows. Native American lore talks about ancestors speaking from the grave. I figure, with my luck, I'd have a jinxed white girl haunt me." He laughed.

"I'm not jinxed," I said.

He laughed again. "You sure?"

I studied the metal bar in my hand; it stood pale next to my white-gold wedding band. Okay, so maybe he had a point.

"I have a favor to ask, and now that I have you on the phone, I'm sure you're gonna say no, so I'll just hang up now." I was second-guessing my decision.

"Just ask and give me the chance to say no. I'm curious." A car door slammed, and the background noise around him disappeared.

"You love saying 'no' to me." I rolled my eyes. He'd been doing it so long, why change now?

"Which means there's room for a yes. Hit me with the request."

"Are you alone?"

"I'm sitting in my car, yes, alone. I'm at a tribal meeting that I have to get back to so make it fast." Irritation was back in his voice.

"A tribal meeting outside?" I'd always imagined them inside for some reason.

"What, you thought we did them in tepees?" More irritation.

I scoffed. "No, I thought you did them around a table

like everyone else did meetings. Jeez, cut me a break. I'm on week two of my new hell."

His voice softened. "We're outside because it's nice weather and we can be. It's not often we have sunshine. If everyone is relaxed, then more can be accomplished. Now, are we going to get to what you want from me sooner or later?"

I went for broke. "I want you to teach me to shoot a gun. Carson gave me the basics, but I need to be less beginner and more..." Well, expert was a reach. "Intermediate."

Leo groaned. "How about you practice with the stun gun?"

"Leo, seriously, I'm scared. I'm locked in my bedroom because I don't feel safe in my own home. So unless you can burn some sage or something to fix that, then help me. Teach me to be a better shot."

There was a long pause. Then he sucked in a breath and blew it out slowly.

"Meet me at the range day after tomorrow eight a.m. sharp. Did Carson have a gun?"

I nodded and said, "We have a nine millimeter in the closet." Locked in a box. I was going to sleep with it next to me, but I was just as scared to have it then to not.

Leo groaned. "For the love of everyone around us, please, I beg you not to use it tonight."

"You're a good Samaritan, Leo Stillman. You're doing a great deed here. Thank you," I gushed.

"Yeah, yeah. A whole slew of people would never forgive me if something happened to you and knew you asked me for help. Besides, as a police officer, it's my job to make sure *everyone* is safe."

"Thanks, Leo," I said, feeling a rush of warmth surge through me. Maybe I wasn't alone. I mean, I had Precious, but what was she going to do? Organize everyone?

"I'm going to regret this," he said then hung up.

What a butthead.

20

SATURDAY

Mrs. Wright lived in the newer developed portion of Ridgefield near Carson's office. Her neighborhood consisted of craftsman-style homes with large porches, some painted funky colors. Driveways were behind the homes accessible through an alley.

I parked in front of the house. Precious came for good luck. The metal bar with the etched numbers was taped to the bottom of LC's driver's seat. Lamest hiding place ever, but I had no better idea. I was keeping it near me.

"So she thinks her cat is cheating on her?" Precious asked while surveying the house from inside the car.

"I think it's a cat. She never said definitely." I held up my camera. "This one I can do, no problem."

Precious nodded toward the house with her head. "Shall we? She's watching us from the behind the blinds. Middle window." The house sported three windows across the front. I glanced, covertly I hoped, in the direction of the middle window. The blinds moved.

Still uncertain how a PI should dress, I'd worn gray leggings, a gray and yellow tunic, and my Birks. In hindsight, Birkenstocks were probably not the best solution should I have to run for my life, but it was too late now.

She met us at the door. Mrs. Wright was a petite woman, somewhere in her sixties, with a short bob that hung like a bell. She had long pink fake fingernails and swipes of blue shadow over her eyes. She wore yoga pants and a Rolling Stones concert shirt.

"Took you both long enough. I thought you were going to sit in the car forever. Maurice is chomping at the bit to get out." She said car like "kah." She crossed her arms.

Introductions didn't seem warranted at this stage. "So, you let him out and I'll follow."

She nodded, her hair swinging. "I'll let you meet Maurice first. That way it won't spook him if he comes across you on the street."

Precious gave me a questioning look. Was I sure Maurice was a cat? I shrugged because I wasn't.

She rushed us inside where we were greeted by the blaring of the TV.

Mrs. Wright gestured to the living room where a gentleman roughly her age sat, a TV tray before him, a game of solitaire on the TV tray. He was bald.

She gestured to him. "That's my husband, Marv. He's a retired cop, used to work the shooting range. Lost a lot of his hearing." She raised her voice to almost shouting level.

"If he wore his hearing aid, he wouldn't have to listen to the TV so dag-gum loud. Turn it down, Marv!" She rolled her eyes.

"Don't tell me what to do, devil woman," Marv said and cranked up the volume. Mrs. Wright glared so fiercely at him I expected laser beams to shoot from her eyes and strike him down. She swung her attention back to us. "He'll be leaving soon. Likes to take his golf cart down to the VFW and talk shop with the old men down there. Come on, it's slightly quieter back here." She gestured for us to follow and took us to the kitchen where the sound was indeed slightly muted.

A large ginger tabby was pacing in front of the door, meowing.

"Look at him, desperate to get out of here. What have I done wrong? I buy the best cat food. I have all kinds of toys, and yet he can't get out of here fast enough."

"Maybe he wants out because of the noise," Precious said.

Mrs. Wright nodded. "I wondered the same thing, but on days Marv leaves early and the house is quiet, Maurice does the same thing."

Precious cut her eyes to me. Cat/Maurice confirmation. Check.

"And you said he goes to Mrs. Wong's? Where does she live?" I asked.

"Follow me," Mrs. Wright gestured and led us down a hallway to the back of the house and into the far corner bedroom. She closed the door behind us, which instantly shut out the noise.

We let out deep sighs of relief.

The room was set up like a home office with a large TV in the corner and a Ma Jong game on the desk.

"This is where I escape to," Mrs. Wright said. She pulled the curtain aside and pointed across the backyard to the houses in the distance. "See the purple house?" She rolled her eyes. "Crazy woman painted her house purple. Not gray purple. But bold and vibrant amethyst. I looked it up. That's what the color is called. Amethyst. I mean, what's wrong with white or blue?"

I didn't have an answer so I peered out the window through my camera, moving the zoom in and out to get a sense of the house. Mrs. Wright's window had an excellent view of the purple house's backyard with only the yard of another house separating them. I zoomed in on the plain back door, painted a lighter shade of purple, and then the windows, one being a kitchen with curtains.

"Could be worse," Precious said. "Could be blood red or poop brown."

Mrs. Wright snorted. "Could be, but the house ain't those colors, and if they were, I'd still complain. That woman is tacky and lives in a tacky-colored house. And just who are you anyway?"

"I'm Sam's friend, Precious."

"You're the tallest woman I've ever seen," Mrs. Wright said.

I glanced over my shoulder to see Mrs. Wright standing next to Precious. Mrs. Wright's head came to Precious's shoulder.

"Or you're the shortest woman I've ever seen," Precious countered.

Mrs. Wright laughed.

I said, "Does Maurice go through her back door?" I lifted my camera and zoomed in on the door, looking for something, anything. I wasn't sure what. But it was your average, ordinary door.

Mrs. Wright joined me at the window. "Yeah, I don't know how Wong knows, but she opens the door and greets Maurice, cooing all over him."

I glanced at Mrs. Wright. "Can you hear her from here?"

Mrs. Wright said, "No, I used this." At her closet, she slid the wide door to the side. Inside were shelves lined with boxes of bullets, a few sets of binoculars, handcuffs, and so much other cop stuff. She pulled out a device similar to a ray gun but with a large dish around it, like those Elizabethan collars that pets wear when they've had surgery and aren't allowed to lick themselves. Attached to the gun were headphones.

"This is a parabolic listening device." She tapped the Elizabethan collar. "This is the parabolic curve that picks up sounds. This baby can get sound from three-hundred-plus yards and that woman"—she pointed her device in the direction of the purple house— "was wooing my cat."

"Where can I get one of those?" I asked, thinking I might need equipment like it. I hadn't seen one in the secret office space. This PI thing had its moments of coolness, and right now was one.

"Why do you have this?" Precious asked.

"I told you. Marv used to be a cop."

We nodded our understanding. Another thought struck me.

"How is it Carson came to do this for you?" I asked. I hadn't noticed a security system when we came in.

"We own your office building. I asked Marv to go handle Mrs. Wong, but he refused. Heaven forbid, he miss out on any gossip among the decrepit man club. He told me go to Carson." She put her hands on her hips. "Then he goes and dies and leaves me with you."

I held up my camera. "I have a really good camera," I said. "How did you know Carson did PI work?"

Mrs. Wright said, "Marv said he'd sometimes hang out with those old windbags."

"I see," I said. Did Carson do that as a means to find jobs? I didn't know. But I now knew *goodwill case* meant he was doing this for free. Smart considering this was my landlord and all. I returned the focus to the case. "So, if you let Maurice out, he'll go straight to Mrs. Wong's and she'll let him in?" I wasn't sure what my role was here.

"She used to. Now he heads in her direction and disappears. Like I said, sometimes for a day or so. I think she put in a doggie door, but I can't get close enough to prove it. It's like that woman has eyes on the back of her house and catches me sneaking up every time."

"So you want me to prove she has a doggie door and Maurice is using it?" Easy peasy. One more notch for experience.

"Yeah, and I want to know what she's using to lure him there. And I want her to stop. So if you"— she scanned me quickly then jerked a finger to Precious —"or maybe your Amazon friend here instead, wants to be the heavy and rough up Wong so that she stays away from Maurice, I'll pay extra."

Extra of zero was what again? I glanced at Precious who was smiling.

"I'd be happy to talk to her," Precious said.

Mrs. Wright shook her head. "Not talk." She banged one fist into the palm of her hand. "Rough up. Wong is smaller than me. You could really put the fear of Jesus in her. I tried. I waved my gun at her and she waved one back."

Before Precious and Mrs. Wright could get into it further, I intervened. "Give me ten minutes to get into position and then let Maurice out. We might be able to resolve this today." I nodded for emphasis and grabbed Precious by the elbow to leave.

We drove around the block and picked a house two down from Wong's purple one. Going around the side we were able to hide behind some shrubs that made a pseudo-fence. I laid on my belly and had a clear shot of Wong's back door and Maurice's path from any angle. Sure enough, there was a doggie door. Maurice came dashing across the lawn and under some bushes to Wong's. I snapped shots of him butting open the doggie door with his head and going inside.

Precious and I fist-bumped, and I sat up. "Except...how do I find out what the lure is?"

Precious pursed her lips in thought. Then said, "You think you could sneak up to the doggie door and push it open? Maybe shove your camera in there and take some random shots?"

Nothing about that idea sounded good. I took stock of the house. "All the windows have curtains so I can't just peek in."

"Which is against the law anyway," Precious said. "Last thing you need people to hear is that you're a Peeping Tom."

"Unlike sticking my head in the doggie door. That's not against the law or creepy whatsoever."

Precious huffed. "It's not like you've come up with anything better."

"You either," I shot back and jumped to my feet.

"What are you going to do?" Precious said, coming to stand next to me.

"I'm going to knock on the door and ask." The idea was just as good as any and probably better.

"You want me to stand behind you like the heavy Mrs. Wright wants? I kinda want to see if I can pull it off." Precious narrowed her brows. "Does this look menacing?"

"Not really," I said. She was too pretty, too put together to look like a bully. "Maybe if you weren't so clean cut, weren't wearing a high-end pantsuit, or maybe if your hair wasn't so..." I made my hands go out in wild waves aside my head to indicate curly. "Big." Big hair just wasn't scary in a menacing way. More like it was scary how much product she used to get her hair to be that big and stay that way.

"Maybe I'll go in like a classy secret agent." Her eyes lit up. "I'll go grab one of those guns from Mrs. Wright and can hold it like this." She crossed her arms but made a gun hand and had it resting against her bicep. "That would scare her."

"Let's save that for a backup plan. Maybe she doesn't need to be scared."

Precious's expression fell, clearly disappointed. "You're a party pooper."

"Remember, we're also supposed to be looking to see if I'm being followed."

"Oh, good point," she said, scanning the area.

The plan was to approach Wong's house from the front. Like normal people. She answered my knock seconds after I rapped on the door.

"What," she said. She was the same height and age as Mrs. Wright with the same hairstyle.

"My name is Samantha True. I'm a private investigator." I dug into my backpack and pulled out one of Carson's business cards and handed it to her.

"This has your name written over another's," she said with a thick Asian accent and frown.

"Yes, I was out so I borrowed one of his. Anyway, I was hired by Mrs. Wright—"

"That woman crazy," she said.

I continued, "To find out why Maurice, her cat, continues to come to your house. You wouldn't want to share that reason, would you?" I hoped my expression looked pleading enough.

"Who's the person on this card?" She waved my business card in the air.

Lie. Don't lie. I wished I knew the right answer. "Er, well. He was my husband," I mumbled.

"Was?"

"He's dead," Precious said.

Mrs. Wong tsked. "Men! My husband had the nerve to up and die last year. Leaving me alone to do this retirement by myself. I paint house happy color so I want to come home." She gestured for us to follow her. "You come in. Come in. I show you what crazy lady's cat is doing here."

Precious and I shared a look. Mrs. Wong was lonely. When I made a sad face, Precious nodded. Her house was immaculate. And quiet. A Ma Jong board was out on the table. One coffee cup was in the sink. Knick-knacks were everywhere.

We followed Mrs. Wong through the house to the kitchen. In a pet bed in the corner of the warm room was Maurice and another cat, a female, with eight little kitties nursing.

"You see why he come. He come to his family." Mrs. Wong gestured to the litter.

Precious and I cooed in unison. I snapped a few pictures.

Wong slapped me against the arm. "You cannot tell crazy lady. She take them away."

I gave the situation some thought. "What if I could talk with Mrs. Wright and explain the situation. That the mom kitty is yours, and you want to keep the babies. You do want to keep them, right?"

Mrs. Wong nodded. "They're my family, too."

"I believe Mrs. Wright would love to know Maurice has babies. She might want to help you take care of them."

"She'll want to take them," Mrs. Wong insisted.

Precious laid a hand on Wong's shoulder. "Do you really want nine cats to care for? That's a lot. They'll be knocking stuff over. Having accidents." Precious grimaced. "But maybe if Mrs. Wright took half and you kept half, you could raise them together. Mrs. Wright loves Maurice as much as you love..." She pointed to the orange and black Calico.

"Moko."

Precious and I cooed again. "Moko, that's so cute," Precious said.

"Mrs. Wright thinks you are trying to steal Maurice away," I said.

"And she's scared," Precious added.

"Is it okay if I go and get her?" I asked.

Mrs. Wong hesitated then nodded.

I opened the back door. Looking toward Mrs. Wright's house I waved for her to come to join us. I met her in the backyard and showed her the nine reasons Maurice was so desperate to get out of the house. Over a game of Ma Jong, the two women worked out custody rights.

Case closed. And what a high, feel-good moment it was.

21

MONDAY

I arrived at the shooting range right on time. Sleep had
been elusive. Maybe because I was jumpy at every
sound coming from outside my bedroom door. Or maybe
it was because I didn't know where to hide the metal bar
when I was home so I taped the thing to my back. I was
scared to let it out of my sight so I slept with the stupid
bar taped to my body, and I drove with the bar taped to
my car. This was ridiculous.

Getting the bar stuck to my back would have won me
money on any of those home video shows. I made a bed of
duct tape on my floor, sticky side up, the bar running
down the center. Then I aligned myself so I could plop
backward onto the tape, affixing it in place. And it worked.
The first five minutes after I'd flopped back onto the tape
and squirmed like a puppy on her back to get the tape to
stick, I'd felt like a super genius. Like maybe I was getting
the hang of this PI thing. Then I tried to sit in bed and

watch some TV only to have the tape pull my skin. The skin under the tape was hot and itchy. The skin around it was sweaty. So between fear and tape discomfort, I barely slept. Around four in the morning, I'd had enough and ripped off the tape, clutched the bar in my hand and fell into an exhaustive sleep that felt like five minutes before my alarm went off at seven.

At the last possible minute, I put on yoga pants, a large Seahawks T-shirt, sketcher slip-ons, and pushed my hair out of my face with a headband. Where the tape had been on my skin was now a large patch of red welts that itched something fierce. I did remember to brush my teeth, thankfully.

Leo was parked in his police SUV and hadn't seen me pull up. I had a moment of pleasure when I startled him by tapping on the passenger window. He wasn't in uniform. He wore dark-washed jeans and a long sleeve dark green T-shirt that showed off his darker skin and light eyes. The color suited him. The shirt did a nice job showcasing his bulky arm muscles and wide shoulders as the material hugged every contour of his body.

"Lemme in." I jiggled the handle.

He pointed to the back where the criminals sat.

I narrowed my eyes, and he unlocked the door.

"Very funny," I said, sliding into the passenger seat.

"Didn't wake up with a sense of humor today?" He eyed me up and down, pausing at my hair.

I stifled a yawn. "Wanna trade lives? Then I get to tell the jokes."

"Did you eat?" He handed me a bag from Freshii, my

favorite clean-eating restaurant. Every ingredient was pure, whatever that meant. I loved their breakfast burritos. Sometimes, though, they didn't love me. The clean food liked to clean me out, if you get what I'm saying.

But I was hungry, and the burrito was good. I pointed to a clear takeout cup half filled with a magenta-colored juice. "Is that their beet juice?" I made a face of disgust.

"Yeah, it's really good."

I side-eyed him because I'd had the juice, and it wasn't good. It needed about a cup of sugar before the drink could be considered tasty. "Thanks for the food." I took a hefty bite.

"Yeah, well, I don't want you shooting a gun on an empty stomach. All kinds of things can go wrong. I got you a coffee, too." He handed me a medium to-go paper coffee cup. "There's more cream and sugar in there than coffee, just how you like it."

I gave him a suspicious look. "How did you know that's how I liked it?"

"I'm a cop. I'm observant."

"You're my hero," I said as I whiffed the heavenly fragrance.

He snorted. "Never thought I'd hear that."

"Never thought I'd say that. Probably because my caffeine levels are low and it's affecting brain function." I sipped the glorious drink, coming alive.

"That I did expect to hear." He chuckled. "So while I sit here and watch you spray food all over my car, why don't you bring me up to speed."

I dusted bits of egg off my pants. "I do not spray food."

Maybe a little when I ate with such ravenous need as I was today.

He gestured for me to go on.

"Hold this." I handed him my coffee then reached for the backpack. I told him about running into Lockett and how people kept asking if Carson left anything behind. I tapped the backpack. "This was sent to me right before he died. He sent it to my dad's newspaper."

Leo arched a brow and waited for me to continue. I filled him in about finding the clue, and with dramatic flair, whipped the bar out from the center pocket.

Leo handed back my coffee and took the bar. He studied it for a second then took out his phone. He typed in the first set of numbers. He showed me the screen.

"A bank routing number?" I should slap myself upside the head. How many hours had I stared at the numbers, wondering what they meant? Too many.

He tapped the second set of numbers. "I'm guessing that's the account number at this bank."

It was the same bank where Carson kept the business account.

He smirked. "You figured this out, right?"

I rolled my eyes. "I'm tired. I would have figured it out sooner or later." Probably later.

"How did you pass the PI test again?" He smirked. "So it was hidden in the backpack and you think that's what they're looking for?"

I nodded.

"What are you going to do with this?" He tapped the bar against his knee.

I shrugged. "Maybe a safe deposit box? I dunno. I can't leave it with anyone because it puts them at risk."

Leo's brow knitted briefly, then he said, "I have an idea. You leave both with me. I have a box in the cargo I can keep them in, and no one would be the wiser. After we finish here, we'll drive down to the sporting goods store and get another backpack just like this one. You carry that one for a day or so and then leave it in your car, doors unlocked, and let them take it."

"Ohhh," I said. "I like that plan."

"Maybe I should be the PI." He gave me a pointed look. One I chose to ignore. "Time to go shoot." He nodded to the range. It was an indoor jobby with several bays for shooting. Which was good considering many mornings in the PNW could be hazy or misty and were typically cooler. Trying to aim and shoot while cold would be good training, it was something I wanted to work up to.

I balled up my garbage and tucked the bar back into the bag, which I wore with both straps over my shoulders. I'd brought Carson's gun, and having that in the pack added to my edginess.

Leo got us registered and hung up the targets. He then laid out a small pistol.

"That's a Sig Sauer P238. It's the right size for you. Accuracy comes not only from practice but being comfortable with the gun. We'll start there." He tapped the small weapon.

I pulled out Carson's Beretta case. "I did some practice with this."

Leo nodded and set that gun out, too.

Being at a range made me nervous, mostly because of how much power to wreak havoc was in one room. Leo ran down instructions then clapped earmuffs over my ears and protective eyewear on my face. He handed me the Sig. I positioned myself like Carson had taught me and got an approving nod from Leo. I sighted the target then squeezed the trigger as I let out a breath. When the magazine was empty, I placed the gun on the ledge in front of me.

Leo studied the target with lips pursed. "Were you aiming at the target?"

"Center mass," I said, repeating the term I'd heard used before. Leo pulled the target in.

"Well, you hit it if center mass is the space under the criminal's right armpit." He pointed to one hole that had hit the outline of the man.

"It's this gun," I said and tapped the little pistol. "I don't like it. I want to try this." I pointed to the 9mm. The Sig was lighter than the Beretta, and maybe I needed more weight. Leo put a new target out then instructed me to prepare the Beretta.

I did, but struggled to rack the slide without getting my fingers pinched.

Leo groaned. "You still have that stun gun I gave you? You need to have that on you at all times."

"Yes, I still have it. Can I shoot now?" I asked with irritation.

Leo tossed both hands in the air. "Just aim for the target. Anywhere near the target would be good," he said as he took a step back.

Like I did with the Sig, I sighted, relaxed my shoulders, and while I slowly let out my breath, I squeezed the trigger. Whereas the Sig went *pop, pop, pop* the Beretta went *band, bang, bang* and had more of a recoil. But I managed it. When the magazine was empty, I put it on the ledge and stepped back.

Leo stared at the target, squinting. Confusion was on his face. Yeah, I'd sucked with the little gun so I was hoping I did better with this one. He pulled in the target and pointed to several holes on the target's chest.

"You're pulling slightly to the right," Leo said, "but I'm impressed."

I beamed at him. "Imagine what I could do if I got a full night's sleep?"

He shook his head, a small smile tilting his mouth up to one side. "Easy, trigger finger. You're not an expert marksman yet. Let's work on the slide some and your aim, and then we'll get out of here. I have an idea of what you really need to practice."

We stayed another hour and a half, and by the time we left, I was more comfortable with the gun than I had been twenty-four hours ago.

Afterward, Leo took me to laser tag where I spent the first twenty minutes laughing hysterically as I tried to run on the trampoline floor and escape being tagged. By the end of our forty minutes, I was able to get some shots in while hiding behind objects or in a kneeling position. I laughed the entire time.

Our last stop was a sporting goods store.

"Let's just hope if you have to use your gun, the target

stays remarkably still," Leo said as he handed me the new backpack he'd just purchased. I handed over the clue and Carson's bag.

"Or that I don't have to chase him across a trampoline floor," I said with a happy grin.

"That, too," he said and fist-bumped me.

22

TUESDAY

T he following day I pulled an early morning shift at Ralph's. Lason seemed moody and was difficult to engage in conversation. After work, I followed up with Shannon. Sean was coming home every night. Which meant I couldn't get the money shot. I called the casino and asked to speak with Kim Mugg and was told she was on the floor working. Sean had two million minus taxes, and no one but the casino employees knew. Soon, they would be releasing his name to the press as was their custom. What was Sean planning? Was Kimmie in on it? Was he home because she had to work? I didn't for one second believe he'd changed his ways. I was in limbo until Sean decided to make a move.

I made plans to meet with Precious at her office at the end of her workday. I'd balanced my account and figured I was going to be short some funds come the end of the next month. And I couldn't count on double-ohs. Precious said I could do more work for her, and I'd be a perfect personal assistant to run errands for some crazy-busy loaded person. Afterward, we were going to yoga. I grabbed a late lunch in downtown Vancouver at one of the food trucks. One last splurge before I went hard-core ramen noodles.

Every day, awesome food trucks lined up around a small business park. Nearly anything could be found from a simple but delicious burger and fries to the fragrant curries of Indian fare. My goal was to work my way through each one. This month I was on truck three of six, Mexican food. I was excited to chow down on my tamales and fish tacos.

The weather was beautiful. The sun was out in full brightness, the temperature was perfect for a good hike or a run. Soon, we would climb into the nineties, and being outside would be pretty but sweltering. Carson had been dead almost two weeks, and I barely recognized my life.

I needed to get back to my routine. As I walked back to my car, I promised myself I'd get back to running tomorrow. Running wasn't something I did because I got some weird high from the exercise. Running and any other form of cardio was something I did for life balance because come winter with its gray skies and endless rain also came seasonal depression. And as wonderful as doing nothing but lying on the couch eating chips for days on end was, seasonal depression did not pay the bills or keep me in the lifestyle I was accustomed. I enjoyed hot water and flushing toilets. So I exercised to keep the doldrums away, and I did it year-round because stopping and restarting months later was *so easy*. Said no one ever.

Carson's pack, hitched over one shoulder, kept slipping down and making food balancing difficult so I slipped it on over both shoulders. I was nearly to my car, not paying attention, my face in the fish taco bag, when I was jerked back off my feet and flung to the side. Bouncing off my car, I smashed my head against the window.

I crumbled in pain, clutching my hip and my head and trying to see past the blinding stars of agony that obscured my vision. I winced and glanced up at the presence looming over me. He cast a long menacing shadow, his face blocked because the sun was at his back.

He reached over me and lifted me up by the backpack. He grabbed me by the front of the shirt.

It was him, the guy who'd knocked me down at Lockett's office, who sat outside Dad's newspaper office, and broke into my house.

"Enough of this game," he said and shook me like a rag doll, causing me to bite my tongue, the metallic taste of blood filling my mouth.

My teeth rattled and clanged against each other. I flailed my arms trying to make contact with something, anything, but came up with only air between my fingers.

My mind went blank, a sensation so weird it took me out of the moment, albeit briefly. I instantly came back to the present when he slapped me across the face with an open hand. A ringing erupted in my ears.

Something bad was going down, and there was nothing I could do to stop it.

"Oh, no," I said, repeating it over and over again like a broken record. I wasn't telling him no, just acknowledging the inevitable. This was not good.

"Do I have your attention?" he said, spittle going everywhere. Then he tossed me up against my jeep, against the door, the pack digging into my back. My head bounced off the sideview mirror and shattered it, shards of glass digging into my skin. I slid down to the sidewalk, my legs bending awkwardly.

He leaned in close, so close I could tell he'd had curry from the Indian street truck. His presence was all around me, larger than life.

"Oh, no," I continued to say.

He whipped out a large knife, like one of those you'd see on the hunting channel. It was larger than my hand with jagged edges, but it likely didn't strike fear in the hearts of wildlife like it did mine. The chances of wetting my pants was high. Tears were running down my face. I swiped at my eyes and came away with water and blood.

"You listen to me," he said, inches from my face, the knife in my periphery. His features must have been carved from granite. A chiseled, unfriendly face with sharp cheekbones and thin lips. He was dark—dark hair, tanned skin. I gasped. He had two different colored eyes. One was brown, the other blue, like David Bowie, only this guy wasn't anywhere near as cool as Bowie. Instead, this guy reminded me of one of those husky dogs with the two different colored eyes. A crazed husky who was about to rip off my face. Like a mad dog, worse than Cujo. He was foaming at the mouth, not so much from anger but from some sick pleasure he got from hurting me. I could see it in his twisted smile. I took this as an omen of impending awfulness.

He said, "You tell your dope-smoking friend to stop poking around. You get this one chance"—he touched the cool edge of the blade to my cheek—"but if you and the caffeine-addicted stoner don't start minding your own business..." He slid the flat side of the blade down my cheek. "If you don't learn to look away right now, there's going to be big trouble for you. Heartbreaking trouble." He pressed the blade into my cheek, the tip pushing into my skin. "You don't want to know who Carson was. Why do you care so much about a liar and a thief? Or are you really that insecure and dumb? Maybe desperate?" His tactic was both physical and psychological, both equally powerful. They worked.

"Oh, no," I repeated, stuck in my loop.

Then with a sudden jerk of my arm, he forced my face down toward the ground. One arm was tucked beneath me, the other behind me being held at an awkward angle and making any movement painful. He ripped at my backpack with a knife, the repeated sawing sound echoing in my head. Finally, the strap on the side of my pinned arm dropped away. He let go of my arm then shoved my head down once more so that it banged on the pavement, causing a second explosion of stars. Twice in one day was a record for me.

I flipped to my side, bringing my hands to my head.

Mad Dog walked away, my backpack clutched in his hand, looking as small and insignificant as a rag doll.

I lay there for what felt like hours, staring in the direction Mad Dog had disappeared, waiting for him to come back. A random thought penetrated my brain.

How odd that no one else was on the street. Not a single person had walked by. I sat up and looked around in confusion. I'd parked a few blocks away from the food trucks because I hadn't wanted to get stuck going around the one-way streets. From where I'd parked, I could easily access the interstate and head home. Where I'd parked was also in the opposite direction of where the offices were. Where the majority of people worked.

Stupid mistake.

With one hand pressed to my temple, I dug my phone out of my pocket. The screen had cracked from when I'd hit the car, but it still worked. Anger flushed through me and returned some of my senses. These people, whoever they were, had no right messing with me or my life like this. At this moment, I was so angry with Carson I could scream.

I found Leo's contact and gave him a call.

"I'm on duty," he said. His way of answering.

"Great, because I'd like to report a crime," I said, surprised that my voice held together.

"What kind of crime?" he said as if he thought I was kidding.

"Assault," I said and started to cry. "I just got my ass kicked by some big guy with two different colored eyes. He said I must be dumb or desperate. He was *not* nice."

Leo's voice softened but had the edge of a cop meaning business. "Where are you? Can you tell me what you see?"

"I went to the Vancouver food trucks. I'm looking at the old Tumwater bank, the one that closed when they opened the larger one closer to the water." I tried to read the sign in the window, but my brain couldn't process anything but the image next to the words. "I think it's going to be a quilt shop. Sign says it's coming soon. That'll be nice. I like how artsy downtown Vancouver is getting. I wish Wind River would do the same." I was babbling.

"Quilts are nice. Where are you? In your car or out?"

"Out, duh! He didn't beat me up in my car, thankfully." I gave a sharp laugh. "I hate getting blood out of leather."

"You're bleeding?" Leo's voice dropped lower.

"Yep, and I lost my food. I was really looking forward to that fish taco." Though the thought of eating made my stomach roil.

"I'll take you to get tacos. Don't worry about that." Leo paused and sucked in a breath. "Sam, is he still there? Tell me about your injury. Are you shot?"

"No, he's gone. I waited, but he never came back. He had a knife, not a gun." I leaned back against the car, feeling dizzy.

"Did he use the knife on you?" Through the phone, his sirens wailed.

"He cut the pack from me. So that plan worked. Yay," I said weakly.

"Sweet mother of God," Leo said. "Hang on a sec, Sam. I need to call in some help."

The noise coming through his phone went silent. He must have put me on mute.

I started to hum. Not a tune, just a low humming sound that was in sync with the trembling of my body.

Leo came back on the line, "How ya doing, Sam?"

I hummed to let him know I was still there.

"Stay with me. Paramedics are on the way. They'll get there before me. I'm ten minutes out."

"Hmmm," I said, my knees knocking together.

"You're doing great, sweetheart. You're super tough," he said.

My teeth began to chatter. Leo kept chatting and encouraging me, but I couldn't process anything he said, my mind stuck on a one-note hum, like a machine indicating someone had coded. A paramedic seemed to come from nowhere and squat before me. He held out his hand for my phone. I didn't have the strength to give it to him but let it drop.

He gave the cracked screen a glance then filled Leo in as he took my pulse.

I closed my eyes but jerked them open when he commanded me to. The entire process was a blur. Next thing I knew, I'm sitting in the back of the ambulance with a Coke in my hand.

Leo stepped in my line of sight and stared down at me, his mouth a thin line of controlled fury. "Please tell me you got some of his DNA under your nails or something. I want to find this guy."

I swallowed hard. "I didn't do a single thing. He was

going to hurt me, and I couldn't stop him." A fresh set of tears broke free.

Leo climbed in the rig and sat next to me. "What you've just experienced is normal. You aren't trained to handle spontaneous stressful situations like an attack."

"I couldn't even think, Leo. I just kept saying 'oh, no' and even after he left, I just sat there waiting for him to come back and finish me off."

"Goofy loop," Leo said. "It's not uncommon. Happens to rookie cops, too. We don't expect these things to happen to us. Only certain people are trained to take themselves out of the situation so they can react. Don't beat yourself up."

I grunted with frustration. "I was so helpless. I hated every second of being his victim. Carson did this to me. He's made me a victim twice now, and I hate him for it." I buried my head in my hands.

Leo placed a strong hand in the middle of my back. "Maybe once you've recovered from this, you can take a self-defense class. Do you think you can identify him?"

"Yeah, I think so. He had two different colored eyes. One blue, one brown."

"Heterochromia," said the paramedic sitting behind me over my shoulder.

"Does that affect his strength, too?" I asked. "Because he was freakishly strong."

"No, sorry," said paramedic.

"I'm just freakishly weak I guess. Maybe a self-defense class would come in handy." Getting beat up was not fun. Why people did it for a living was baffling. I told Leo about seeing this same guy at Lockett's office and outside my dad's newspaper.

Leo leaned forward, resting his forearms on his knees. He looked badass in his uniform with the eagle tattoo that took up his whole forearm.

He said, "Now they have the pack, maybe this can be over."

I stared at Leo, incredulous. This was nowhere near over.

He surveyed me, the muscle in his cheek working on overdrive. "Please tell me this is over. They have the pack. Not to negate what's happened here, but the end goal has been achieved. I was hoping you'd just leave it at your house or car and let them break in to get it while you were out."

"Hm," I said. "That would have been a much better plan than me walking around with it." Hindsight twenty/twenty. "I can't walk away from this Leo. They threatened me."

"All the more reason to walk away," Leo pointed out.

"But how do I live with that? How do I not have the answer to these questions?"

He stared at me, long and hard. Probably trying some Native American mind control or something. Finally, he gave up with a heavy sigh. "Oh, no," Leo groaned with a shake of his head.

I laughed. "That's what I said."

23

TUESDAY

Leo dropped me off at Dad's newspaper since my car was being processed as part of the crime scene. Though I'd adamantly proclaimed I was fine to go home, Leo seemed to think otherwise. The entire ride to Wind River, I sat in the cruiser, holding my broken phone and trying to sort out everything in my head. I had a palm-sized bandage on the right side of my temple where several shards of the mirror had cut me, coupled with small cuts along that side of my face. Bruises up and down both sides of my body were blossoming every few minutes, and my head throbbed so hard it could explode at any given moment.

"I need a new phone," I said.

"Take it to Chucks," Leo said. He'd grown silent after pumping me for information about the attack. I'd told my story so many times now I was sick of it. I was also aware of how many unanswered questions there were. Lots of black moments I couldn't fill in. Mostly, those happened when the guy was whipping me around like an empty plastic bag on a windy day.

"Yeah, Chuck's. Good idea." Behind Chuck's market was the used electronics store he ran. Get your Apple fixed while getting your apple fix. That was Dad's favorite joke.

My stomach growled. "I need a burger," I said. "And a shake."

Leo drove through BurgerTown, a locally run chain, and hooked me up. I'd devoured everything and licked the lid of the shake before he pulled alongside the curb outside the newspaper.

"Samantha," he said, facing me and leaving the cruiser to idle. "I don't know who Carson was before he came into your life. I never really got to know him." He shrugged. "Maybe he was running from someone. Maybe he was a con. Maybe a thousand different scenarios, but none of them are good, and you're stuck in the middle."

The burger churned in my stomach from his cautionary words. "I know." The bandage at my temple tugged at my skin. "I also know I'll never be able to put this behind me if I don't know why he did this to me."

"What if you never know?" He arched one brow.

He raised a question that had been niggling at the corners of my mind. The other version of this question was, what if I found the answers but didn't like any of them?

I shook away the fear. "What do you want me to do? Hand them the routing number and dust off my hands?" I made like I was doing so. "Because I've seen enough TV to know that's not how these things work."

Leo crossed his arms. "This isn't TV."

I crossed mine, too. "Okay, I've seen enough true crime TV to know whoever Carson was running from isn't going to shake my hand, say thanks, and wish me well. And deep down you know it, too. That's why you put your number in my phone. That's why you took me to the range."

Briefly, he closed his eyes then groaned. "That's why I'll show you some self-defense moves when you're feeling better. But I want you to keep that stun gun on you at all times. If you go outside, it's in your hand. You understand?"

I nodded and beamed at him. "Thanks, Leo, you're a pal." I widened my eyes. "Whoever thought I'd say that to you?" I laughed and reached for the door handle.

He reached across me and pushed the door open. "Get out of my car."

I laughed then followed it with a groan. I'd stiffened up on the ride home, and my muscles were screaming as I stretched them to get out of the car.

"Yeah," Leo said before I closed the door. "I hope you like feeling like you do right now. Because if you think this was bad, try the alternative."

"Which is what? Kicking their ass?" I joked, but secretly wished I could.

"Getting dead," he said straight-faced. "I don't want to work you up as a homicide."

His words cut right to the heart and sent a bolt of fear

up my spine. Not wanting him to see how successful his warning was, I rolled my eyes and said, "Cops, you guys are so dramatic." Then slammed the door.

He gave a short BLURP of his siren that caused me to nearly jump out of my skin and sent my entire body screaming from the sudden movement. I caught his expression through the window, expecting him to be laughing, but he wasn't. Instead, his dark eyes bore their cautionary message.

I nodded, taking his warning seriously. I was uneasy, and apprehension was a good thing. Undaunted meant dead.

I brushed at the gooseflesh running up and down my arms and steeled myself for what was about to come next. I wasn't going to turn away from this situation. I would face it head-on, even though the consequences could be dire. The last two weeks had been effective in knocking me off balance, tipping me upside down. And those feelings of helplessness would eat me alive if I continued to let these outside forces dictate. Good or bad, I needed to grab and hold my own power, or this day and Carson's lies would forever negatively impact my life.

I waved him off, and just as I was turning toward the paper's office, I caught sight of Sean's work truck parked in the center of Riverfront Park. He was working on the giant planters that surround the theater portion of the park. Finally, I was going to get face time with Sean.

I did an awkward shuffle-like-hobble as I made my way into the paper. Stella was at her usual helm, the front desk.

She stood, and her mouth fell open. "What in all that's holy has happened to you?"

"I went for fish tacos and tamales." I tried not to groan as the stitch in my side throbbed. I handed her my phone. "Can you take this to Chuck for me real quick? I see someone I need to talk to."

She held out her hand and narrowed her eyes. "What's going on?"

"I'll fill you in in a minute. Do you have a camera?"

Stella held up her phone. "Just this one. I'd have to run to the back to get a company camera."

Using my eyes to plead, I asked, "Can I borrow it?"

"Only if you return it in the same shape I'm loaning it to you."

I whisked hers up. "I'll do my best." I shuffled from the building and down to the park, clutching my side with my hand.

Sean Kleppner looked no different from high school, only less hair. Blond, blue eyes, and sun-kissed from working in landscaping most of his life. He was tall, but showing the beginnings of a potbelly, and he sported a chin curtain. What once had been a soul patch was now a full beard with no mustache. Personally, I didn't get it.

"Hey," I said, collapsing on the half wall that ran around the perimeter of the outdoor theater. I tried not to pant but was failing miserably. "It's been forever since I've seen you. How's Shannon and the kids?"

Sean was stuffing dirt into a large pot. He glanced up at me and, hand to heart, I swear he grimaced.

"They're fine. Busy." He glanced between his pot and my face. "What happened to you?"

"Fish Tacos." I said. "Super popular." I admired his handiwork. "I like what you've done here with the bigger pots." Which was true. Sitting on top of the half wall were eight evenly spaced pots of overflowing plants. Sean was changing two of them out to a larger pot. The larger the pot, the more plants and flowers and the grander the design.

"I've been asking the city for years to change these pots into bigger ones, but they're too cheap," he said.

"What changed their minds?" Lots of older folks sat on the city council. Cheap was their motto.

"They haven't, so I took it upon myself to show them how much better it would look if the pots were bigger." He swept away the dirt that had fallen from the freshly planted pot onto the wall.

"You bought these?" With his winnings? If so, his actions puzzled me.

"Yeah, and once the council gets lots of compliments and tells me how much they like it, I'm gonna ask them to pay up or I'm gonna take my pots and go." He pounded the dirt in frustration.

Ah, there's the Sean I expected. In high school, he'd always been the one to bum rides, bum a cigarette, or whatever he could get for free. Silence hung between us.

Had I come over here with a plan, this moment might be going better. "You heard about my hus—uh, Carson, didn't you?"

Sean glanced at me. "Yeah, Shannon told me. Rotten

luck." He heaved a large bag of soil onto his shoulder and turned away toward another pot. Leaving me with a view of his profile.

I snort-laughed. "You're telling me. But speaking of luck, I was at the casino the other day. I actually won, but not as big as you did, I hear."

Sean fumbled the bag, bumping it along his side before dropping it into the pot. Something small and square popped out of his pocket and bounced toward me.

"Who told you that?" he asked, not once looking at me. He paused, presumably gathering his wits, then stabbed a spade into the bag, splitting it open.

By my calculations, Sean had two weeks before word leaked about his winnings. I eased from the wall and said, "The guys I was sitting with at roulette. They were talking about a big slot machine winner. Turns out it was you."

"Did they tell you how much?" He poured some of the soil into the pot.

With much pain, I reached down and scooped up the box. It was a jewelry box, the kind that typically held rings and earrings. I flipped the top open and was surprised to find a ring with two entwined hearts. Diamonds, microscopic ones at that, dotted one arch of each heart. The ring looked familiar, but I couldn't place it. Sean was focused on the soil, allowing me to snap a picture.

"They just said it was a lot. I'm surprised you're still doing this and not living the life of the independently wealthy," I said. "I can't even imagine what I'd do if I won money."

Sean paused and stared out at the river. "I'd run a fishing excursion company," he said in a rush of words.

"Hey, you dropped this." I held the ring out, lid open. "It's pretty. What's the occasion?"

He glanced at the ring box on my palm and paled. Sean dropped the bag and whipped the ring from my hand. He narrowed his eyes. "Not that it's any of your business, but it's for Shannon." He ducked his head. "I've been an ass lately, so I thought I'd make a grand gesture and apologize." He cut his eyes to me and sighed heavily. "You know my dad, Sam. He's not the easiest man to be around and sometimes Shannon catches my grief." Sean's shoulders slumped. His dad was one of those guys who was quick to ignite, blaze a path of destruction, and then ask questions later. My dad did not hold him in high regard.

Even when someone knew their parents were a piece of work, it didn't help to hear others agree. I said nothing.

Sean shoved the ring back into his pocket and kicked the wall. "If he'd just retire already. But no, he has to micromanage every step I make. I'm so sick of it. Sick of him." He picked up a rock and chucked it across the length of the park toward the water.

Being disgruntled with one's job did not excuse infidelity or lies. But I was pretty much done with trying to understand human nature. Also, I was in no place to talk. I didn't know what it was like to have a demanding and demeaning parent, not really, though I'd been the subject of teasing as a kid. I hadn't enjoyed it. Who was I to make assumptions about Sean and the journey he was on? I made a note to see if Shannon was wearing the ring next time we met.

"If I see Shannon, I'll keep this to myself," I said, pointing to his pocket.

He gave me a half smile. "Please do," he said before turning his back to me.

I nodded once and shuffled back to my dad's business. Before going in, I gave the park one last look. The new planter stood tall and large, extending upward like a middle finger. Sean's eff you to his dad and the town. I bet there was some satisfaction that came with creating a look that people were going to love but secretly had a double meaning. Ugh, I was empathizing with a womanizer. I needed a video on how to read people if they were lying.

24

TUESDAY

S tella was waiting for me inside the lobby when I returned. She handed me my phone. Before returning her phone, I texted the ring picture to myself.

"You owe me thirty bucks," she said. "Also, Evergreen Jewelers called. Your necklace is ready. They said they've been trying to reach you. You need to pick it up or they're going to put it in their consignment display to cover the cost of your bill."

I groaned. I'd forgotten all about that necklace.

I paused by Stella's desk to catch my breath and pressed my hand to my side.

"I could use some water," I said, then mumbled, "or a stiff drink."

Stella's gaze swept over me, and she crossed her arms. "Russ!" Her voice boomed throughout the building. I supposed the anger in her voice spurred my dad into action. He came flying out of his office, papers in his hands, his glasses perched on his lower nose like an old schoolmarm.

He did a double take when he saw me. He peered over his glasses. "Samantha?"

"I'm fine, Dad. I was mugged downtown. They stole my backpack and knocked my fish tacos out of my hands. Can you believe that?" No need for him to worry more than he had to.

"You shouldn't lie to your father," Stella whispered. "He can handle the truth."

I couldn't meet her gaze. "I'm going to lie down on your couch, if that's okay."

Dad helped me into his office and cleared off a box of papers taking up space on the end of the couch. I stretched out with a groan and a sigh.

He stood over me and stared down. "Did you call the police?"

"Yep, I even saw the paramedics. I was cleared." Letting my body relax into the cushions felt oh so good.

"Are you okay, Sammy? Do you need help? Is this about the money Carson owed?" Dad's bushy brows were pushed together as he studied me, clearly worried. I hated to see him like this. He'd never been the parent who did the worrying. That was Mom's job.

"I'm good, Dad. Seriously. I was mugged. Next time I won't fight back." I held my gaze steady with his.

He grunted as if he didn't believe me, then ambled back to his desk where he shuffled papers.

"What are you working on?"

He loved to talk about breaking stories, and doing so

would take his mind off me. "Remember that fire that happened up in the Olympics. A senator's son was killed?"

I wracked my brain for the story. I'd read it when I was looking for information on Carson's accident. "Vaguely," I said.

"It happened on Tuesday, the day before Carson died," he continued and stared at a paper. "It seems the senator's son, an aspiring politician himself, was staying in the family cabin, going to do some hiking. He was a big outdoorsman." Dad waved his hand as if to bring himself back on track. "Anyway, looks like the fire started when the son, a man about your age named Benjamin Fulton, fell asleep smoking in bed."

"Not unusual," I said and closed my eyes. "These things happen more than we like."

"True," Dad said, but something in his voice made me open my eyes and look at him. His cheeks were pink and his eyes bright from the scent of a story. "Except the son didn't smoke. The senator swears by it. Said Ben might have tried it when he was younger, but he was too much of a health nut to smoke. If that's true, it would also beg the question of why there was a handful of empty whiskey bottles in the cabin as well."

"I'm not fully following," I said, wondering if it was because I did have a concussion.

Dad sighed like he was sad his youngest child was daft. "Both police and fire marshal reports claim Ben likely passed out while smoking in bed. The senator says that's impossible. Look at these." Dad came around and tossed two large photos on my chest. I held them up.

Dad pointed to the first one. A man in his mid-fifties stared hard and tired at the camera taking his picture. He had a large, bulbous nose, the type one gets from drinking, rheumy eyes, and red splotchy slack skin. "That's the senator about twenty-five years ago. He was early-forties. At the height of his career. When I exposed the sports world for pushing performance-enhancing drugs, Senator Fulton came out as a recovering alcoholic and talked about how poor our medical treatment for addiction was. That it was shameful corporations were doing this to players because there's no treatment. He's still an advocate. Even for Indian Health Services, he's trying to make sure Native Americans have options."

He held up a second picture. "This is the senator now." The hard expression remained, but the Senator was healthier. No red booze-nose. No slack skin. No blotchiness. The picture of a fit man in his sixties.

"The senator believes that his kid would never drink and smoke because of his own addiction?" I shrugged. Lots of kids hide things from their parents. Like me, right now, not telling Dad the entire truth about what happened today.

"Exactly. And he makes another good point. What avid outdoorsman gets toasted the night before he's about to take on a sixty-five-mile hike in the Olympic mountains?"

"An alcoholic one?" I'd learned that nothing was as it seemed in life, and people were great at hiding what they wanted no one to know.

Dad bopped me on the head with one of the photos. "Think about it, Sam. This kid, Ben, he's hiked Rainer.

He's done the Pacific Crest Trail, the Appalachian Trail, and the Continental Divide Trail. He wants to do Everest. Is that the kind of person to get soused the night before? I can see him having a few beers on the trail or even keeping a flask during the hike, but I can't see him drinking a bottle of scotch the night before. It doesn't sit right in my gut." To prove his point, he jabbed his fingers into his midsection.

I pushed to a sit with a groan. "I know it doesn't seem likely, but Dad, Carson seemed like a dream come true, and he left me with a mess. Besides, what are you going to write about that's fact? It's the senator's word against the police. And the senator is grieving. He doesn't want to believe his kid could have been an alcoholic."

Dad leaned against his desk. "I always listen to my gut, and it says there's more to this story than we know. And I'm going to get to the bottom of it."

I shrugged one shoulder and grimaced. "I might be able to help you with that. Do you know Toby Wagenknecht?"

Silence from his part of the room. "I do. Are you trying to get your old man to buy you pot?"

I laughed and felt the ache in my ribs. "No, but I need to talk to him. I also think he can help you do some digging." My phone was on the other end of the couch, and I made a halfhearted attempt to reach it.

"I'll call him." He picked up his phone and dialed. "But I doubt he's available. It's his high time."

I glanced at my watch. It was smack in the middle of

high time and it was disturbing that Dad knew about these things.

But Toby must have answered because Dad identified himself, told him I was there, and asked him to come to the paper. Then he hung up.

His expression curious, he said, "He'll be right here."

"Did he sound high?" I asked, wondering if this was the best time to tell him he was in trouble, too.

"He always sounds high," Dad said.

True. I situated myself in the corner because I needed the support on both sides. I kept my expression bland so I wouldn't worry Dad further.

The good thing about downtown Wind River was that from anywhere in the city limits, town was only a ten-minute drive. The bell over my dad's front door chimed, and he went out to inspect, returning a few minutes later with Toby in tow. The bell chimed again, and Dad groaned as he left to handle it. I'm sure he sniffed a story with me, too, and thought this was his chance to hear it. I gave a silent thanks to whoever had come in behind Toby.

"Dudette! What happened to you?" He sat on the edge of the couch, his vape pen swinging from the lanyard around his neck.

I kept my voice low. "You know that research I asked you to do?"

He nodded vigorously then took a hit from his pen. "Yeah, I did some simple searching. No biggie because I noticed someone was following me."

"What do you mean?" When it came to tech, I was an ignoramus.

"I mean someone was following my searches. I had to go deep web and try to cloak myself. They also tried to scan my files. I shut them down lickety-split."

"You need to be careful. They"—I pointed to the bandage—"know who you are. They told me to tell you to knock it off."

Toby, naturally pale, went gray. He took a long inhalation from his pen. "Sssshhhheeeet," he said, drawing out the curse word the same time as he let out the smoke. "I hate bullies."

He had a history of trouble with bullying so I understood where he was coming from.

"I'll admit that they spooked me. Couldn't even get high today because I was so busy trying to figure out who they were." He took another puff.

I sniffed the air. "Is that s'mores?" The aroma was a bit chocolaty with a cinnamon smell. Reminded me of camping.

Toby took another puff and blew it out. "Called Cowboy Campfire. I picked it because things are about to get real western around here." He made like he was shooting dueling guns, stopped to blow off their tips, then tucked them in imaginary holsters at his side.

"Well, if you're up for it, for more action, my dad needs some help, too."

"Oh, I'm up for anything." He then pulled out his laptop from the knapsack on his back and said, "Let me tell you about Tyson Lockett and when I became aware of being followed. Our story starts in Seattle."

"Seattle?" The city was close enough for Carson to make a day trip without me knowing.

Toby continued, "Your lawyer friend is currently under investigation by the Office of Disciplinary Council. He could be suspended and possibly disbarred. He's charged with using fear to force clients to pay thousands of dollars to keep him on retainer and then not following through."

25

WEDNESDAY

L C was still hanging with the crime scene people, which meant this gave Precious a chance to jump back into the fray. She'd given me a scathing set-down when she learned about what happened. Mostly, she was upset because I'd kept her out of the loop and claimed she could have been there, could have been watching my back, and this might have been avoided blah blah blah. Basically, she was right.

"Where to first?" she said with her high ponytail almost touching the roof liner of her high-end SUV. Her makeup was perfect. I hadn't bothered, figuring any color I chose would be in direct contrast with the purplish and green bruise alongside the right side of my face. Feeling naked, I swiped clear gloss over my lips.

"Let's go by Keys Bank, main branch. I'll make a deposit into the business account and see if this account number from the clue is a checking account or what." I tapped the picture on my phone of the bar with the account number.

"Are you sleeping?" she asked as we pulled out of my driveway.

"Not really. Last night I stayed up late watching videos on how to tell if someone is lying."

"Stayed up late for work, right? Not because you're scared to go to sleep?" Typical Precious, getting right to the point. There was no reason to deny it.

"Maybe I should have let them have the townhouse. I lie in bed and see images of someone moving through the house, or I wait for the alarm to go off." I settled back against the soft leather of her car seats. It was another beautiful day in the PNW. Too bad my mood didn't match.

"You *have* to sleep," she warned.

"Well, duh," I said.

She slammed on the brakes, and I jerked forward, grimacing as my body ached from the sudden strain against the belt.

She swirled toward me. "Don't say 'well, duh'! You know I didn't mean it to state a fact." She slugged me slightly above my knee. At least it wasn't in the shoulder.

"Ow."

"I said you need to sleep, *and* my next question was what are you going to do about it? Keep staying in your place, hoping *one day* you'll feel safe again?"

I gestured for her to drive, and she did. "I don't know what I'm going to do. I hope when this is over I'll feel better staying there again." I had a niggling doubt that would be true. The townhouse felt violated. It also felt like the shell for the I of my life.

"You have to get ahead of them, Samantha. You have to own this," she said and whipped the SUV through the roundabout that would take us to the interstate.

"I've been trying, *Erika*," I said, using her given name to make a point. "I'm doing the best I can." I mumbled the last part because I wasn't sure I was doing my best. My gut told me I was missing something obvious.

Precious sighed heavily. "I know you are. It's just I feel so helpless. And I don't like the way it feels."

I snorted. "Try being me."

"You're doing a great job, other than the sleep." She gave me two thumbs up then returned her hands to the wheel. "You could stay with me. In fact, I'm kinda hurt you haven't asked."

"Because I don't want to bring my troubles to my friend's doorstep." I pointed to my face.

Precious snorted. "I have a state-of-the-art security system, and I've taken kickboxing classes for years."

I had a vision of Precious being whipped around like a rag doll, like I had been, her breasts clobbering her in the face. She had a hot temper when riled, and I had a morbid curiosity to see how an event like that would play out.

"Okay," I said, "I'll stay the night at your place."

She exited into Vancouver downtown and toward the main Key Finance bank. "Sweet, we can watch action thrillers and maybe pick up some tips."

As if real life would be as smoothly coordinated as a film. *I wish.* Besting Mad Dog, Heterochromiac man, would have been awesome.

"Circle through the parking lot and see if you notice anything odd," I said when she pulled up in front of the building.

A customer walked in front of the car. She was an older woman wearing brown tights stretched to an inch of its threads, a flesh-colored tank top imitating a second skin, and black crochet Ugg boots.

"Odd like how?" Precious sighed. "Where does she keep her ID? How about her keys?"

We both stared for a moment, then in unison said, "In her boots." We fist-bumped, then I got out of the car.

The line to a teller was short, and I deposited my new winnings into my business account. Not being able to pay Toby was a constant fear. I'd looked up his hourly wage in the secret spy cloud and was shocked to discover he made more than I had working at Toomey's Photography Studio. A true clue into my business prowess was that I had no clue how many hours Toby had racked up to date. I sucked at this job.

When the deposit was complete, I showed the teller a piece of paper with the secret bar account number written on it. "My husband left me this account number for this bank. But I'm not sure what sort of account it is."

Her nameplate identified her as Trista, and she looked barely out of high school with wicked long fake nails painted vibrant red except the ring fingernails. Those were gold. She glanced at the paper like it was an imposition.

"That's not a savings or checking account number." She smiled to the customer over my shoulder.

"Okay, I kinda figured. Do you have any idea what sort of account it is?" I smiled, hoping she would take pity on me.

She slid the paper to me, not bothering to give it a second look. "You can see a manager. The lady at the front reception will call one for you. They can help you." Her expression asked me if we were done here. Anger flared through me. I was tired of people not being helpful. Just once I wanted someone to give me a straight answer.

I pointed to my bruised face. "See this," I said, not waiting for her to nod but continued when she glanced at my head. "I got this at the taco stand. Guy was seriously unhelpful. So I taught him a lesson. You should see how he looks." I slid the paper off the counter while staring her down, then took two steps back. I pointed to my face then to hers before swiveling on my heel and exiting the building in a fast jog-walk, afraid she'd tapped some secret button under the counter to sic the security guard after me.

Precious was idling where I left her and flirting with the security guard. He didn't look to be in any rush to rescue a teller from a madwoman.

Precious gestured to the guard as I got into the SUV. "He asked me to move, and I told him I was only going to be a moment. We got to talking about what he wants to do long-term because this gig isn't working out." She faced the guard. "Bart, right?" He nodded. She handed him a business card she kept on her center console. "I'm Erika Shurmann, and I can help you get your life on track in the direction you want. Give me a call."

I didn't have to see her to know she was giving him her dazzling smile. Bart looked like a man who'd been offered a three-tittied woman.

"I sure will," he said in awe, staring at Precious's chest region.

"Let's go," I said and punched her in the arm. "Sorry, Bart. Have to get going. Nice to meet you." I pushed at Precious's knee to get her to put some pressure on the gas.

"Bye-bye," she said as she eased from the curb. When we were back on the main road out of Vancouver and headed back to Wind River, she asked, "Why are you shaking?"

"I maybe threatened the teller," I said and chewed my lip. I told her the story. "I think I'm losing it. I lost my temper and still didn't get the answer I wanted, but I can't go back there today."

Precious snorted. "We need to bring you back around. And you know how we do that?" She didn't wait for me to answer. "You need a win. Where are we with the cases you're working on?"

I ignored the use of "we." "I need to talk with Shannon." I glanced at my watch. "Perfect timing. We'll get there right as school gets out."

Precious gunned it. "Hold on to your titties, kitties, we're on the case."

We made it to the school five minutes before the dismissal bell rang. "Let's go to her classroom," Precious said.

Shannon's room was empty so we waited for her to return.

"Oh, my word," Shannon said as she blew into the room. She put her hand to her heart and stared wide-eyed at me. "You got the picture, didn't you? I knew it. That rat bastard is cheating." She collapsed into a kid-sized chair.

"You were hoping he wasn't?" I asked.

She nodded and put her palms over her eyes. "He's the father of my kids. I don't want what comes next."

"What does come next?" Precious asked.

"I don't know. Now that I have to decide." She groaned.

On Shannon's hand was a silver ring, and I moved closer to check it out. It was two entwined hearts with flecks of diamonds on the outer arches. I touched the ring. "Tell me about this."

She pulled her hands away and stared down at her fingers. "Sean gave it to me a week ago. I was hoping he was turning a new leaf, ya know? He said he was sorry for being a half-assed husband and father." She choked back a sob.

It was yesterday Sean had the ring. If he'd lied about giving it to Shannon who was he really giving it to?

"Shannon, I don't have the money shot yet, but I did see him with someone. Your suspicion about his extra-marital—*ahem*—activities was spot on." This part of the job sucked. I really wanted that win Precious mentioned earlier.

Shannon made a sound that was half nervous giggle, half sob. "I'm glad you don't have a picture. I don't think I want to see one anyway. I don't want to know what this woman looks like."

I was sitting across from a real wife. Knowing I was another "this woman," also known as the "other woman," was uncomfortable. Never mind what else I needed to tell her.

"I have something to ask you."

She gestured for me to continue, her expression ragged from disappointment and grief.

"You said he's been acting weird. Did he tell you yet about the casino?"

She shook her head.

"Not even that he won?"

She shook her head again.

"Has he bought any big purchases?" How a man sat on nearly two-million dollars as long and as quietly as Sean had was baffling.

"No, in fact I had to call him because he hadn't put his pay in the account, and the mortgage was about to come out."

I paused, thinking, trying to make sense of it. He gave Shannon the same ring he was carrying in his pocket. Everyone at the casino thought he'd hooked up with Kimmie, and I'd seen them together. He hadn't told a soul about the money, and it wasn't showing up in their joint account.

"I ran into Sean yesterday. He's really miffed at both the city and his dad."

Shannon rolled her eyes. "He's always mad at his dad. A few years ago, he decided to quit and start his own land-scaping company. We talked to the bank and everything, but when it came time to pull the trigger, he chickened out. Said he'd rather not compete with his dad and he'd probably be more successful owning a fishing excursion boat. I was so mad because, of course, I had to do all the legwork. He's such an ignoramus when it comes to some-thing as simple as opening a bank account." Clearly, her stages of getting over something cycled faster than mine. She was past shock and denial and moving fast into anger.

"Sean's been coming home every night?" Trying to think like a shady ne'r do well was coming easier by the day. I was getting an idea about how things might play out.

"Mostly, but he left today for another camping trip."

My gaze settled on her two-hearts ring, and I suddenly put the pieces together. I jumped to my feet. "I believe I know where he is. I think he's going to split town. He won over two million at the casino about four weeks ago."

Shannon's mouth fell open. Shocked.

"Yeah, well the casino won't release it for two more weeks. It's their policy to give the patron privacy and time to put security into place. Do you want me to stop him or let him go?" The decision was hers, but I was hoping she'd want me to intervene.

Shannon jumped to her feet, too. "Stop him. I want some of that money."

I glanced at Precious.

She nodded. "Let's go. I've already started the car," she said and showed the key fob.

"I'm going too," Shannon said. "I'll just swing by my car and get our son's baseball bat."

26

WEDNESDAY

Our first stop was the casino. I needed to confirm a suspicion I had. I made Shannon wait in the car and Precious her keeper. But I took her ring with me.

The hour was early, and I wasn't sure if any of the people I needed to see would be there. A quick scan on the floor showed no Jessica, but there was another blonde working the table next to hers who could be Kimmie. Lisa Harper walked by, and I snagged her by the elbow.

"Hey, remember me?" I quickly let go when I caught sight of her hostile expression. I didn't have time to mingle with security. "I'm Sean's friend."

Her expression changed to annoyance with a tad of disgust. "That piece of crap."

"Yeah, tell me about it. He hasn't been in, has he?" I watched her closely for any signs of lying. Not that I was an expert by any means, but my gut was telling me something was off.

"He hasn't been in since he won." She smiled thinly.

Maybe it was the type of questions I was asking. Too specific. I tried another one just as practice, not expecting anything to come from it. "Have you seen him at all? Not at the casino, but maybe in town or something?"

Lisa stiffened. She crossed her arms, her hands gripping her biceps. She paused as if she was thinking hard about the question, but her body language spoke for itself. She was hiding something. "No, I don't think I have. In fact, I don't think I've ever seen Sean outside the casino."

I glanced at her fingers and was rewarded with my answer. "Except for when you used to meet him at the cabin behind The Chief." I pointed to the two entwined hearts ring. "Looks like he gives those out as parting gifts. Even gave one to his wife."

She stuffed her hands in her pockets. "I have no idea what you're talking about."

"Sure you don't. Shame on you hooking up with a married man." The words tumbled out before I even gave them thought. I was such a hypocrite. I glanced out at the casino floor. I'd come during a shift change.

"You think you're so high and mighty. But you would, too, if you were in love," she said, unknowingly pushing my shame button.

Lucky for Carson he died before I could kill him.

"I'm done here." She pivoted and fast-walked away from me toward what I assumed was the staff-only area of the casino. The portion behind the walls, inaccessible to customers like me.

I did my own version of fast-walking to catch the blonde leaving her table. "Kimmie?" I asked.

She faced me. Yet again another version of Shannon, this one squeaky clean. No piercings, but like the Shannon of our teen years. "Yes?"

She was holding a tray of balls and chips, I assumed the house winnings. I couldn't see her hands.

"I'm Samantha. I believe we have a mutual friend. Sean Kleppner? He gave me this." I showed her Shannon's ring.

Kimmie gasped. "He gave me one, too. Yesterday."

"That's because he's going to dump you, you nitwit," Jessica said from her table. Our attention went to Jessica. She waved her hand in the air, pointing to the exact ring.

Kimmie shook her head. She was a soft-spoken little bird, and I hated Sean for using her like he did. "No, he's going camping. I'll see him in a few weeks when he gets back."

Jessica snorted. "Doubtful. The only way you're going to see him again is when he comes back in here to gamble, and he won't be doing that until he blows through his winnings."

"Yep," I said pointing at Jessica. "She's right. Sorry, Kimmie," I said, backing away. "Thanks for your help, ladies."

I hustled out of the casino then jogged to the car. Precious was peeling out before I had the door slammed. Our destination? The cabins behind The Chief.

Sure enough, Sean's work truck was parked at number three. Parked perpendicular to it was a brand new Ford F-

350, a vehicle big enough to tow a house. A paper tag was stuck to the back window. The truck bed was partially loaded with camping equipment, fishing rods, and rope. Precious pulled longways across the road, blocking the way out.

"So he really is going camping?" Shannon asked, puzzled.

"I don't think so. He's leaving town for good. I'm guessing he bought that new truck with some of his money and is using the rest to buy into a boat excursion company in Mexico." Sean would need to leave the country if he wanted to run from his wife and obligations. "He might even be going someplace like Punta Cana. Anywhere, really, that doesn't extradite."

Shannon picked up that bat. "No, he's not."

But before she could reach for the door, Sean ran out to the back of the F-350. He was shouting at someone in the cabin. "Hurry, she said they might know we're here. We have to go now!" He stopped short as he caught sight of Precious's SUV, his eyes going wide.

"I can't wait to see who his bimbo is. How I'm not going to clobber her, too, is going to be a miracle," Shannon said and got out from the car.

I fumbled in my bag for my stun gun. I tossed my phone to Precious and told her to call Leo and give him the rundown.

"Now, Shannon," Sean said, his hands up, palms out in self-defense mode. "You know you aren't happy with me. Do you really want me to stay?"

"No," she said, "I don't. But I want some of that money. It's the least you can do for your kids."

He gave her a spiteful look. "I spent it all."

Shannon tossed the bat from hand to hand. "On what? This truck and rings for the bimbos? Who's in the cabin, Sean? Hmm? Is she afraid to come out? She should be." Shannon's voice was menacing as she crept toward him.

"It's me," a male voice said from the small front porch of the cabin.

Both Shannon and I stopped in our tracks. Then Shannon laughed.

"Of course, it would be you, Orville. You two can't take a poop without telling the other about it."

Orville stood at the doorway of the cabin. "Just give her some money, Sean."

Sean crossed his arms. "Nope, not doing it. She wants to act all high and mighty and accuse me of affairs, but why not tell us about the one she's been having with the sixth-grade math teacher?"

Both Shannon and I gasped. Likely for different reasons.

"How did you know about that?" she asked.

"I'm not as dense as you think," Sean said. "I'm not going to make that math geek's life cushy." He jabbed an angry finger in her direction. "You both can go to hell."

With only a yard between them and both staring each other down, I moved around Shannon to stand below them but in between them, forming a triangle, and positioned myself so I could reach either or be between them in a flash if need be.

"I only hooked up with him because you were already cheating. I'm so lonely, and you're never around," Shannon said.

"Whatever." Sean took a tarp out from the back and whipped it open, preparing to tie it down to the top of the bed to keep everything contained. He then slammed the tailgate closed

"Where's the money, Sean?" Shannon tapped the tip of the bat on the gravel.

His tarp deflated and fell, crumbled on the truck bed. "Uh, what money?" He shifted uncomfortably.

Shannon picked up the bat and walked toward the front of his truck. "This is a pretty new vehicle. You know my minivan needs brakes." She tapped the bat to his front driver's headlight.

I moved to the side of the truck, staying between them. "Listen, you two, I bet we can come to some sort of agreement without breaking anything."

"After I bust up your truck, I'm gonna crack open your head like a watermelon," Shannon said and did a couple practice swings toward the truck.

"Don't be crazy," Sean said. He had a hand out, as if that would stop her.

"Me? You don't want *me* to be crazy? You're about to blow out of town with two million dollars and leave me here with our debt. Never mind your children. What about them? Don't you care about them?" Shannon was clearly disgusted. "You know what? Never mind. You deserve everything this bat has to dish out." She stepped back and took a high swing position and came in fast, smashing one headlight in a deafening sound of crumbling glass and plastic.

"Jesus, Shannon, stop!" Sean screamed and ran to stand between her and the truck. "It's brand new!"

Shannon stared at him with a crazy-eyed look that scared me. I flipped the switch on my stun gun to turn it on and kept my finger there ready to unleash volts.

"It'll be a piece of shit just like you when I get done." She raised the bat, and Sean bum-rushed her.

They slammed to the ground with a grunt and swear words, rolling and clubbing at each other. I dashed in, trying to decide who to send electricity through. Maybe both.

"There has to be a better solution," I yelled down at both of them. Leo's cruiser pulled into the area. "Cops are here," I shouted, hoping they'd come to their senses.

Using the bat, Shannon bonked Sean in the head with a loud clunk.

"Ow," he screamed.

"You're an awful turd of a man," Shannon hollered and tried to bean him again. An opening presented itself. Sean had rolled away, giving Shannon a moment to collect herself and raise the bat for a good hard swing.

I jumped in between and blocked him with my body. "Stop!" I said and sparked up the stun gun. It emitted a loud crack, much light lightning does when it strikes. "Or I'll take you down. This has gone on long enough."

Shannon tossed the bat from hand to hand. "Get out of my way, Sam. I'm going to end this today."

I tried to reason with her. "Shannon, take a moment to think about what you're doing."

"He's going to leave me high and dry. Well, I'm tired of being a doormat. Get out my way. You work for me. You have to do what I say."

I shook my head. "Not when you're going to do something crazy."

"Thanks, Sam," Sean said behind me. "I appreciate you going to bat for me. No pun intended."

I spun on him. "I'm not doing this for you. I'm doing it for Shannon."

"Come on, though. You kinda understand where I'm coming from, don't you? If you had a sudden windfall of money, wouldn't you split town and leave your husband's creditors high and dry?" He gave me a pleading look, but there was something behind it that showed his insincerity.

"Actually, I don't understand. And in fact, this is how I feel about it." I put the stun gun to his gut and pressed the button. Nine million volts ran through him, and he dropped to the ground like the bag of dirt he was.

27

WEDNESDAY

L eo came to stand next to me. My hand trembled, my thumb still on the trigger.

"Did you have to stun him?" Leo asked.

I did a one-shoulder shrug. "Goofy loop. All I could think about was making him shut up. I couldn't break the cycle of thoughts. That's my defense."

Leo chuckled. "That's not exactly how goofy loop works, not that you need a defense. What you did instantly defused the situation. Maybe not how I would have done it, but it works."

"Would you have pistol-whipped him?" I asked. "Because next time I'll wait for that."

Leo gave me an odd look. "That knock on the head has made you bloodthirsty."

"Being a victim did that," I said and clicked off the stun gun. Sean was twitching on the ground, coming around.

"You'll make a good PI," Leo said.

I startled, looking up at him, mouth agape. "Huh?"

"What?" he said, feigning confusion, then pointed to Shannon. "Put the bat down, Shannon." There was no way I was going to get that compliment again.

"Is he dead?" she asked. "Or at the very least, did he wet himself?"

"She tried to kill him," Orville yelled and pointed to Shannon. "And then she electrocuted him." He pointed to me.

"He's fine. He's just had some sense knocked into him." Leo told Orville then turned to Shannon. "Now, you want to tell me what's going on here?" Leo stepped forward and took the bat from her hands. The story spilled from Shannon with some small interjections from me for clarity. Sean roused and struggled to sit up. I offered him a hand. He looked at it warily, so I waved Orville over to help his friend up.

After Shannon was done, Leo gestured to Sean. "Now your turn."

When he'd finished interviewing everyone, Leo stuck his thumbs over his service belt and sighed heavily. "What we have here is a domestic dispute and, typically, I arrest someone."

Shannon started to cry. "I have two kids at after-school care I have to pick up."

"You should have thought of that before you came out here to attack me," Sean said with contempt.

"You should have thought about that *just once*, and

maybe I wouldn't have come out here," she retorted and lunged for the bat.

Leo moved it out of her way, and I moved closer to her. Leo held up a hand. "You both have a choice. How are we going to solve this without me taking someone to jail? If I take someone to jail, then I have to fill out paperwork. Sam has to fill out paperwork. Orville has to fill out paperwork. You both have to—"

"We get it," Shannon said. "Because I'm the bigger person here—"

Sean snorted. I made my stun gun crackle, and he shut right up.

"As I was saying, I'll be the adult. Sean doesn't want me or the kids. That's clear. All I want is some of the money. Enough to set us up a little so we don't have to struggle so much." Her lower lip quivered. "That's not a lot to ask for. My son is really good with soccer, and I'd like to be able to keep him in that."

Sean nodded. "He is really good," he mumbled quietly.

A tear fell down Shannon's face. "If Sean were to give us some of the money, then I'd happily do the paperwork to get a divorce. All he'll have to do is sign the papers."

Sean gave us a disgusted look. "There isn't any more money. I spent every dime."

Shannon gasped. "You spent two-million dollars?"

His body shifted so he could turn his back to her. "I had to pay taxes, you know," he mumbled.

My gut said he was lying. No, it fairly screamed it at me. Sean was the epitome of stingy. Not even providing for his kids. I found it hard to believe he'd *spent it all*. A lot of it? Yes. But not all.

"What did you spend it on? Has to be more than this truck." I stood over him and showed him my stun gun.

"Well, I have a gambling problem, you know. So I lost a lot of it back to the casino." His attention was on the ground.

He was lying. Lisa said he hadn't been in the casino since he won.

"And The Chief has a card room so..."

"So you dumped how much into cards? One thousand? Ten thousand?" I asked, incredulous.

He scoffed. "Don't be stupid. Of course not." His eyes widened at his mistake. Sean hadn't gambled the money away.

I shook my head in disbelief. A car pulled into the drive leading to the cabins, and Lisa Harper got out. Precious and I made eye contact, an unspoken message passing between us. She waylaid Lisa.

Then it hit me. Lisa had said she'd hook up with a married man if she loved him. Lisa with her tan. Sean's talk about fishing boats. "She's hooked you up with doing fishing excursions, hasn't she? New truck, big enough to tow a large boat. Leaving town. It adds up."

Sean flushed. "Yeah, so what if she did? I'm out of this stupid town and away from my nagging wife and demanding father. Orville and I are going to live large in the sun, drinking beer, and taking dumb tourists out to catch giant fish." He raised his voice and directed his next words to Shannon. "And that's why there's no more money left."

"You're an idiot," she said. "Have you forgotten how seasick you got when we went on that whale watching excursion? I hope you barf your brains out every single stinking day." She waved her hand dismissively and said to Leo, "I'm done with him. Can I go?"

He held up one finger. "Sean, I'm going to escort you and Orville out of town, right to the Oregon border. And then I'm going to have another cop friend escort you to the next district and so on until you and Orville are states away. You want out of here, let us show you the door. You leave now or you go to jail."

Sean climbed to his feet, dusting off his seat. "Okay, but I gotta go into town first."

Leo stood firm. "Nope, you leave now or you go to jail. It might take me some time to figure out how I want to charge you, so you'll sit in jail long enough for Shannon to go tell your pops what you're up to."

Sean kicked the rocks before looking from Lisa to Orville then back at Leo. "Come on, man. We played ball together in high school. Don't bring my dad into this. You know what a tyrant he is."

Leo gave a gallant shrug. "That would mean something if you were trying to do the right thing. Make your choice." He tapped his watch.

Sean huffed and sighed, but no one capitulated. We waited him out.

He faced Orville. "We packed up in there?"

Orville nodded. "Only our bags are left."

Sean waved at him in annoyance. "Well, bring 'em out. I guess we're leaving town now." Orville shuffled into the cabin and came out seconds later with two large duffle bags.

Sean said to Leo, "I really need to swing by downtown."

"For what?"

Sean hemmed and hawed, then said. "Well, to go to the bank."

Leo wasn't buying it. "You have a debit card?" When Sean nodded, he said, "Then use it when you get to where you're going. You fellas ready? Load up. Let's go." He pointed a finger at Sean. "If you so much as pull any kind of funny business, I will shoot out your tires and arrest you on the spot. Your broken headlight gives me cause. You understand me?"

Sean nodded. He took the long way around the truck, passing in front of Shannon, who was by the passenger side. He stopped to tie down the tarp, but before he moved around the tail end of the truck, he said something to her in a lowered voice and ended it by shooting her the bird.

She lunged at him, but Leo was quick to intercept her. "Why don't you three get out of here. Tell his friend there that she should scram, too, unless she wants to be pulled into this mess and possibly arrested." He said the last part so Lisa could hear it. She said something to Precious then got into her car and backed out. I escorted Shannon to Precious's SUV and helped her into the back seat. I slid in next to her, unwilling to leave her in the back by herself.

"Hey," I said. "I know you're in shock, but do you have another account that he can't access that you can move your money into?"

Shannon was momentarily puzzled, then realization dawned. "You think he'll take from our joint account?"

"Totally," Precious said, climbing into the front seat. "He doesn't care about taking care of you or the kids."

Shannon pulled out her phone and worked her banking apps. "You know what's odd. He kept saying he needed to go downtown, but we don't bank at the one downtown."

Precious said, "Maybe he opened an account down there."

"He wouldn't know how to do it," she said bitterly.

I asked, "What did he say to you before he flipped you off?"

Shannon scoffed. "He said that there's still some money left, but he'll never give it to me and I'll never find it. He's a piece of crap and a liar. How could he spend all that money?" She gave a bitter laugh. "Though if anyone could, it would be Sean."

My brain was stuck, trying to catch a thread of something. A point I was missing. As we drove in front of The Chief where Graycloud was outside working on his planters, it struck me.

"What if he does still have some? What if he hid it?" I asked.

Shannon rolled her eyes. "He would totally hide it. He's so afraid of people trying to steal from him. Ironic, right?"

"Precious, drive to downtown Wind River. To River-front Park." That's where I'd seen Sean redoing the pot. "What we have to do would be better done at night, but who cares? We can ask for forgiveness later," I said more to myself.

I explained to them my theory. When we got downtown, I loped across the street to the hardware store and bought two buckets. All this activity was making my body ache.

At the park, there were a few moms with little kids around, but we ignored them and proceeded with our plan.

"Look," I said pointing to the two larger pot. "Doesn't it stick out like a middle finger?"

"Sean's favorite form of communication," Shannon said. "We have to make this fast. I have to get the kids from after-school care." She clapped her hands to her cheeks. "What will I tell them about their dad?"

Both Precious and I were at a loss for words. "Maybe your parents can help. Or his parents," I offered finally.

We took the plants from the pot and placed them gently in the bucket in the same arrangement they'd been in the pot. Then we dumped the dirt into the other bucket. Sure enough, at the bottom of the pot was a large dark cloth, much like cheesecloth, sitting on a pile of rocks.

Shannon pointed to it. "That's nothing. That's just a barrier," she said with disappointment.

The cloth was wrapped around something small, shoebox-sized. Because it was wedged between more dirt and rocks, I tore open the cloth. I spread the gap wide, and the three of us gasp.

Wrapped in plastic were packages of hundred-dollar bills. I pointed to one. "This is called a brick. It's my understanding that one of these is a hundred grand." I took pictures of the money and the people in the park as some sort of proof.

"How many are in there?" Shannon asked in awe.

"Looks like three," I said and opened the purse on her shoulder. I put the bricks in her bag.

Shannon sat on the wall in shock while Precious and I repotted all the plants to the best of our ability.

"How do I deposit it?" Shannon asked, still stunned.

"I'll help you get a paper trail so you can show it's legit," I said, thinking I was going to owe Toby even more money after he helped me figure out how to do what I just promised.

We repeated our actions with the second planter and found two more bricks.

"Come on," I said. "Let's get you home so you can put that somewhere safe."

She stood and faced me, tears running down her face. "Thank you, Sam. Thank you so very very much. You have saved my life."

I hugged her. "I wouldn't go that far, but I'm glad I could help."

Precious was right. A win did go a long way to making me feel good.

28

THURSDAY

A plan was a good thing to have. I really should get one.

My body was desperate for a rest, and I a firm plan of action, but time didn't seem to be on my side. I had the advantage of knowing the secret account, but for how long?

To add to the time pressure was Marni's case. I had nothing solid on Lason, and she'd been putting him off for nearly two weeks.

I was working again today and hoped Lason would be on the schedule. Too bad there was no gadget to detect bad men, including the con, the wimp, the liar, the momma's boy, the couch potato, the player, and the cheapskate. To name a few. I was half tempted to just flat-out ask him.

While dressing, I was struck with the simple fact that there was no way I could fully tease out Lason's intentions.

Only he knew those. At some point, Marni would have to take a chance or not. I could, however, give her as much info as possible.

A PI's job wasn't always so black and white as I originally thought. The job was more than snooping into people's business. It was answering hard questions and making even harder decisions. But whatever I discovered or uncovered had enough weight to it that my client would have to carry it with them always.

Just as I would carry Carson's choices and actions. I pondered what Toby had told me about deep web searches into Lockett. A trip to Seattle was inevitable. My gut told me this trip would provide the answers I sought.

But decision-making was on hold until I had what was in the account at Key Financial. One goal per day was my limit. Okay, maybe two for today, but that was max.

My shift at Ralph's started at noon, and even though dressing casual for the job was allowed, I wore a black flowy knee-length skirt with cropped leggings underneath and a white peasant shirt with pink and light green threads running through it. I kept my shoes simple and chose ballet flats. I blew out my hair to come toward my face, mostly to hide the ugly purple bruises on my temple. Nothing, not even good concealer, could hide the ring of black under my eye. Outside, it was currently overcast but sun was predicated. Until then, the weather would be cooler so I grabbed a gray cardigan. I'd reverted back to using my old backpack since Leo had Carson's and the fake was with Mad Dog.

Key Bank and Finance was a local west coast chain

serving California, Oregon, and Washington. Their marketing used various looking keys. Skeleton keys were brandished on ads that said *Looking to do some home remodeling?* and the like. My journey began with the receptionist.

She was an older woman with bright red lipstick, heavily plucked eyebrows, and a pack of mints at her ready. She popped two in her mouth before I could get my question out.

"I was given this account number by my husband. He's now deceased. I'll need to access the account." Ugh, I needed a better presentation. I'd given her too much information.

"Do you have the death certificate?" The mint cracked between her teeth as she bit down.

"Do I need one?"

"If you're trying to access an account that's not yours." Chomp. Chomp.

"I don't know if the account isn't mine. I have no information. Just that it's in your bank and the account number." I kicked myself for not asking for a manager right off the bat. I made a mental note to think things through next time. Heaven forbid there be a next time.

She stared at me as if trying to figure out what to do with me. She took her role as gatekeeper seriously.

"How about I see a manager or someone who could help?" I suggested.

She popped another mint, squinted at me, then jabbed a lipstick-matching red polished nail onto the phone's keypad.

"You busy?" she said to the person on the other line, then paused. "Good, I got one for ya." She arched what I guess was her brow at me. It was hard to say, so little was there to arch.

She punched another button then pointed to the leather chairs in the waiting area. "Have a seat." She tossed another mint in her mouth.

I returned her steady stare-down then moved to the waiting area. Moments later, a large man with Popeye arms strode toward me. He wore his hair short, military cut, khaki pants, and a blue polo that matched the company's logo. A Bluetooth connector appeared glued to his ear. The polo strained across his chest and his biceps. In a few years, when the man got lazy and stopped taking steroids, he would go to fat. He would also look far less intimidating when that happened. I cursed my rotten luck.

He stood over me and stuck out a beefy hand. "Dan Burke, branch manager. Let's go to my office and talk." His handshake turned into a boost up from the seat, whipping me up so fast pain shot through my right side.

"I'm sorry," he said at my sudden intake of breath, but not an ounce of remorse was in his tone.

"I was in an accident. With my car. Two days ago." I don't know why I was bothering to give him any information. He wasn't giving me the same courtesy, and I paused, wondering if once again I was two steps behind whoever Carson had been running from.

He led me into a corner office and took a seat behind a large desk. He cut right to the chase. "My receptionist tells me you're trying to access an account that you don't have rights to."

I sat with a plop, my mouth dropping briefly. "That's not true," I protested. "I don't know anything about this account except it's at your bank and the number. I'm trying to find out what the account is. I should also tell you that I have a business account with your bank." The receptionist must have filled him in while I was going to the waiting area. I didn't like being treated like I was doing something wrong. Of course, finding this information etched on a bar, hidden in a backpack that was sent to me on the day Carson died, didn't make me feel like I was on the up and up either. I hoped my cheeks weren't pink from embarrassment.

"I can't give you any information—"

I waved him off. "Mr. Burke. I'm not asking you to break the law. I'm not trying to take something that isn't mine. I have an account number that was left to me, and I only want to know more."

"Do you have a death certificate?" He crossed his massive arms over his chest.

"Do I need one if the account is in my name?" I crossed my arms as well. It was a long shot, but since the business had been in my name, maybe this one was as well.

He stared at me. I stared back, not blinking. I was a master at this. Rachel and I had done it for hours as children and teens. I'd perfected it every time someone accused me of pretending not to know how to read to get out of work. All it took to win this game was to let your vision go fuzzy. I could drag out a stare for minutes.

He continued to assess me, but blinked, so I did as well, which was a huge relief as my eyes were burning. I was not going to break. I would be late for work if it meant waiting this guy out and winning. I'd had it up to my eyebrows with people railroading me and bullying me. This big lug wasn't going to be added to that list.

His phone rang, and he tapped the piece in his ear, his gaze flicking over my shoulder. He made a few yes and no comments before tapping his ear again.

I continued to stare, solid in my resolute.

He sighed and looked away first. "What do you want Mrs...."

There was no victory in my success, only fury. "True. Samantha True," I said. "I want you to look up the account and tell me if my name is on it. If my name or my company name isn't on it, then I'll happily walk out of your office and this building. I will be moving my business account to a friendlier bank after this. Just so you know."

Burke didn't seem to care. He'd written me off as a scammer or something, for reasons unbeknownst to me. He probably thought I didn't have a business account with his bank.

"What's the account number?" He made no move to access his computer.

"The number combination is weird," I said and told him the sequence, dashes included.

"That's because it's not an account," he said, still not budging.

"What do you mean?"

"That's not an account number."

I tossed up my hands in frustration. "All I have is your routing and transit number and then this number combo. If it's not an account, what is it?" I leaned forward angrily. "Just a little help would be nice. But if you want me to bring in a lawyer or the police, I'd be happy to do that." Mentioning the police seemed to soften Burke.

"You wouldn't run out of here if I called the cops?" he asked.

I gave him a puzzled look. "No, why would I? I'm just trying to get some answers to questions I have."

Burke let his arms fall to rest on his desk. "Key Bank and Finance is a large institution that handles several accounts for many well-to-do clients. We often have family members come in and try to gain access to those clients' accounts."

I kept my arms crossed. "And you assumed that's what I was attempting to do?"

He shrugged. "When we mention the cops, these people usually find an excuse to beat feet. I assumed your husband roughed you up." He pointed to my face. "And you were here to clean his clock through monetary means."

"My husband is dead. I told you that," I said flatly.

"But you don't have a death certificate."

With a deep sigh, I reached into my purse and took out my identification, placing it before him. "This is who I am. And all I want to know is if that account has my name on it."

"It's a safe deposit box," he said while looking at my license. "The last digits after the dash are an access code." He faced his computer, hunting and pecking at the keys with stabbing fingers.

I sat back, puzzled. Cooper had asked if there was a safety deposit box.

"Do you have the key?" He picked up my identification and handed it back to me.

The key. A key. Was there a rouge key somewhere? "I'll have to look. When I found the banking information, I wasn't looking for a key." Could it still be in the backpack? I didn't think so.

"The box is in your name, Ms. True."

Even though I had hoped the account would be in my name, I was surprised it was. "Really?"

"Come back with the key, and I can let you have access to the box," Burke said. His tone had gotten friendlier, though I suspected he wouldn't formally apologize. Being nice was his way of doing so. What a douche.

I searched my mind for possible keys. I stood to leave and said, "I'll be back." Then another thought struck me. "Is anyone else on the account?"

He glanced at the screen and shook his head.

So Carson had set up a safety deposit box that only I could access. Not even himself. Strange for sure. Then I was hit with worry. I gathered up my pack, met Mr. Burke's gaze, and said, "Mr. Burke, I hope that if someone else should come asking about this account, you'll be a complete horse's ass to them as well."

His lips twitched slightly. "You can be assured of it. That's my job."

"Good," I said. I only hoped I could find the key and get back here before anyone else. This other player had more resources and skill than I did. "Be particularly wary of a tall man with two different colored eyes." I pointed to the bandaged side of my head to emphasize how serious this matter was.

29

THURSDAY/FRIDAY

I was sporting my dad's mini cooper for the day. This little beast, painted red with a white racing stripe, could dash in and out of traffic like an attention-deficit kid jacked up on sugar. I liked it. Made me feel in charge.

Designated employee parking at Ralph's was behind the building, and I quickly found a spot. As I approached the back door, the hushed, angry voices of an argument between a man and a woman made me pause. Interrupting would be awkward. It was Lason and Tara. The words were fast and jumbled, but the intent was loud and clear. Tara wasn't happy, and Lason was getting the brunt of it.

She was pointing at his face but, as fast as lightning and with a crack louder than thunder, she went from jabbing her index finger to one hard slap across his face.

I gasped.

Tara stormed off, pushing past me with a bump to my shoulder.

Lason fell back against the wall and slid down to the ground, his hand over his cheek.

"Yowza," I said and crouched before him. "Should I pretend I didn't see any of that?"

He hefted out a weary sigh. "I give up, Samantha."

"On life or her?" I gestured in Tara's direction.

"On being a good guy. They say good guys win, but so far that ain't happenin'." He moved his palm from his face and looked at it. She'd slapped him so hard we both expected he'd find blood or something.

I moved to sit next to him. "I wish I had the answer to that. I still believe good guys can come out on top."

He glanced at me, pausing as he took in my bruised face. "No offense, but you don't look like you're coming out ahead either."

I laughed. "None taken." Was I the good guy in this scenario Carson thrust me into? I gave the question thought. I was still unsure because I'd been the fake wife, the other woman. Neither of those came with a positive connotation. Something inside me stirred, an acceptance maybe? I knew the answer. Yeah, yeah I was the good guy.

I pointed to my face. "The guy who did this to me? He's not gonna get away with it. Good guys don't have to lie down and take it. My intentions are true. My intentions aren't aimed at greed or inflicting harm." I tapped my chest. "In here, I know I'm on the right side. I don't know what Tara's problem is with you. But if you love her and doing right by her, then maybe you need to talk some more. But keep a table between you for your own safety." This was my way of gently probing him for Marni's sake.

"I do love her," he said.

My stomach plummeted in disappointment for Marni.

"But she's nothing but trouble. Always has been. Ever since we were kids. I may have to love her because we're family and all, but I don't have to like her or even do what she says."

I curled my lip in confusion. "What? You're in love with someone you're related too?" Ew.

Lason's expression matched mine. "Gross, no. Tara's my cousin. And she's a pain in the butt. Can't keep a job to save her life, and now it's my responsibility to help her be an adult and do the right thing. And it's my fault when she doesn't." He pointed to the empty space where Tara had been. "You know what that fight was about?"

I shook my head.

"She's mad because I don't clock her in and out. Because I don't help her lie and say she's here when she's not."

I gasped. "Seriously?"

"Yeah, I even went so far as to transfer her to a different store. She lasted two weeks before the assistant manager was begging me to take her back. She's pulling me down, man," he said with heavy frustration.

"Let her go then," I said. "Sometimes people only learn when they have to."

"My mom and aunt will lose their minds." He dropped his head in defeat, his chin on his chest. "You know what, Samantha? I met the nicest woman. A woman I could really like. But how do I involve her into this mess that's my family? 'Hey,'" he said, as if he was talking to someone in front of him. "'Want to go out and have a fabulous time and see if this develops into something good? Then maybe we can get married and you can enjoy this insanity that is my family, too!'"

What advice could I give? I had a great family. Our version of crazy worked well together. "I don't have any tools to help you with that. Sorry. The last year of my life was a lie."

"Not all of it, I'm guessing," Lason said. "I bet what you felt wasn't a lie."

I nudged him with my shoulder because no truer words had been spoken in days. "If you like this girl, tell her up front. Tell her what she's getting herself into. Let it be her choice."

Lason snorted. "Sounds so easy when you say it."

"Nothing about taking a chance is easy," I said.

A moment of comfortable silence passed between us. A new friendship had formed.

"You're late for work," he said.

"I know. If my boss were a decent kinda guy, he'd clock me in on time instead of sitting outside feeling sorry for himself." I nudged his shoulder again, and we laughed. Lason climbed to his feet and helped me up.

He said. "I'll make a note in the computer. Don't worry about it. Thanks for listening, Samantha."

"Any time." In my pack, my phone whirred with a text message. I pulled it out and glanced at the screen. It was from the jeweler where I had taken my necklace. The message wasn't friendly, and there were too many excla-mation points for my liking, so I was inclined to let them have it. Good riddance.

The necklace, presented as an act of love from Carson was probably from guilt. Two stupid keys and one heart, implying I held the key to his heart.

I paused at the door Lason was holding open for me. "Two keys," I said to him.

"What?" He appeared confused.

"I have two keys." Maybe what was in the box was his heart. Not his real heart, that would be gross, and unless he was a machine, he couldn't have put that in there anyway. But maybe *I* wasn't the key to his heart. Maybe I just held them, and whatever was in the safe deposit box was. Boy, that thought really depressed me.

Lason was still puzzled. "Did Tara slap you, too? What are you saying?"

I shook myself from my thoughts. "Never mind. Listen, I know I'm the worst employee ever, but can I take a little longer break today. I need to run an errand."

"Sure," he said. "It's not super busy. But how long is a little longer?"

Our meal breaks were thirty minutes. "I might need forty-five. I have to run to Mill Plain to pick something up."

"Fine with me," he said, and we went inside.

Now, if I could get through the next few hours without constantly checking the clock. I kicked myself for not asking to just go right then, but I made good use of the time. When I got out on the floor with an order, I slipped into a quiet pocket and gave Marni a call. I told her what I'd learned about Lason, leaving out the crazy family. I figured he could tell her that.

I didn't sleep that night as I stared at the ceiling, holding the necklace in my hand. Any minute now I expected Mad Dog to burst in and fight me for the keys. I was up before the sun, I was dressed before the rooster crowed, and I was at Precious's place, drinking coffee and jiggling my leg as I waited for her to dress. There was no way I was going to open that box alone. We were at the bank when they unlocked the doors, and I was the first to step up to the receptionist and ask for Mr. Burke.

His greeting was much nicer this time. His attention was more on Precious whose expression of cold disdain must have intrigued him. She was desperate to give him a set-down for the way he treated me.

"Do you have the key?" he asked.

I nodded. Words stuck in my throat. He asked for my identification and the account then walked us to the back. We entered into a private room with bars and a secure door. Once he had us locked in, he opened the door across the room that led to the vault. Like mailboxes one sees at the post office, several small doors with numbers lined the wall. He guided us toward mine.

"Insert your keys."

I stared at him since he'd said keys, plural. I inspected the box. There were two keyholes. "You have a different way of doing things."

He gave a half-smile. "We *are* Key Finance."

I took out my necklace with the two keys. I shared a glance with Precious before I snapped the keys off, removing them from the heart and the chain. Burke said nothing. I slid one small skeleton-like key in one slot and the other in the second, surprised it had gone so smoothly since my hands were shaking something fierce.

The door swung open, and Burke slid out a small metal 8x11 box with a lid on hinges. He set it on the table.

"I'll give you some privacy," he said and stepped from the room.

Precious took my hand. I squeezed hers in thanks. I reached out to the metal box with trepidation, as if it might bite or electrocute me. I slid my thumb under the lid and pushed in the button to open it. The lid released with a *pop*. I jerked my hand away in surprise, expecting it to spring open or something to leap out or...anything jump scare to be honest.

Only, nothing happened.

With trepidation, I eased the lid up like a large yawn.

Precious and I leaned forward and peered into the box.

"What the duck is that?" she asked. "Totally not what I was expecting."

I pursed my lips. Me either.

Inside the box were three severed thumbs and two credit cards with sticky notes that read *copy.*

30

SATURDAY

We decided to drive Precious's SUV to Seattle. My gut told me I would find answers there. Starting with Lockett. Toby wasn't happy to be missing high time, but I was compensating him well so he couldn't complain. We stopped long enough to grab two take-out pizzas, one Meat Lover's, the other a Hawaiian.

Turns out the severed thumbs in the box were thumb drives and on the bottom of two, someone, I'm assuming Carson, had written *copy*. They were disturbing to see rolling around in the box. The two credit cards were actually storage for mini SD chips that slid out from the corner. Kinda cool in a covert way.

Afraid Mad Dog and whoever he worked for might be outside watching, I had stuffed one finger down Precious's bra and another in my boot. I didn't have the chest to disguise the finger. I had added a gel cushion sole in each of my boots and placed the key under one in my attempt to hide them. I left the rest behind in the safety deposit box for safekeeping.

"Paranoid much?" Precious said as she adjusted the finger down her shirt.

"Scared," I said.

Now, Toby, disgruntled because I wouldn't let him work remote from Carson's high-tech secret space off the office, was working his tech magic on the drives in the back seat of Precious's SUV and grumbling.

"Okay, I'm in," he said.

I climbed in the back seat next to him. "Keep driving," I told Precious, "I'll fill you in."

Toby scrolled over images of blue file folders. "These are filled with news articles about Indian Services and Indian Affairs. Some of these files are encrypted, which I'll have to break to figure out what's inside."

I gave him an expectant look.

He shrugged. "I don't know what any of this means."

Deflated, I pointed to the icon of a film reel. "Start that."

Toby clicked on it, and a grainy video popped up and began to play. We leaned in closer to the screen, and Toby turned up the volume. We watched it seven times before I started putting the pieces together.

Two men on the screen, a slender, fit man and a round, older man. One did not appear to work for the other. They also did not appear to be friends. They were outside, the backdrop a nighttime forest with a full moon and a dark swath running through the trees. A river perhaps? Humpty was talking, and the thin man was leaning toward him and nodding. This is where being a dyslexic came in handy. I'd spent my life learning to read body cues.

"This one," I said pointing to the slender one, "is going to do a job for Humpty." Humpty's casual stance with one hand in his pocket told me he was a man who got stuff done.

"When?" Humpty asked in a booming, demanding voice. Most of the sound was too quiet, but the odd loud word was picked up crystal clear.

"Next week." Garbled words and then, "...make the news." Slender man said more but it was muffled. Same thing with what Humpty followed up with. When they shook hands, I felt dirty just watching. Something awful had just been decided.

"I wish I could make out the rest of what they're saying," I mumbled.

"Let me see if I can enhance the audio," Toby said.

I rolled my eyes. "While you're at it, could you zoom in on this guy?" I tapped the image of slender man. "Something about him is familiar. I'd like to know who he is."

Toby huffed. "What? Do you think I have facial recognition or something? Like I'm the FBI. Had we done this in Carson's computer room, I bet I could do amazing things with this video."

I punched him in the bony knee, but not too hard. Only hard enough to make him flinch. "I need you here, not there." I pointed to the screen. "This works better face to face. And are you seriously gonna sit here and tell me a computer junkie like yourself doesn't have at least a simple recognition program on your computer?"

He lifted his vape pen, refusing to make eye contact. He clicked a few buttons then pushed his computer onto my lap. He'd drawn a box around a slender man, and the computer was working on enhancing it.

"No smoking in my car," Precious said from the front. "I don't want that nicotine smell in my car."

"Nicotine!" Toby said. "Get out! I don't do that crap. Have you seen people going through nicotine withdrawal? My Uncle Thomas stopped smoking and gained over forty pounds that year," he said as he reached forward to the front then lifted the lid off the pizza box I'd left on my seat. "I allow for one vice, and I choose an herbal one." He took one slice of pizza and stacked it cheese side down on another before taking a bite.

He flicked the air freshener hanging from Precious's rearview mirror and said with a full mouth, "Just think of me as a walking, talking version of this. Only my stuff smells way better than that manufactured crap. I'm my own aromatherapy."

I laughed. I glanced back at the screen and gasped. "It's that guy Cooper that I met in the park."

"You said he knew Carson," Precious said.

"He was just one of many looking for something Carson left behind. We need to figure out the other man. Maybe that will help me connect the dots. Cooper said Carson helped him with a client. Maybe this guy was the client. "

Toby wiped his greasy hands on his pants and made

some more clicks. The man's face enlarged, but the angle was never right and he was too pixelated. Or maybe that ugly.

I tapped Cooper's face. "See if the program can pick up this one's real name. When we get to Seattle and track down Lockett, we can ask him what Humpty's name is. I have a feeling he'll know."

I watched the screen as it worked on searching for Cooper's identity. Trouble was, he would have to be in a federal database for anything to pop. Criminal, prior military, school teacher, or federal employee were areas it would search. My bet was on him being some sort of criminal. He'd said Carson was working with him, but now I wonder if Carson discovered Cooper working something illegal. Had Carson's untimely death been Cooper's good fortune? I paused as a sick thought burst through the others. What if Carson's death had been planned? What if he'd died because of whatever was going down in this video?

"You guys," I said quietly, "What if Carson died because he was working with Cooper? I can't ask you to put yourself in danger for something that doesn't involve you. You should go back home." Distance between me and them was the only way to keep them safe. Even though going at this alone was terrifying.

"Like h-e-double hockey sticks. We aren't leaving you. At least, I'm not," Precious said. She gunned the SUV.

"Precious," I said. "I'm serious."

"I am, too," she said with such determination that changing her mind would be impossible.

I was both appreciative of and scared for her.

She tapped her temple. "I'm visualizing a successful resolution as I drive."

Toby was on another helping of pizza sandwich.

To him I said, "We can take you to the train station, and I'll get you a ticket home."

He paused, pizza halfway lifted to his mouth. "Dudette, whatever Carson was into might not be good, but he was good to me. He took me seriously from day one. Gave me a job I love and understood my schedule. If someone killed him because of this stuff"—he gestured to the screen—"then I owe it to him to finish what he started." He chomped on the pizza.

I wish I could be as clear cut about Carson's motives toward me as Toby was toward him.

"What if Carson was a bad guy, too, and was using you for some reason?" I asked this question to Toby but myself, too.

"What reason?" He continued to eat.

I stared at the computer, shifting my focus from the men to the scenery behind them while I searched my brain for some sort of link that connected me, Toby, and Carson. If Carson put in security systems, if he charged large amounts of money for top-notch cybersecurity, then what did he need Toby for? Wasn't he capable of doing all this himself? In photography, we learned how to use the negative to check elements of the image. I applied this to the video. I let the men on the screen fade to the background and brought the scenery forward. The forest popped and the dark ribbon between the trees reminded me of the Windy River. The answer figuratively slapped me upside the head. Then I literally slapped myself on the forehead.

"Land," I said.

"Huh?" Toby said, pre-pizza bite.

"Up by Graycloud's place. There are several parcels that overlook the river. Your parents own a parcel. So do my parents. The Kleppners. My landlord, Chuck, the Stillmans." I fumbled for my phone and accessed the secret cloud, pulling up client files, but didn't find what I was looking for. Toby's computer was still in my lap, and I clicked on the external drive. A file labeled WR/LD was listed. Wind River/ Land maybe? I clicked on it and was shown a list of the landowners.

When I clicked on my parents' name, files about them, me, and Rachel popped up, including several pictures of me and notes I couldn't bear to read. A cold sweat broke over me. I swallowed hard and clicked on Toby's parents' name. Pictures, information, even tidbits that went back to high school. The same was for the Kleppners. Carson knew about Sean's womanizing proclivities before he even met Shannon or Sean. Marni Edgar was listed because her firm had handled the sale all those years ago. Carson's notes on her were about her being lonely. Leo's file was the only one that lacked personal information. No weakness that could be exploited.

Carson had played us. From moment one, we were targets. Carson had played me.

"Toby," I said. "Carson wasn't your friend. Or mine. We were tools he was using for a greater gain." I spun the computer so he could see the screen. "We need to figure out what the objective was and get Carson and this mess behind us. See if you can find any connection between the land and Carson." I filled Precious in on what I found in the file.

Toby scanned the screen, the two slices of pizza drooping in his hand. After a few minutes, he closed the laptop then tossed the slices back in the box. "I've lost my appetite."

I squeezed his knee. "Me, too. I got your back."

He tapped his chest. "It hurts, man."

Because I'd been wondering how deep Carson's deception went, I was more prepared than Toby. Still, this discovery cut to the bone. The sooner this entire mess was behind us the better. I deleted the files. There was no purpose for this information to be in my possession.

I said, "When we get to Lockett's law firm, I'll go in solo. Toby, you keep working on those files and, Precious, you keep the car running in case we need to get away fast."

"Roger," she said and eyed me from the rearview mirror.

"Works for me," Toby said. "I'm a big scaredy-cat."

"Maybe not a *big one*," I said and elbowed him. He was staying after all. "Maybe just a little tiny scaredy-cat."

Seattle was an amazing city. My parents used to bring my sister and me here to watch the games, Dad being a big sports guy. For me, the city had nothing but wonderful memories and good food. I was prepared to throat punch any bad guy who might try and change that for me. My stun gun was in the back pocket of my jeans, fully charged.

We passed the Space Needle and the glass museum, Mom's favorite, as Precious's GPS led us to Lockett's law offices. Precious pulled to the curb of a seven-story brick building much to the frustration of several cars behind her. Many blew their horns and gestured with fingers. Precious blew them kisses.

From the top floor, some lucky devils had views of the sound, the needle, and the wheel. I was in and out in under seven minutes, three of those waiting for the elevator.

I climbed into the back seat with Toby. "That was a bust," I said, slamming the door in frustration. "He's taken a month-long vacation. They said he's in Australia."

"We know that's not true because he was at Ralph's," Precious said.

"Maybe I should have hung out there. Probably had a better chance of finding him that way." I crossed my arms in a huff. "Sorry about wasting your time, guys."

"Actually," Toby said turning the computer to face me. "I'm working on breaking another one of Carson's encrypted files, and look what I found."

On the screen was a picture. Clearly, it had been taken through a window looking into what appeared to be a coffee shop. In the picture were Carson and another man's profile. They were sitting across the table from each other but leaning in close.

"I can pull up the time stamp and geocache for a location. Someone took this with their cell phone," Toby said and pointed to some data he made pop up on the screen. "This was two days before Carson died. And it was sent to him in an email." He pointed to a line of odd characters and nonsensical words. "I ran a search on these files for this geocache stamp and found it several times in another file." Toby did more clicking, and screens popped up. "See all this?"

"Yeah, those numbers repeat in a column." The geocache code was showing up two dozen times, easy.

"Yep, that's the location. The numbers next to it are dates and times. And they come from Carson's cell phone."

"He tracked his own whereabouts? Why?" I hated not knowing what I didn't know.

Toby shrugged. "Your guess is as good as mine."

"Who's the guy?" I asked, tapping the picture.

"No idea, but they're at the Daily Grind Coffee shop," Toby said. "Carson was a frequent patron of this coffee shop." He ran his finger down the column of location code.

"Which is right down the street," Precious said and pointed to her GPS.

"Let's go," I said. "Maybe we can find this guy and get some answers. They look to be having a serious conversation."

"I could use a coffee," Toby said. "A double shot Americana sounds exactly like something I need to help steel my nerves." He held out his hand to show it steady, but floppy. "Look at me, I'm a mess."

Precious, who was backward in her seat, arched a

brow. I chuckled. She spun around and readied herself to pull out into traffic and said, "Hold on to your titties, kitties. We're going to get some answers." She whipped into traffic and gunned it, cutting off a Prius in the process.

I clutched the computer to keep it steady. Toby grabbed his pecs and held on tight.

31

SATURDAY

T oby waved my phone in my face. "I sent the picture to the cloud storage. And I loaded an RFID app. You see someone suspicious, open the app and press the button."

"That feels illegal," I protested. "Don't those apps scan the person and swipe their information?"

Precious said from the front, "Next time you're getting the shizzle stomped out of you, make sure to ask for the bad guy's name."

She had a point. If I had Mad Dog's name right now, we'd be further along.

Toby said, "There's no guarantee with it. RFID tags are everywhere so the app will pick up a lot of info we don't need. It's the whole needle and haystack thing."

I nodded. "I'll use the app."

"We're here," Precious said, coming to an abrupt stop

and sending both Toby and me into the back of the front seats.

The Daily Grind took up the corner of a block-long brick building. Large glass garage doors came together at the corner. They were rolled up, letting the sunny weather in.

Precious had pulled up to the curb, her front passenger wheel riding up on the sidewalk. "I'll circle around. Text us if you need backup support, and I'll try to find a spot. The closest parking garage I found was two blocks that way." She pointed behind us.

"Okay," I said and fidgeted with the cloud, pulling up the picture.

"I'll be going that way, north, around the block," Precious said, pointing to the front of the SUV. "So if you get spooked, don't run north, run south, and we'll intersect sooner."

"Roger," I said. Directions were difficult for me so I stared down the street in the direction she called south and tried to commit the image to memory. My face was still a discolored mess so I put on a Seahawks cap, pulling my hair into a ponytail through the size adjuster in the back. Maybe the shadow would disguise something. "Double shot Americano for you, Toby, and for you, P?"

"Oh, get me something frilly and fun. Hemp milk if they have it."

I jumped out of the SUV and took a deep, calming breath as I strolled into the cafe. We had no other leads, and I hoped this one would play out.

The line was short, and I surveyed the crowd as I

waited. Typical hipsters. PNW men seemed of two types. The men with bushy mountain man beards and men without. That was it. One could never assume the guy with the clean-shaven face and Mariners jersey was a sports nut any more than the man with the full beard was outdoorsy. That was the beauty of living here. Nothing was predictable.

Except maybe the coffee shops had customers with open laptops and expressions of grim concentration.

At my turn, I stepped up to the counter and ordered. The barista, a woman my age, had a high and tight haircut, dark heavy eye makeup, a sleeve of tattoos on both arms, and a friendly smile. I wanted to be friends with her. She oozed confidence. After paying, the opportunity to go fishing opened.

"Do you work here a lot?" I asked. With my luck, she could be a brand-new employee. Tabby was the name on her badge.

She eyed me. "Yeah, why?"

"I'm looking for someone. It's a shot in the dark, but maybe you can help." I held up my phone and showed her the picture. I pointed to Carson. "I know this guy." I pointed to the other guy. "But not this one."

"Why you want to know him?" She crossed her arms, and then her eyes darted to a corner of the room. I glanced that way. She was looking at the table that was in the picture.

"And why not ask this guy what his friend's name is." She pointed to Carson.

"Because he's dead," I said matter-of-factly.

She gasped, then whispered, "So is his friend."

"What?" I said, even though I'd heard her. What were the odds? Maybe this guy had been in the car with Carson when the tree fell on it.

She gestured for me to move down the line, and she did as well. "You need a drink carrier?"

I nodded.

"Listen, I don't know you—"

"I was married to Carson." I rolled my eyes heavenward. "Well, I guess not really married since he had a wife he wasn't divorced from but I *believed* I was married to him. But he left me a mess, and I'm trying to clean it up." I figured the girl was the sort who could sniff out a lie and had her share of bullcrap from men.

She narrowed her eyes, and with disgust, she said, "He did not!"

I grimaced. "Which part makes you angrier? The wife or the mess? Because I'm kinda torn. Feeling them both with equal anger."

She shook her head. "The audacity of some people. I didn't know Carson well. Met him when he started coming in and talking with Ben. That's the other guy in your picture. Ben Fulton. He was a nice guy. Big on the environment. Always complaining to me about the waste the coffee stirrer and cups made." She rolled her eyes but in a good-natured way.

I connected another puzzle piece. "He's Senator Fulton's kid, right?"

She nodded.

"Big outdoorsman, too. You think Senator Fulton is

right? About how there's no way his kid could have fallen asleep with a lit cigarette?" My dad's instinct for a story trumped again.

"Yeah, totally. Ben's only vice was coffee. Real health nut." She pointed to some bars stacked on the counter. "I carry these gluten-free, preservative-free, only five ingredients health bars just for him." She sighed heavily. "I'm gonna miss him."

"I'm sorry," I said. "By chance, do you know why they were always meeting?" I was hoping she'd managed to catch some bits here and there.

She shrugged and continued to make our drinks. "Not really. Something about land and wetlands and preserving. That was Ben. He wanted to preserve anything and everything. He could make a cup of coffee last hours." She chuckled.

I did as well. Ben Fulton sounded like a nice enough guy. Not that I was a good judge of such things. Regardless, how did he get mixed up with Carson?

She glanced over my shoulder and said in a frosty voice. "Can I help you?"

The hairs on the back of my neck stood straight up. The ones on my arms, too. My inner alarm system was pinging madly.

No doubt, something was about to go down, and I was going to be in the mix of it. I don't know how I managed it, maybe from sheer nervousness, but I clicked on my photo app then slowly turned to see who stood behind me.

Mad Dog.

I nearly wet my pants. "Oh, no," I said weakly. I raised

my phone and pressed the photo taking button. Never looking at the screen, only at Mad Dog's two differently colored eyes.

"I knew you were too stupid to listen to good advice," he said, his tone laced with distaste.

"Stay away from me," I said. I couldn't believe he was confronting me like this in a public place.

"Come with me," he said and reached for my arm.

I jerked back. "Oh, no," I said, stuck in that same stupid goofy loop.

From over my shoulder came Toby's large Americana. Reflexively, I took it.

"Toss it at him!" Tabby said.

So, I did. The scolding cup of coffee splashed onto Mad Dog's arm since he'd moved forward to block his face at the last minute when Tabby had shouted her instructions. The drink spilled over to his chest. He howled, his attention on pulling away his shirt.

"Kick him in the dick," Tabby shouted.

So, I did.

Mad Dog must have needed a moment to process what she said. As my knee was one second from making contact with his groin, he jerked his attention to me, and realization dawned across his face. Had the moment not been so scary, I would have called it beautiful. Using as much force as I could, remembering that this was the guy who'd flung me around like a rag doll, I sent my knee as high into his body as it would go.

And I took pictures of the whole thing, too.

Mad Dog doubled over. I stood stunned.

"Run!" Tabby said. And I was propelled into motion.

"Thanks," I said. She was lifting up a phone, hopefully to call the police.

I dashed out the door and ran up the street with no thought to what I was doing or where I was going. I was a block away when it dawned on me I'd done the opposite of what Precious had told me to do. I was running behind the SUV and not toward it. But there was no way in heck I was going to turn back.

I whipped around the corner, not paying any attention to where I was going and ran smack into a tall, solid wall of a person.

I screamed and covered my head with my arms.

"Samantha!"

I looked through my arms to discover it was Lockett I'd run into. I stopped screaming, but was panting heavily.

"Come on," he said and dragged me toward the building. "We need to get you out of sight."

We ducked inside a paper store, and Lockett pushed me away from the window against a wall of journals.

Dear Diary, please don't let me die.

Lockett moved closer to me and peered through the window from the edge.

"What were you thinking going into that coffee shop?" he asked incredulously.

"I was thinking I could get some coffee and maybe find out who this guy was in a picture with Carson," I whispered. Though I wasn't sure why I was. I did feel like I might cry, though.

"What guy?" His attention traveled between me and the window.

Using the same dexterity a pig might with a smartphone, I was finally able to pull up the picture. "This guy."

Lockett glanced at the screen, his lips a thin line. He finally said, "That's Ben Fulton. Senator Fulton's kid."

"Oh, I'm so glad you know that. I, of course, had to travel here and get chased by Mad Dog to find that out." I blew out a breath, then shoved him in the shoulder. "Why are you here?"

"You're in over your head," he said.

"Really? You think? No thanks to you."

"Why the coffee shop?" He glanced from the window to me.

Should I share what I'd learn? Was he trustworthy? I hesitated, but he clearly knew more than me, and any information now would be a good thing.

"Apparently, he and Carson were meeting a lot at this coffee shop."

Lockett nodded. "That explains a lot."

I narrowed my eyes. "What does it explain? Enlighten me. It seems everyone in this game knows more than me, and I'm sick of it."

"Well," Lockett said, hemming and hawing. "It's hard to explain."

"Try me." I crossed my arms.

The store clerk walked up to us. "May I help you?" She appeared perturbed. Either that or the bun she was wearing was tight and pulling back her facial features, creating a put-out look.

"No," I said and waved her off. I didn't want Lockett distracted.

"Is there a back door out of here?" he asked.

"No," she said.

He arched a brow. "Really? So you're telling me that should a fire break out in the front of the store, you're doomed because there are no other exits?"

"Yes," she said looking down her nose, though her head was tilted back as if he was several feet taller than her.

"I find that hard to believe," he said.

"Why do we need to go out the back? Don't you know karate or something. You were wearing a black belt, remember?" I poked him in the arm.

He faced me, his expression haughty. "We are not to use our skills on others unless justified and provoked."

I rolled my eyes. "Gosh, I hope that doesn't happen. That would be horrible," I said in mock horror. Then I pointed to my face. "I think this is justification and provocation."

Lockett sighed. "You might have a point."

I contemplated stomping on his foot. Instead, I called Precious. She answered on the first ring.

"Where are you?" She sounded worried.

"In a paper shop on—" I glanced at the clerk, wanting her to fill in the rest.

"On fourth," she said with bite.

"On fourth. Middle of the block. It'll be on your left."

"Okay, I'm rounding again. One block away. I'll go slow on Fourth."

I ended the call and pushed Lockett aside to watch for Precious.

Lockett said, "We might as well go stand out there. They're probably following her anyway."

"Speaking of which, how is it you managed to come upon me at such an opportune time?"

Lockett huffed. "I've been following you. And let me tell you, it has not been an easy task, which is a good thing I guess."

That explained the feeling of being watched.

32

SATURDAY

Lockett and I made it to Precious's SUV without getting shot. Not that I thought there were gunmen or snipers around us, I just wasn't going to put anything past these crazies. Whoever they were.

Leery of taking the ferry and getting trapped, we aimed for the interstate. With no specific destination in mind, we drove toward Kitsap County. Lockett wanted to see if we were being followed; odds were high. Once we were cruising at high speed, I turned to Lockett and pummeled him in the upper arm. Frustrated with getting no response, I whipped out my stun gun and made it crackle. "You better start talking."

Lockett's eyes went wide. "What do you want me to say?"

"I'd like the truth. Start there." I clicked the stun gun's button twice more, making it pop.

"Can someone fill me in on what's going on?" Precious asked as we cruised down the interstate.

"And where's my drink?" Toby asked.

"Mad Dog popped up. He's actually wearing your drink, Toby. Sorry. We can drive through someplace when we get off the interstate."

Toby pouted. "I was really looking forward to that drink."

"Oh, just puff on your vape pen," I said in frustration and tossed him my phone. "Here, got some pictures of him. See if you can run the program and find out who he is."

"You could have used the RFID program," Toby mumbled, messing with my phone. He looked at me, puzzled. "There's no pictures on here."

"What?" Incredulous, I tried to stretch over Lockett, who was trapped in the middle, to look. Impossible! I'd pressed the stupid button one point five million times. There had to be *one* picture on there.

Lockett leaned toward Toby and checked. "Nope, nothing."

I slapped myself in the forehead and plopped back against my seat, dejected. I was the world's worst PI, and let's not talk about my inability to take a picture. Of which I had been doing successfully for ten years.

"But wait," Toby said and held up a single, bony finger. "What you did do was access the RFID app." He showed me the screen. "It's right here next to the photo app. And you pressed the heck out of the button."

"Really?" Hope sprang eternal.

"Totally. Give me a second to run it."

Lockett and I stared at him, waiting.

"By a second I mean a few minutes." He lifted his vape pen and worked his keyboard with a laziness that drove me berserk.

I narrowed my gaze and locked eyes with Lockett. "Tell me about Ben Fulton."

Lockett sighed. "Ben Fulton is...was...Senator Fulton's only son. Do you know who Senator Fulton is?"

"Somewhat." Thanks to my dad's investigative prowess. "He's been on the news, raising a stink about the manner of his son's death. Police think Ben fell asleep with a cigarette in his mouth, but Senator Fulton said his son didn't drink or smoke. Tabby, the barista I just met, confirmed that. Said Ben was a real health nut," I said, bringing Precious and Toby into the loop.

Lockett stared out the window. "Yeah, he was, which is why I'm inclined to agree with the Senator. Ben died in a fire a day before Carson died. I didn't put it together at the time because I didn't know Carson was meeting with Ben."

"But Carson drove into a tree that fell on his car and killed him. How can that be staged?" I asked.

"Did he drive into a tree or was he driven into a tree?" Lockett asked, letting the implications hang there.

Toby chimed in. "Our bad guy's name is Vincent Ricci, and he works for Carson and Cooper Security. And get this. This is the same guy Carson asked me to look into right before he died."

I tensed. Two things came at me at once. The name of

the company Mad Dog worked for and that Ricci had
been on Carson's radar. Lockett swore under his breath
and buried his face in his hands.

"Carson *was* his real name, his last name." It made
sense really. When I'd said Carson to Tabby, she hadn't
blinked.

Lockett mumbled something.

"What?" I asked Lockett. From Lockett's reaction, I
knew this wasn't gonna be good. "Give me my phone,
Toby." I wiggled my fingers as if to say hurry.

He tossed it to me. I pulled up the search engine and
typed in Carson and Cooper.

"Don't do it," Lockett warned. "You can't undo it."

I chose to ignore him. Carson and Cooper Securities
popped up on the screen, a longstanding firm that special-
ized in providing protection to some of the most influential and or famous people in the world. The firm offered
security and threat assessment training to police forces
and universities across the nation and had contracts with
many governments, including ours.

I clicked on the *About Us* tab and up popped a photo of
ten people standing in a V pattern. Carson and the guy
who had called himself Cooper stood at the point. I read
the caption.

Carson and Cooper was founded by Jake Carson (top right)
and Joe Cooper (top left).

After spending eight years in special forces, Jake realized he
liked to play by his rules and left the armed services. He's
applied the skills he learned while serving by offering protection
to some of the most influential people in the world. Jake Carson

recently left his position of CEO at Carson and Cooper to pursue other interests.

Joseph Cooper (top left) is a behavioral analyst who's made it his life's work to understand the dichotomy between good and bad. He graduated from Harvard and spent a decade working for the FBI's Behavioral Science Unit.

I enlarged the screen to look at Carson. Jake, I guess, since that was his name. The picture was taken before we met. Here was a guy with a wife, a multi-million dollar company, and essentially the world at his fingertips. Why change his name? Why commit bigamy?

"Explain," I said to Lockett. My patience was thin, and time for digging around for the truth was gone. I wanted answers and I wanted them now.

Lockett pressed his lips together in a thin line, as if he was contemplating what to say. His silence was infuriating. I was desperate for answers, and here was someone who had them. Withholding them was not an option. I whipped out the stun gun and stuck it in his side.

"Times up. Maybe when you come to, you'll be quicker to speak."

"Wait," he said as I pressed the button. He twitched and slumped back against the seat. We rode in silence until the stun wore off him. It felt like hours, but was only a few minutes. In the meantime, I ate a slice of pizza.

I offered him a water bottle.

"That was unnecessary." He snatched the bottle.

"Was it?" I asked and looked at Precious. "Was it?"

"I don't think so," she said. "Next time he wants to sit there and say nothing, you can stun him again and we'll leave him on the side of the road. He is, after all, a man who could be disbarred for ethical reasons."

I looked at Lockett. "There's an idea. And that's what truth sounds like."

"Fine. I just want you to know I'm not withholding information because I want to. I'm trying not to further complicate your life."

I scoffed. "Let me be the judge of that."

"And the charges against me are trumped up by Cooper, my guess is to render me incapacitated." Lockett looked away as if lost in a memory. "A little over a year ago, Joe Cooper engineered a coup of sorts. He had Carson kicked out of the company by using a no-confidence vote. Carson was allowed to keep his stock, but essentially was persona non grata at the company he and Joe started. He also found out that Cynthia, his—ahem—wife, was having an affair with Joe. When he filed for divorce, things became even uglier. That's when Carson came to me and said he wanted to start over. He had a new identity and kept saying he wanted a fresh start."

I snorted with contempt. Learning Carson's wife had cheated only made me feel slightly better because, ultimately, the selfish acts of these people changed my life forever. "And you helped him become Carson Holmes."

Lockett nodded.

I shook my head. "No, there's more to it than that. If he simply wanted to start over, then why is Carson's partner trying to hurt me? Why is everyone looking for something?"

"I wasn't sure Cooper was behind this until right now," Lockett said.

"You mean you've had thoughts that he might be?" I wanted to strangle him but feared if I put my hands on his throat he'd stop talking, and getting information from him was hard enough.

"I didn't know. Carson—Jake—kept me in the dark. Likely to protect me."

"From whom?" I shook a finger in his face. "I swear to everything that is holy, if you don't stop talking in circles, I'm going to use my pistol." To emphasize my point, I lunged for my bag and rifled through, pretending to look for the gun I hadn't brought.

"You have to understand something," he said. "If I tell you what I know, I can't take it back. I don't know if I can protect you, either. I've been following you like a shadow, and Ricci still got past me and roughed you up. You're lucky he didn't kill you. Next time, he won't be so nice."

I snorted.

Lockett put up a hand. "This is no joke. Whatever it was Carson discovered probably got him killed. It probably got Fulton's son killed. It will get all of us killed if they think we know what it is. And they won't stop at me or you or Precious there. They'll take out your parents and sister and niece just in case. This is the big leagues."

Lockett was forgetting one simple fact. There was no way I could undo the past. There was a good chance Cooper already thought I knew whatever it was. I was in danger. And by default, my friends and family were in danger, too. I might go down in a ball of flames, but I was going to take Cooper with me. No one, and I mean no one, messed with the Trues.

My stomach churned with unease, my palms sweating. "Toby, Precious? Are you sure you don't want to cut bait and run?"

"Are you quitting?" Precious asked.

I shook my head. "I think Cooper already knows I have something. Or that I'll lead them to it. There's something really bad going on here, and I'm going to do my best to see it through. You two, on the other hand, can get while the getting is good."

"Not a chance," Precious said.

"Count me in," Toby replied. "Though I could use a coffee. My nerves are shot."

Precious chuckled. "Mine, too. I might need a hit off your special vape pen. If I'm going to die, then I at least want to knock one thing off my bucket list before I go."

We chuckled.

"Before I die, I want to skydive," Toby said.

"I want to surf Australia," Lockett said. "I was supposed to be there now but, well, Carson had to go and die and jacked up my plans."

Gallows humor.

"You two must have been really good friends," I said. Because it would take a strong friendship for Lockett to get involved as he had done and possibly lose his livelihood, too.

He smiled sadly. "The best. He's been my best friend since the first day of kindergarten when Tommy Smith stole my lunch and Carson knocked him down and took it back. That was the kind of guy he was." Unshed tears glistened in his eyes. "But after Cooper kicked him out of the company, Carson changed. In hindsight, I see how he was spinning out of control. I was the sole person who could have changed his trajectory. Had I picked up on his anger and need to get back at Cooper, I might have stopped him from getting involved in your life, Samantha."

There was no mistaking the guilt that pulled at Lockett's haggard look. I had two choices. I could continue to doubt my instinct and have Precious kick Lockett to the curb, or I could bring the man into the fold. If I did the latter, I'd first have to remove his need to shield me from the truth. That damage was done. The horse had left the barn.

"Toby, show our lawyer friend the video."

Lockett looked puzzled. "There's a video?"

"Yeah, and when it's over, you're going to fill in more blanks and hold nothing back," I said.

There would be no going back from here, but deep down I'd known that already.

33

SATURDAY

W e gassed up then grabbed coffee from a drive-thru hut that was prevalent in the PNW. Precious parked in a lot of a sporting goods store and positioned the SUV to face the street. There was no telling if we were being followed or not. We'd done a crappy job of paying attention. We needed a game plan, and driving around endlessly wasn't an option. I'd gotten sucked into an internet search of Jake and Cynthia Carson images. Cynthia Carson, the real wife, was a tall, leggy redhead who dressed impeccably. In the pictures, she clutched Carson possessively. And in the pictures of Carson and Cooper with her in them, she had hands on both men. Like they were both hers.

"That's Senator Bolt," Lockett said, touching Humpty on the screen of my phone, drawing my attention away from my dark thoughts. Thoughts that wouldn't help me get my questions answered or put all this behind me.

"What do you think he and Cooper are up to? My guess is Cooper is doing a job for Humpty, um...Bolt. I also think land is involved." I explained the family files we found. Toby was still working on improving the video's sound and slowly breaking Carson's encryption.

"I got one open," Toby said and swiveled his laptop to us. "More geo-tracking off Carson's phone." Toby's brows furrowed in confusion. "Why would he do that?"

"To show us where he's been. It could be used in a court of law," Lockett said.

"He did another number, too. I'm backtracking the number now." He swiveled the computer back toward him.

Lockett said, "Senator Bolt is on the Appropriations Committee, Homeland Security, Government Affairs and one or two more. His state has military bases and a large company with a government contract, so it's not out of the realm of possibility that he would do business with Carson and Cooper."

Precious said, "Maybe Bolt needed protection."

"Then why meet outside, at night, in a remote location?" I glanced at Toby, who shrugged. The motive for Carson taking the video wasn't pairing with the information we had. "There's something diabolical about this meeting."

"Got it!" Toby said. "The other number belongs to Ben Fulton. Since the tracker shows latitude and longitude, I tried to match both of the numbers up and see when or if they intersect. Carson and Ben met twelve times over the three-month period. They met the day after the video was taken, too."

I pointed my finger at him. "Keep trying to open those files. I need to call my dad. Besides telling him to watch his back, he might know some things." I was about to step out of the car for privacy when Lockett stopped me by grabbing my arm.

"Look," he said and pointed to a dark SUV at the light. We faced the main road that led to the interstate. "He's gone around three times now."

Precious asked, "How can you tell it's the same SUV?"

"The tags. I started watching for cars and repeats." Lockett leaned forward between the passenger and driver seat. "I'm happy to drive if you want. But once the light changes and he takes off, I want you to wait until he's turned the corner to come around before you shoot out of here. Take the interstate." He pointed to the onramp toward Seattle.

Precious blew into her hands as if warming them, then slapped them together and rubbed them gleefully. "I totally got this." She looked at Toby, winked, and said, "Hold on to your titties, kitties."

"Yeah, yeah," Toby said and gripped the computer in one hand, coffee in the other. I buckled in and watched the light.

Thankfully, Precious had left the engine to idle so there was no indicator we were planning to move. When the car was out of sight, she crept forward. The tail of the other SUV turned the corner, its taillights fading.

"Green," I said with maybe too much apprehension.

Precious gunned it. Her SUV shot out of the parking lot, jumped across the divider that separated us from the road, cut off a bread delivery truck, drove across four lanes, and fishtailed as she righted the vehicle into the lane. We took the on ramp at over seventy miles per hour, and I prayed there'd be no cops nearby. We needed all the lucky breaks we could get.

"Get off at the next exit," Lockett said. "We can head to Seattle through back streets and see if we're being followed again."

I said, "We need a place to regroup and get organized."

"I wonder if, like in movies, they can track us with our credit cards. I used mine at the gas pump," Precious said.

"Can we hole up at your office?" I asked Lockett.

"My partners and I agreed for me to stay away. For client integrity until my case is decided."

The world suddenly felt very small. No safe place to hide was a knee-quaking, scary feeling.

"Let's find a parking garage in case there's drones out," Lockett said and searched his phone. After finding what he wanted, he directed Precious to a hospital parking garage in downtown Tacoma. We parked on the first floor in the middle so we could see cars coming and going from both exits. I stepped out to call my dad. I needed to warn him. And who better to tell my mom than him. Hearing her voice would wreck me. The others got out as well.

The call was excruciating. How does one tell their parents to be careful but not worry? I explained how Carson was meeting with Ben Fulton but left out the part about Carson being wealthy and kicked out of his company. Though, he'd find out soon enough with his own digging.

"I knew it," Dad said excitedly. "Senator Fulton may be a ballbuster, but he's always been a good guy with good intentions. I know a parent who loses a kid is grieving and might react from that grief, but the few times I covered politics and him, he was always a stand-up guy. He's stayed true to his word and done our Native Americans right."

"What do you know about Senator Bolt?"

Dad was a wealth of information. He growled. "That greedy SOB? He'd sell his mother if he thought it would make him buckets of money. He has his hand in all kinds of projects. Why do you ask?" Papers rustled in the background.

Oh, boy, time to show more of the ugly Carson. "I found some of Carson's files, Dad, files on people of Wind River. Their secrets."

"Carson had these?"

"Yeah, he did some PI stuff for a few people and kept copious notes." I was hedging.

"That sounds normal. I'm not sure what you're getting at, Sammy."

I blew out a sigh. "These notes were more a list of people's skeletons. And his file included notes on us. Our family."

A long pause. Dad was working it out.

I continued, "The common factor is that everyone he had notes on owns land near Graycloud. Or is connected to that land somehow. Like the land broker named Marni

Edgar. She's with Ogleby's International Realty. Her name sound familiar?"

More rustling. "Wait," Dad said. A drawer slammed. "Here it is. Yeah, the last two offers that came in for the land came from Ogleby's, and the broker's name was..." I could picture Dad scanning the page. "Marni Edgar."

"Graycloud has been there forever. Why now? And why this land?"

Dad was silent except for his pen tapping on his desk. "The last offer was from the shell corporation that was building those fancy resorts. Our land butts up to the reservation but also a portion of the wildlife refuge. It has views of Gifford Pinchot National Forest. The land has access to the river, is an easy drive to St. Helen's, Adams, and Mt. Hood, so the outdoor opportunities are large. Hunting in that area is exceptional. And the interstate is close enough to get to the cities. Seattle, Portland, and Vancouver. There's nothing like this land to the south, and as you go north, you might get more remote and better hunting, but you move away from the city and finer living."

"Seems extreme to go to such lengths to get this land when surely others would do." Everything about this seemed petty and unnecessary.

"Nothing is extreme when large sums of money are to be made," Dad said. "The things I've seen people do for fame and fortune would astound you." He sighed wearily.

Maybe not so much anymore. I told Dad about the video. "I think this video is the key to everything."

"Send it to me if you can."

I leaned against a wall and closed my eyes, willing strength to come find me. "I don't know what to do, Dad. I'm in over my head."

"You need contingency plans."

"We need a plan, first," I laughed.

"If what Senator Fulton says about his son is true and Ben was all about the environment, then perhaps Carson was talking to him not about developing the land but conserving it," Dad said. His wheels were spinning.

"Yeah. I could make that leap." If the land were conserved, then development would halt in its tracks.

Some clicking sounds from a keyboard were in the background. "Ben has a history of protesting commercial growth. I'm looking at several stories here about Ben, and it would seem the senator's son was a member of #Conserve. You know who they are?"

I shook my head. "No." Though I'd seen the occasional sign, I never followed up with researching it. I'd just written it off as another social media suck-in.

"#Conserve is young by standards of time spent fighting the government. They're taking a different approach. They're trying to talk to the government and reason with them. 'Use what we have' is their motto. Their platform is to conserve and retain history. They want companies that build these giant mega stores or malls and eventually abandon them for better locations to be held responsible for that abandoned property. Meaning they can't go unless they demolish the building and return the land to its natural state or have a new company come. In theory, it's a nice idea."

Carson trying to turn the land my parents' and others owned into conserved land didn't jive. Wasn't he supposed to be a bad guy in this scenario?

"Okay, I get it," I said, straightening. "Do you think the Senator was helping Ben?"

"Give me the dates Carson met with Ben."

I did.

"The senator was in DC during those times. He's home now for Ben's funeral. Hard to say if he knew about Carson, but he already suspects foul play. Let me say this, Sammy. If someone came to me and had evidence that my child might have been murdered, I'd move hell and high water to bring that culprit to justice. Senator Fulton has just the power to do it."

"You're right, Dad. Thanks," I said. A black SUV passed in front of the garage, same make and model as the one we'd seen earlier.

"I love you, kiddo. Be careful," Dad said with a hitch in his voice.

Tears filled my eyes. "I love you, too, Daddy-o. I'm sorry I'm causing so much drama," I said, walking toward Precious and the others.

"Baby, you're doing what's right. I couldn't be prouder."

"Call Rachel, Dad. Tell her these people could have access to the base, and she needs to watch her back. Tell Mom I'm sorry." The SUV entered the garage. "Gotta go, Dad. Love you," I said and disconnected. Taking in the scene, I brushed the tears from my face as I jogged to Precious's SUV.

Toby was leaning against the passenger side back door messing with his vape pen. Precious was by the driver's side texting. Lockett was standing a few feet in front of the SUV and was on the phone, too. I pointed over my shoulder to the SUV moving down the first lane, only four lanes separating us. He swiftly returned to Precious's SUV while disconnecting his call. Not wanting to yell and call attention to us, I ducked low between cars and rushed Precious, pulling her down.

The loud concussive boom of a gunshot sounded through the garage. Precious and I gasped, clutching each other as we pressed our bodies into the ground.

"I've been hit," Toby yelled.

Precious and I watched in horror as he collapsed to the ground, the SUV between us. Toby writhed on the ground, his hand over his shoulder, blood filling the space between his fingers.

"Where's my vape pen? I could use a puff. This hurts like all get out. Jeez, I'm gonna die," Toby moaned. "I didn't think you were serious, Sam, when you said we could get hurt."

Lockett appeared next to Toby. He inspected the wound, all the while telling Toby to bring it down a notch.

"Pst," I said. He turned and looked under the SUV. I asked for details by raising my brows.

"It grazed him. He'll need stitches." Lockett said.

"Snitches get stitches," Toby whined. "Help me, Lord."

I was on the driver side, Lockett and Toby on the passenger. I gestured to the SUV and then mimicked like I'd drive. I pointed to Toby and then the car.

"We're at a hospital," Lockett hissed.

"Yeah," I said. "And the emergency room is way over there." I pointed in the other direction.

"Just shut up and get in the car," Precious said.

"On three," I whispered. Which in hindsight was stupid because they knew where we were.

I held up one finger, then two, and before three, Precious jumped to a low crouch and opened the driver's side passenger door. I climbed into the driver's seat.

"Stay down," Lockett said and shut the passenger door behind Toby. Lockett got up front with me.

Toby was sprawled half on the floor and half on the seat, whimpering.

Leaving was a risk, but being a sitting duck bothered me more. "Precious, I'm going to drop you and Toby off at the ER. You should be safe there."

"We'll all be safe there," she said.

"But it's temporary, and I need to end this once and for all." I glanced in the rearview mirror. Precious looked worried and ticked off. I sighed. "No matter where we go, they find us."

"Geo-tracking," Toby said through gritted teeth.

"What?" I asked. I scanned the area and threw the car in reverse. The SUV following us was to my left, two lanes away.

"Like Carson did, he geo-tracked his steps. They're probably doing that to us."

Toby was right. How could we be so dumb? Or maybe it was naive. "Everyone turn off your phones." I tossed Lockett my phone to turn off.

I whipped out and aimed the SUV at the exit. "I'm going to speed out of here and across the lot to the ER. I'll get as close to the door as possible for you, Toby."

He gasped. "I'm to go in *by myself?*"

"I'll go with you," Precious said, sounding angry. I tried not to personalize it, but they were here because of me. "But you have to come back for us," she said and pushed at the driver's seat.

"Absolutely," I said.

Toby grunted. "Good thing I grabbed some tools from the office the other day. In my bag is a black puck. Basically it acts like a hot spot, gives us access and routes our location to the office in Wind River." Precious picked up his bag and ruffled through it before coming out with a round black puck. She placed it on the center console.

Toby continued, "Use it to stay in touch with us. Stay off your network. Keep your phone in airplane mode until you need to contact one of us and then use the puck."

I was speeding down the lanes, hoping no one was planning on backing out of their spot. The tires squealed as I took the curves hard and fast.

"He's following us," Lockett said.

I exited the garage going over thirty, which was really fast when you were in a parking lot with speed bumps. I hit one and our SUV caught air.

Toby howled when we bumped hard back to the ground.

"Oh, for goodness' sakes," Precious said. "You haven't been shot. You've been grazed. Like a skinned knee. Stop being so dramatic."

"Why don't *you* get shot and tell me it doesn't hurt," Toby said angrily.

"Bring it," Precious said. "Visualize the pain going away."

"Or I could visualize you going away," he said through gritted teeth.

"You can go into the ER alone if you want," Precious retorted.

Wisely, Toby said nothing.

I fishtailed out of the parking lot, the ER a straight line ahead of me. The curved drive up to the ER had only one ambulance but was clear of other vehicles. A cop car sat outside the drive, the cop standing next to it. I sped toward it and came to a screeching, sliding stop at the entrance doors.

"You drive," I told Lockett and watched in the rearview mirror as the black SUV came up behind me. I jumped out of the car and ran around the front to the ER entrance pad that opened the automatic doors. Inside were the hospital staff and two more cops. Maybe one was a security guard.

"Help," I yelled. "My friend's been shot." I ran back out to the passenger side of the SUV and opened Toby's door, hospital staff and cops following me.

Mad Dog, AKA Ricci, got out of his SUV and narrowed his gaze at me. He was dressed in dark colors with a blazer. There was a bulk of something under one arm.

I gave him a smile, pointed my finger at him, and yelled, "Gun!"

People around me dropped to the ground. Ricci froze. The cop by the patrol car used it for cover and pointed his weapon at Ricci.

"Hands up," people in uniform were yelling.

Toby and Precious low-shuffled into the ER with Toby's laptop bag flung over Precious's shoulder. I slowly stepped to our SUV and opened the front passenger door. Lockett was in the driver seat. Ricci had his hands up as the cops surrounded him. One patted him down and removed a gun from what I guessed correctly was a shoulder holster obscured by his blazer. Another man was being escorted out of the black SUV. Everyone's attention was on them. I climbed into Precious's SUV and turned to Lockett. He was my ally now. He better be on the up and up.

"I need a destination," Lockett said.

"Senator Fulton's house. We need some bigger guns on our side, and I'm thinking he's our best hope."

34

SATURDAY

We drove to Bellevue, Seattle's most expensive suburb. The senator's home was on the water facing Lake Washington with views of Mercer Island, the Seattle skyline, and both the Olympic and Cascade Mountains. A small cottage in this area sold for over a million.

Today's "excitement" had me sweating something fierce, and there was a good chance I smelled. That with my bruised face were gonna make looking authentic tricky.

Knowing Precious and Toby were in the ER, I accessed the Wi-Fi puck. Instantly, a text message came in.

One from Toby had a video attachment. The message read. *We're doing nothing but waiting. Managed to get audio.*

I shared this with Lockett.

Lockett pulled into the parking lot of a fancy pizza restaurant. "Let's hear it," he said.

The video started.

Bolt: It has to be this land. No other parcel offers access to the highway or river like this land.

Cooper: The Indian is causing lots of trouble. You might have more problems and attention than you want.

Bolt: Get rid of him and anyone else in our way.

"Carson and Cooper didn't run a legit firm?" I asked Lockett.

Lockett looked puzzled. "Their company is legit. This is probably some sort of side hustle."

"A side hustle doing what? What does land have to do with protecting people?" I thought about Carson and Cooper's security business.

Lockett grunted in frustration. "Well, I could see their business protecting the landowners getting harassed."

Which Carson had sorta done with Graycloud and the security system he'd provided.

I said, "But this meeting was clandestine and about taking out the landowner."

Lockett nodded. "Seems extreme to kill a landowner just so you can put up a fancy resort. There has to be more to it."

I recalled what Dad had said when I'd met him and mom for dinner. "Drugs maybe?" I shared the stories about how these resorts were going up in various towns near reservations and main interstates but were shells for drug running. My gut told me I'd hit the nail on the head.

"That makes sense. And while it sounds good that Carson was trying to stop Cooper and Bolt, my guess is it wasn't for altruistic reasons. When he came to me for a new identity, revenge was the only thing he wanted. I think I knew that then but didn't want to believe it." Lockett looked sad. It would seem that while I was learning the true nature of the man I married, Lockett was learning the same about his friend.

Senator Fulton's house clung to the side of a foothill and sported both a pool and a tennis court. The driveway was long and approached the house from the side. Several cars were parked along the drive. We were met by a beefy man in fatigues, standing outside a guardhouse next to a set of iron gates.

"Senators don't have government assigned security, do they?" I asked.

"Nope," Lockett and.

So Fulton hired private security. I found that interesting, only because I was now aware of Carson's original company. Was this beefy man an employee of Carson and Cooper? I was nervous about Senator Fulton being our white knight, and seeing this security guy added to my doubts. We were gambling that he was an ethical man, basing our assumptions on his actions in the Senate and the recent statement he made about his son.

The man came to the driver's door. His gaze swept through the car, assessing us.

"Do you have an appointment?" he asked in a no-nonsense voice. His hand remained on his hip where his weapon was located. I'd seen enough movies to know this could go sideways fast.

I leaned across Lockett. "No, we do not. My name is
Samantha True. I need to speak to the Senator about his
son and a person we have in common." I didn't want to
give everything away.

He blinked once. "The senator has had a lot of crazy
people coming here to say they know things about his
son." Unspoken meaning, he thought I was another crazy.

"Could you please call the senator and tell him that I
have a video he might want to see that could prove his son
was murdered."

Another blink.

I clapped Lockett in the shoulder with the back of my
hand. "This man was the best friend of Carson Holmes, I
mean, Jake Carson. I ah...had a relationship with Jake. I
have"—I held up the severed finger hard drive—"something here from Carson to give to the senator."

Something flickered in the guy's eyes. Maybe it was
the finger or mentioning Carson's name. He said, "The
senator is hosting a wake. Now isn't a good time."

Our timing sucked, but I pressed on. "I'm just trying to
do the right thing here," I pleaded.

The man hesitated, then said to Lockett. "Don't move
this car an inch."

"No, sir," Lockett said.

At the guardhouse, the guy picked up a phone. He
spoke with someone for several minutes then returned.
"Let me see your ID," he said to me.

I dug through my purse with nervous hands and
retrieved it.

Guard man glanced at the ID, then passed it back. He pointed one finger at me. "You and only you can go in. The senator is entertaining, so you'll only have a few minutes of his time."

"Wait, no," said Lockett.

"That's the deal," guard man said.

"It's okay," I said. This was mine to handle anyway, without backup.

"Park and wait for her over there," guard man told Lockett while pointing to a turn-around spot in the long, wide driveway. I climbed out and gave him a parting look over my shoulder. While guard man was directing him to turn around, I turned on my phone's voice recorder.

Guard man walked me halfway up the drive and pointed to a door where guard guy two was waiting.

The inside of the house was overwhelming. Overstated in some rooms, simple in others. Opulent and extravagant with TVs that came down from the ceiling. Built with traditional PNW flair, the motif was expensive lodge house with local granite and a tree growing in a room I assumed was the solarium. We walked by it on the way to the room where I was told to wait, the senator's office I presumed.

The walls were lined with shelves and books on local tribes, Tony Hillerman novels, Stephen Ambrose history novels, and several pictures of the senator's family. Ben appeared to be the only child. A surge of grief coursed through me as I considered his loss and how hurtful what I was going to share would be. I held a picture of Ben standing next to the PCT southern terminus post. Two thumbs up, a sun-faded backpack at his feet, a full, scraggly beard on his face. Ben had nice eyes. And his desire to do right was what probably got him killed. We were all pawns in this game started by Cooper and Bolt.

"Ben wanted to be a public servant as well. He loved the outdoors and felt they needed to be conserved," a man behind me said. The senator had slipped into the room from a different door.

"I'm sorry for your loss. I didn't know Ben. But I think I would've liked him." I sounded so lame.

The senator, a tall, broad-shouldered man, looked haggard. He was dressed in casual slacks and a polo shirt but grief etched his face.

I stuck out my hand. "My name is Samantha True. My dad covered you a few times for his paper. He speaks highly of you." Credibility would go a long way with the senator. Even if it wasn't my own, but my dad's.

Confusion ran across his face, then he said, "You're Russ True's kid?"

I nodded and smiled slightly.

The senator nodded once. "I read his sports stuff every day. Pick my fantasy football team based on his predictions. He's never let me down."

I chuckled. "He takes his league seriously."

An awkward moment of silence hung between us.

I cleared my throat. "Senator Fulton, I was...um...in a relationship with Carson Holmes, I mean Jake Carson. I believe you know who he is."

The senator nodded, leaned against his desk, and crossed his arms.

I continued, "When Carson died, he left me a safety deposit box with some files and a video in it. There's a picture of Carson and your son talking at a coffee shop called Daily Grind." I pulled the photo up on my phone and showed him. "Carson also geo-tracked his own movements and those of your son's. Over the past three months, I can show them meeting several times. I think Carson was trying to stop a land grab by his former partner, Joe Cooper, and Senator Bolt. Because of Ben's work with #Conserve, my guess is Carson was trying to get development restrictions on the land." I pulled up the video. "What I have here is upsetting." I pressed play and handed it over to him. "I can't speak fully about the conversation in the video. I only have pieces. But I do know that both Carson and Ben were killed a few days after this was shot."

He watched the video, expressionless. When it was done, he handed over my phone. "I've seen a different version of this video, Ms. True. The version I saw had a different audio track."

"Shot from a different angle?" I asked.

He nodded.

Man, Joe Cooper was good. All along he'd been looking for this video and, afraid he'd never find it, had preempted its viewing by creating a different "version."

"As far as I know, mine is the real deal. The guy who gave it to me is dead. I think that speaks to its authenticity as well." Using my expertise in photography and my visual memory skills I pointed to the video. "Does your video have a full moon? Are the men dressed the same?"

He thrust my phone back to me. "What do you want me to do with this?"

I was stunned. Not by his lack of response, but by the heart of the question. Because if he didn't know what to do with it, how could I be the one to guide him?

"The right thing, I suppose. I mean, that's what Ben was trying to do." There was a small flutter in the senator's blink. A tell. My dad, the poker king, had taught me that. Something I'd said had hit its mark.

A knock came at the door, and the senator beckoned someone to enter.

Joseph Cooper stepped into the room.

With a whoosh sound, all the air left the room as panic flooded over me. Thankfully, he left the door open behind him because the urge to run was so overwhelming my knees shook.

"I hate to interrupt, but the other guests are asking about you, Senator Fulton." He nodded his head once at me. "Miss. True. Good to see you again. Though it looks like you've had some trouble."

Anger shot through me like a flare. "No thanks to you and that goon you hired. What's his name?" I made like I was thinking hard. "Vincent Ricci? Tell him next time I'll be more prepared."

"I have no idea what you're talking about," Cooper said.

I rolled my eyes. Disgusted by the simple fact that his greed had caused all this chaos in my life. "Shame on you.

Once upon a time you were probably a good man. Carson was your friend. Your company gave people peace of mind. But I get that means nothing to you. Money is your master. I have what you want, and I'm taking it public. Let the chips fall where they may." I faced the senator. "Thanks for your time," I said and moved to leave, but paused to stand in front of Joe Cooper and looked him square in the eye.

"What?" he said, clearly miffed.

"I just wanted to know what a traitor looks like so that next time one sits down beside me and tells me lies, I'll be able to recognize their brand of crazy."

Joe snorted with a smugness I wanted to knock right out of him. Spurred by anger, I stomped really hard on his foot. It was all I could come up with. I then strolled from the house, trying to look confident...but I was desperate to run.

I walked past the gate with a wave to the guard, beelining straight for the SUV.

Lockett jumped when I whipped open the door.

"Let's get out of here," I said and tucked my trembling hands under my legs.

"So?" Lockett said, heading down the drive.

"So the senator was entertaining Joe Cooper, who I just threatened. We're on our own. The Senator has been corrupted or always was." Though I found it hard to believe he'd be okay with sacrificing his only child to whatever cause.

I'd just played our one hand. Now, Cooper knew everything I had. In my head I'd imagined a David versus

Goliath situation, but in this story, the Goliath was going to win. They were too cunning, too powerful.

"So where to now?" Lockett asked.

"We need to pick up Precious and Toby. Then home," I said. "Maybe Dad will run a story in his paper if he can verify facts. There's going to be fallout. Now we just wait for it to come."

35

SUNDAY/MONDAY

By the time we made it to Wind River, it was Sunday morning. Lockett was sticking with us, mumbling something about the adventures Carson forced him into and how he should be in Australia hanging ten. Toby and Precious were abnormally quiet. Toby wasn't even puffing on his pen. My guilt about his injury and subsequent four stitches was massive. He made a point of saying he was still helping because he didn't want there to be a next time, afraid if he were shot again, the bullet would do more than graze him.

We huddled at the newspaper in Dad's office and combed through the files Toby had decrypted. If Carson's notes and stolen emails from an account that belonged to Cooper were to be believed, Cooper was diversifying into the drug trade. Apparently, he was using Carson and Cooper's staff for murder for hire and protection of scumballs. Senator Bolt had been the first client. Who was the target? Carson hadn't figured it out, but Graycloud's name was on the list he'd started.

Lockett explained that if Bolt, a senator who sat on the Appropriations Committee, Homeland Security, and a ton more, wanted to have someone rubbed out, Bolt could own the political climate. He would have politicians in his pocket and so much pull on the inside he would basically be creating his own wealth. Never mind the money he would make from the drug trade.

It was hard to say definitely what Carson's motives were. Initially, it looked like he was acting out of revenge toward Cooper for kicking him out of the company. Like he wanted to sabotage Cooper's new business stream.

The realization of this fact was sickening. Little comfort was found in the fact that somewhere along the way he had changed his approach. Emails to Ben Fulton showed Carson was trying to get the land my parents and the others owned protected through environmental measures. But this was just Carson's newest approach to stop Cooper from getting what he wanted. Revenge. Spite. Retaliation. His hatred and anger were at the core of his actions.

Of course, sharing all our information about Carson meant Dad learned about Carson's real wife but had been gracious enough not to say a thing. He wrapped me in his arms and told me how much he loved me. I was under no illusion that we wouldn't have the conversation about Carson's other life, when the timing was better.

Dad studied us over his glasses. "I'll get this story put

together the best I can. I need to call in some old contacts and see if anyone is talking."

"This could explode or go flat. Either way, watch your backs," Lockett cautioned.

Dad dropped an arm around my shoulder. "You need to get some sleep. Tomorrow..." He glanced at his watch. "Today, rather"—he cleared his throat—"is Carson's celebration of life ceremony."

I'd completely forgotten.

"Is it okay if I crash on your couch here?" I wasn't up to going home just yet.

"I'd prefer crashing here, too," Precious said. "We can share the couch." Her high ponytail was sagging, her lipstick long chewed off.

"I'll take a spot on the floor," Toby said.

Dad held up his hands. "Go upstairs, take the apartment. I don't have any tourists staying there right now."

"Beds," I said to everyone and gestured for them to follow me.

Lockett paused at the door. "I'm going to stay and help your dad. I can call in a few favors as well."

I glanced at Dad, who gave me two thumbs up. Then I led my friends to a set of side stairs tucked along the back wall of the newspaper office. At the top, a door opened to a small landing on the building's roof. This brought us to the backside of the apartment. Encompassing the apartment was a small terrace that I'd used to sunbath, people watch, and grill when I lived here. It took us to the front door.

Dad had installed an electric keypad on the apartment, and I keyed in my mom's birthdate to open the door. We trudged in, each exhausted and on edge. Both Toby and Precious watched me lock and bolt the door. Afterward, Precious drew the curtains.

The space was simple. Living room and kitchen up front. Bathroom in the middle, bedroom right behind it.

"You can have the couch. It pulls out," I told Toby.

He flopped down, feet hanging over the armrest and waved us off.

"Look at us," Precious said. "My ponytail is flat, I have a sweat stain under my boobs, and I don't feel like I want to wash my face even though I've washed my face every day for the last fifteen years." She faced me, looking a little wild-eyed. "And I'd use a stranger's toothbrush right now."

I nodded in agreement.

"These are dark times, Sam." She cupped her hands over her mouth then blew out a breath, sniffing immediately after, her way of smelling her own breath. She closed her eyes. "Disgusting."

Precious and I collapsed on the king-size bed in the back. Neither of us bothered to take off our shoes or do anything beyond relieving our bladders.

If Cooper wanted to kill us, now would be the perfect time. I was too tired to care.

I woke to the soft hum of a conversation in the other room, the smell of coffee, and cinnamon buns. The latter was enough to drag my tired butt out of bed. Precious was still zonked out. I shuffled into the living room/ kitchen combo. Toby was sitting on the couch, feet resting on the coffee table and crossed at the ankle. He'd changed from his previous ironic T-shirt to a new one that had five commas before a chameleon. He wore jeans with no holes and lace-up shoes.

"What's this?" I said, pointing to his attire. The Culture Club song from his T-shirt was running through my head.

He puffed on his vape pen. "Today's the ceremony. Did you forget?" He blew out a wonderful smell of baked cinnamon, bread, and sugar.

I leaned in. "I smell cinnamon rolls. Please tell me it's not your vape pen but real rolls."

He grimaced and said nothing.

"Is it your pen?"

His brow furrowed, he said, "You told me not to tell you."

I slapped myself on the forehead. I needed more sleep, food, and a run to reset my system. Not in that order.

"I have hot coffee," Lockett said behind me.

I grunted with irritation. "That's a start." I took the mug and sat in an armchair. "What's the latest," I asked, rubbing my eyes.

Lockett sat in the armchair across from me, dressed in clean clothes that looked brand new. "Your dad finished the article. He sent it to Fulton to give him a heads up and asked for a statement."

"And?" I already knew the answer. We were in limbo, the next actions out of our control.

"We wait."

I groaned anyway.

Lockett said, "We go about life as usual. We have

Carson's celebration of life ceremony, and the article runs tomorrow. Your dad said he has to send it to the printer in an hour." He shrugged one shoulder nonchalantly.

How he could be so cool and calm was baffling. Inside, and probably outside too, I was a dumpster fire.

"Wait," I said. "Dad sends the stories to bed in the evening. What time is it?" To bed meant to press.

"Dudette, you have an hour," Toby said.

When I sat up quickly, coffee sloshed over my cup and onto my leg, burning me through the fabric. "Seriously? We slept all day?"

Toby and Lockett nodded.

"I gotta get dressed," I said. "Precious!"

She hopped into the room as she was putting on her shoes. "I heard. You know it takes at least an hour to get this package to sparkle," she said.

Lockett stood. "I'm escorting you home," he told her and glanced at me. "Your dad is covering you. So far, everything has been really quiet."

"Now you just jinxed us," I said. "Where will you be?" I asked Toby.

"Here." He relaxed into the couch, looking comfortable.

"Okay," I said. I opened the front door, but then slammed it suddenly.

I spun to face them. "I need an urn!" I'd almost forgotten. I stared at Precious because she was my best option to come up with a solution. The one she'd bought had been thrown at my intruder a couple weeks ago. She nodded to something over my shoulder and smiled. I turned, a decorative white and gray marble canister with a matching lid rested on a pedestal by the front door.

"I can't use that. It's not even an urn." But as I said it, I picked up the canister. It was half a foot in height and a little less in width, making it squatty. The lid sucked on tight. Little chance of it coming off without a good tug thanks to the plastic seal around the lid's lip. I didn't have any other options or time to shop for an urn.

"It'll have to do," I said. "Now I need to fill it with something."

"Give it to me," Precious said. "I'll take care of it"

We split up, with the exception of Toby who was staying at the apartment, and agreed to meet at the Frontiersman.

Dad drove me to my place. I showered, blew out my hair, applied makeup that didn't contrast with the fading bruises, and wore my one black dress. A simple number, cut at an A-line with a sweetheart neck and hidden pockets. I touched my throat where I always wore Carson's necklace. Even if I hadn't pulled the keys off for the safe deposit box, I wouldn't have worn it. Instead, I put on one my mom and dad had given me for my sixteenth birthday, a solitaire diamond bezel.

I carried a small clutch, big enough for my driver's license and some money. Definitely not big enough for my stun gun. I didn't want to leave it behind, so I tucked it into my pocket and found the swing of the skirt hid it well.

When I came downstairs, Dad gave me an expectant look. I gave him a puzzled one.

Dad said, "Ah, I hate to ask, but what's being done about Carson's...ahem...remains?"

I plopped onto the bottom stairs. "Oh, Dad. I'm sorry I kept the truth from you and mom."

He sat next to me. "Sweetheart, I don't know if I'd have handled it any better. I'm sorry you now have to go through with this charade. We need *something* to take to this ceremony. Maybe a picture of Carson?"

A picture! Man, that would have been *way easier.*

"Ah, well, Precious is bringing *the something.*"

He looked like he wanted to say more on the subject by wisely decided to let it go. "Ready?" Dad asked, looking somber. His was a loaded question.

"Do I have a choice?"

As Sherlock Holmes would say, the game was afoot.

36

MONDAY

Dad was right. A ceremony for Carson would go a long way for closure. I was ready to put him and our life, and all the lies, behind me. Reconciling the man I thought I married to the real man was painful and, frankly, I didn't like pain. This ceremony would shut the door on my life with Carson. Now, if I could get through this event with no one else the wiser to Carson's skeletons, that would be awesome.

Precious was waiting for me outside with the canister urn. It was noticeably heavier.

"What's in here?" I tested the weight by moving the canister up and down.

"I don't want to know anything." Dad covered his ears and went into the building.

"Some planter sand Lockett and I picked up at a craft store on the way here. My fireplace was cleaned for spring." She rolled her eyes. "I totally forgot. But look at this. You're gonna love this." She looked around the empty parking lot before taking the lid off the canister.

Inside, colorful wisps of shimmery confetti sparkled back at me.

"Take some out." She didn't wait for me to do it, but instead reached in and took a small handful. "I had a client who found out her husband was cheating. To celebrate her new life after her divorce, she bought this confetti and sprinkled it on his car and yard. She had a few bags left over so I took them because they're bad juju in her new house." She opened her hand, the confetti on her palm.

Liar, the little pieces read. The words were in blue, pink, gold, green, purple, silver, and black. They begged to be tossed in the air to fall to the ground like happy rainbow-colored snowflakes. They were very cheerful.

"You just think about this being inside your urn." She put the lid back on.

We laughed and went inside. The room was surprisingly crowded.

My mother rushed up to me. "You doing okay?" She brushed her fingers across my bruised cheek.

"Yep."

She reached for the urn, paused midway, and cocked her head to the side. "That's a canister."

I shrugged. "Same thing. It's very pretty and looks like something Carson would have liked. So I went with it."

Her gaze met mine. "Is that from the apartment? It looks just like the one I have on the pedestal by the front door. I got it for pennies at Home Goods."

I swallowed. "Nope, different one." She wouldn't look on the bottom for the tag. Not in public at least. Mom took the canister from me. *Please don't let her look at the bottom.* "Go mingle."

I scanned the room and took in the guests. Mrs. Pullman, who owned the liquor store. Carson had set up her security system. Chuck, Mr. Linn, the elder Kleppners, Precious's parents Otto and Bridget Shurmann, her sister Heidi, and so many others from town. Likely in support of my parents.

Some of the guests showed up for me. Lason came with Marni, and both thanked me for what I'd done. Lason made me promise I wouldn't quit. Mrs. Wright and Mrs. Wong came as well. Both hugged me and showed pictures of the kittens. Shannon Kleppner came, escorted by a nice looking gentleman with wire-rim glasses and a pocket protector. The math teacher, I assumed. She cried and thanked me profusely. These were the wins I desperately needed. Their timing was impeccable.

My sister had left a tearful voicemail apologizing for not being here for me in my time of need. I would tell her the full story when this was all over.

The Frontiersman Bar and Grille was at max capacity, and though the vibe was somewhat somber, laughter could be heard. People would walk by and squeeze my arm in support. Tomorrow, the good people of Wind River would put Carson behind them, and we'd all move on, no one the wiser to who he really was. The sense of achievement I had from pulling it off made me stand taller. Now, if the issue with Cooper could resolve as easily, then I'd call this entire shit show a win and happily never look back at it again. I had faith that Dad's article focused on the nefarious plans of Bolt and Cooper. After all, Graycloud was at the center of this thing and might not want the attention either.

Chuck moved to stand next to Carson's canister. "Toast," he said and raised his glass.

Others raised their glasses. Personally, I found the toast ritual an excuse the men used to drink whiskey because they did this at every event. Weddings, births, football games.

Chuck continued, "Death has become his sleep from which he wakes to a new life." The toast was an old German saying.

Lockett moved next to Chuck and, with his glass in the air, said, "Whether at the gates of heaven or hell, may the trip there been worth it." He met my gaze and nodded. Sadness and bitterness were at the heart of Lockett's toast, but only a few of us knew that. Others laughed, unaware.

Then my dad stepped up. "Here's to absent friends." He and Chuck laughed and elbowed each other. Dad tended to become slightly juvenile when drinking.

My mom hissed my father's name. "That's not appropriate."

"Okay, okay," Dad said, holding his glass in the air. "So long as he lives in our heart, he will never die."

When I scoffed, those standing around glanced curiously at me. Toby rushed to the small circle of men near Carson's canister.

"I want to toast," Toby said.

"How about we take Carson to the river and release his ashes there while we toast," Chuck suggested.

"No," Precious and I shouted.

Everyone looked at me. "I mean, that's so permanent, and I'm not sure I want to do that yet. Feels like a big decision." I went to the canister and took it off the table, tucking it alongside my body.

"Okay, darling," my dad said. "We won't do it."

I stepped backward away from them. "Maybe another time if it feels right."

"Samantha," Dad said and pointed behind me.

I glanced over my shoulder and realized I was about to collide with a chair. "Whoops," I said and sidestepped around the chair, but not fully because my toe caught on one of the back legs of the chair, and I stumbled. I put my free hand out to catch myself, finding balance by placing my palm on the seat of the chair. Only the angle of my back and the placement of the chair were at odds. As I spun and tried to stop my fall, the back corner of the chair caught the canister just right and sent it flying out of my arm, soaring high like a bird freed from its cage.

"No," I screamed and lunged for the canister.

"Sweet Jesus," Precious yelled.

The crowd gasped as the canister hit the floor, bounced once, the lid flying off, bounced a second time, and smashed open on the floor. Beige sand and colorful confetti exploded out in a wide-spreading radius.

Some people covered their eyes. Others their mouth.

"Is that confetti?" Mrs. Wright asked and bent to pick up a piece. "I kinda like the idea of confetti at a funeral."

"Is that sand?" my mom asked, looking at me puzzled.

"The confetti says liar," Mrs. Wright said.

"Oh, dear," Mrs. Wong said. "That's not good."

Mrs. Pullman said, "When my Homer was cremated, they gave me his remains in a plastic bag. This does not look the same. I wasn't given the option of confetti."

"Samantha?" my mom said. "What is this?"

"Is your Carson really dead?" Mrs. Wright asked. "Because I see some scams like this on the true crime channel."

I glanced around the room at the questioning faces. I blew out a sigh and plopped onto the tripping chair. "As far as I know, he's dead. I don't have his body." I pointed to Lockett. "He's the one that told me he was dead."

Everyone's attention swung to Lockett. He said, "Er, well, he is dead. I can assure you." He coughed nervously.

"How?" my mom asked.

Lockett looked at me in panic. My mom was watching me and waiting for an answer. I looked at my dad for help but all he did was shrug. I groaned and looked up at the ceiling, searching for the right words. But there weren't any.

"Carson was married when he married me. She got his body." I continued to look at the tiles overhead. "Apparently, Carson came here for revenge against his partner, Joe Cooper. It's a long story, and you can read the heart of it in Dad's paper tomorrow."

Mom gasped. "This is about the land?"

I lowered my head and nodded. "Yeah, he came here to try and get the land, and when he couldn't, he stayed because he wanted to make sure his old partner wouldn't get it. He lied to us about everything."

"But he helped me find my brother," Chuck said.

I gave Chuck a grimace. "Yeah, he did. But he also gathered personal information about you in the meantime that he might have used against you later. I'm sorry."

The room was quiet as people processed the information. Finally, my mom slapped her hand on her leg and said, "Well, nothing we can do about it now. Let's clean this mess up." She went to the hostess and brought back a broom and dustpan.

"I like the touch with the confetti. Priceless," Mrs. Wright said and clapped me fondly on the back.

We cleaned up the sand and confetti and placed it all in two large brown grocery bags.

"Toast," Dad said. "Drinks are on us." He raised his glass, and people scurried to get one of their own.

"I'm going to take this to the dumpster," I told my mom. I needed a moment of fresh air.

"Come right back," Mom said.

The dumpsters were kept on the side of the Frontiersman facing the street that led to the pier. I tossed the trash then leaned against the wall, pressing my hands to my hot cheeks. I closed my eyes and counted to ten seven times before I'd come to accept my humiliation. When I opened my eyes, I was not alone.

Standing before me, blocking any way of escape was Joe Cooper.

"Had you just given me the video, you could have gone merrily on your way."

"As if I believe that," I said.

He grabbed me by the arms, spun me around so I was facing away from him, then pinned me to his side by wrapping his arm around my neck in a chokehold. "Scream, and I'll shoot anyone that comes to your rescue."

He poked what felt like a gun into my back. From there, he pushed me away from the building, not going up to the main street or down to the river but perpendicular to the Frontiersman. Behind the post office. Behind Jankowski's realty office and to the parking lot the office shared with the library. There, a large dark SUV waited, engine idling.

"You won't get away with this. The story is already going to press." I was really worried he would absolutely get away with it. I chewed my lip and searched for an exit strategy.

"I'm confident I will. If you think some small town unheard of newspaper can destroy me, you've seriously underestimated who I am. You don't think I have a few journalists on my payroll that can't punch holes in your story?" He shoved me toward the car.

Ricci got out from the driver's seat and came around the car, opening the passenger door for me.

"I warned you," he said darkly and followed it with an ominous chuckle.

I tried to twist away, but Cooper closed the space between his arm and my throat, making breathing hard. I swallowed the sounds of my pain in several gulps. When I had control, I said, "So you'd risk everything you built with Carson for money? Your reputation, your friendships, your company."

"I can always get new friends. Now that Jake is gone, I can sell Carson and Cooper or do whatever I'd like with the company. I'm beyond wealthy, and bad boys get the chicks. I'm not seeing any risks."

Cooper shoved me into the car, and I automatically scooted across to the other side and tried to escape. The childproof lock was on my door. When I turned to Cooper, he had a 9mm Beretta pointed at me.

If I could get the gun from him, I could use what Leo taught me at the range. But odds weren't in my favor. Cooper was far more skilled than I was. The stun gun rested against my leg, and since my hands were free, I played it cool and slipped them into my pockets.

Cooper said, "Everything is about money. Money gives a person power. Power gives me great happiness."

"You have a sad idea of what happiness looks like," I said with disgust.

Cooper barked a laugh. "Such ignorance. You think good can beat bad, but you don't realize that good is what people pretend to be. Everyone, and I mean everyone, would do exactly what I'm doing if it meant endless wealth."

I rolled my eyes. "You keep telling yourself that if it helps you sleep at night."

"My Posturepedic pillow and blanket of hundred-dollar bills are what help me sleep at night. I'm a stomach sleeper, and the pillow really helps my neck. The money keeps me warm. See? Happiness."

Man, I hated him.

"So what are you going to do with me? Kill me and have a tree land on my car?" I needed confirmation about Carson's death.

"Clever, weren't we?" Cooper's smile was creepy. "You're going to take us to those copies of the video and turn them over."

If Cooper wasn't worried about my dad's small town paper, then why did he want the copies of the video?

"Can't. They're at the bank, and the bank is closed." I relaxed in the chair and feigned a level of confidence I didn't have. What I could muster would fit on the tip of my pinky nail.

"We can manage that small obstacle." Cooper made like he was dishing out dollars. "Everyone wants some."

I shrugged to show that he bored me. "Not everyone."

"Jake was no hero," Cooper said.

"I'm not saying he was. I'm talking about me. I'm prepared to die than let you have these videos." Antagonizing him came naturally. What didn't was working out a solution on how to stun gun him. I couldn't send the volts through my clothes and his for any effect. He was wearing a thick pullover. Combine that with my dress, and I feared the thickness would decrease the volt impact, something I couldn't afford.

"You're very stupid. No wonder Jake picked you for his scam."

I rolled my eyes.

Ricci said, "We might have a tail, boss."

When Cooper glanced out the rear window, the gun

he had pointed on me wobbled. I glanced behind me. Leo, in his police cruiser, was a car length away. We had just taken the first roundabout out of town. Two more, and we'd make the interstate. It was time to fish or cut bait as my dad would say.

I slipped the stun gun out of my pocket and held it close to my leg, letting the folds of my skirt cover it.

"Maybe it's just a coincidence. Do the speed limit. Let's see if he peels off somewhere." Cooper asked me. "Where's the police department?"

"Back in town." I pointed behind me. Cooper was right. Leo being behind us might be sheer coincidence. He might be headed home or to see his mom for all I knew.

Time was even more of the essence. If we made the interstate and Leo turned off, I'd lose all opportunity. We were coming up to the second roundabout. Housing was to the far left, an empty field with a thicket of trees to the right. We would enter the roundabout to the right. Cooper or Ricci. Who should I go for first?

Sucking in a deep breath, I said, "Did he just turn on his lights?" while simultaneously turning on the stun gun then sliding my finger to the tab that would release the volts.

Cooper swiveled in his seat, and Ricci's eyes went to the rearview mirror. I lunged to my left, out of view of the mirror.

I pressed the gun to Ricci's neck and depressed the switch. Ricci grunted and twitched like a fish out of water as I sent bolts through him. The SUV lurched forward in a burst of acceleration. The electricity must have sent a spasm through Ricci's leg, causing him to push harder on the gas. His head slumped against the steering wheel. The SUV jumped the curb, aiming for the copse of trees. The vehicle rocked from side to side like a crazy carnival ride.

It was do or die time.

37

MONDAY

I tried to hold onto the headrest of Ricci's seat but the force of jumping the curb threw me toward Cooper. I banged my head on his window before falling to the floor. A burst of stars clouded my vision.

I don't know how or why, but guessed impact alone caused Cooper to pull the trigger. Glass from the window I'd been sitting by shattered in an explosion of sound. Ringing filled my ears. My eyes were clouded by tears of pain, and the acrid smell of spent gunpowder filled my nostrils.

I lunged for the door and fumbled to reach the door handle, hoping the childproof lock had been applied only to my door. A blur of black came into my periphery. Cooper had swung the gun toward me. My space was small, so he didn't need to aim to hit me should he pull the trigger. I released the handle just as the side of the pistol and his fist punched the side of my head twice.

Blackness was all I could see as a burst of pain exploded in my head. I lunged forward into nothingness, trusting my options out of the car were better than in.

I plunged headfirst from the moving car, Cooper with me, and had just enough wherewithal to tuck into a roll at the last second. My left shoulder scrapped across the earth. Something jagged, likely a rock, ripped my dress and the skin underneath, tearing away layers of both. Propelled by momentum, I tumbled away from the vehicle, dirt, rocks, and brush scraping up my body.

I came to a stop and laid there stunned. My body screamed against any movement. But my mind screamed to run.

"Freeze, police!" came a command from a distance so far away I probably imagined it.

I rolled to one side. Leo was twenty feet away at the curb. I followed his line of sight. The SUV with Ricci had crashed into a tree. I couldn't see Ricci, but Cooper was lying on his stomach, a handful of feet away from me. He lifted up on one elbow with the barrel of the gun pointed right at me.

"Gun," I yelled and rolled away, hoping to get out of range. Cooper would have to come up off the ground to level the gun at me. I tried to stand, but my body raged in protest, and I fell over twice but forced myself up again each time, clenching my teeth.

"One by the car has a gun, too," Leo yelled at me and moved wide, trying to cover both men. Ricci was out of the car and had a weapon, too.

The situation was not in our favor. I'd lost my stun gun

in the fall out of the car. I had nothing but nubby finger-nails and a few rocks to use as a weapon. Neither were good options against a gun.

"You shoot me, and she dies," Cooper said. "You shoot my associate, and she dies. You see where I'm going with this?" The fall from the SUV hadn't been easy on him either. Blood ran down his face on one side that was covered with serious road rash. The blood was occluding his vision on that side, and I needed to use that to my advantage.

"Don't move," Cooper told me as I tried to shuffle to his blind side. "I should have had you killed, too. You're a pain in the ass."

"Thank you," I said and glanced at Leo for guidance. He was in what I called the stand-off position. Both hands on the trigger, feet wide apart, ready for action.

"Sam," Leo said, "laser tag."

Laser tag. Laser tag. I'd sucked so bad at firing my fake gun and scoring points. The only way I'd survived was by hiding behind objects.

I made eye contact with Leo, who then glanced toward the woods beyond the wrecked SUV. I did the same.

Here's the thing. If I ran for cover in the woods, Leo was going to get shot. Cooper would be targeting me, but he'd have to roll over and take aim, which would give Leo a chance to shoot him. And Ricci a chance to shoot Leo. These guys were killers. Cooper had admitted he killed Carson.

Leo's predicament brought tears to my eyes. "I can't," I said to Leo. "What about you?" He might have a bullet-proof vest on, but his head wasn't protected. I wouldn't let him take a bullet for me.

"You have to," he said.

I started to cry.

"Samantha," he said in that infuriatingly calm voice of his. "My people believe that when an eagle takes flight to soar, it watches the wind, not because the eagle is worried about getting dirt in his eyes or that he might not see, but because he wants to ride to the highest peak. He wants to soar. You understand what I'm saying?"

I nodded, not liking what he was saying one bit.

"What the hell is he talking about?" Ricci said. "Crazy Indians."

"Hey," I yelled, furious at our situation. Ricci was dogging on a guy who was telling me he'd take a bullet for me. "He who has two different colored eyes shouldn't be calling anyone crazy. You know your eyes make you look like a rabid dog? Or maybe that's just your face."

"Shoot her," Ricci told Cooper.

"Shut up," Cooper said, and for the briefest moment, glanced over his shoulder at Ricci. I took that second, that pause in his vigilance, and ran toward him. When I was inches away, I kicked a massive pile of dirt and pebbles into his face. Then I bolted for the woods, tears streaming down my face.

Shots rang out behind me, and I ducked and weaved my way into the trees. When there were enough trees behind me to block me from the guys, I used a tall maple as cover. I could see everyone from where I was.

Leo was on the ground, lying on his side. I couldn't see

where he'd been shot. Ricci was down too, clutching his lower leg and rolling on the ground. Cooper was running toward me but hadn't yet made the trees. He was limping.

I suppressed the urge to run to Leo. If I did, then all this would be for nothing. I turned my face upward, praying a solution would fall out of the sky.

And one did. Well, it didn't fall but hung there. A large branch the diameter of my head hung across the path Cooper would come down. The foliage was thick and would offer good coverage. I scurried up the side of the tree, swinging up from limb to branch until I reached the one I'd seen. I perched on it like a bird, my skirt tucked between my legs, balancing like my life depended on it, which it did. If anyone ever said to me that yoga was useless, I would forever refer to this moment. *This one time when I was running from a killer...*

My breath was ragged, and I needed to calm it or else he'd hear me. The plan was to jump on his back and knock him down, wrestle the gun from him, and shoot him. Plans like this worked in the movies. I was hoping a one-off in real life would happen. After all, I was due some good fortune.

Cooper stalked through the woods, looking behind every tree. I wasn't too worried about him tracking me. His expertise was on being an asshole and schmoozing people. Carson had been the expert in tracking from his special forces days.

Cooper moved from under me and took two steps then paused, his head slightly cocked to the side as if he was listening for me.

I didn't second-guess a thing. There was no time or purpose for it. I lunged from the branch and went flying, skirt whipping around me in the wind, arms out wide like one of those soaring squirrels.

He was mid-turn when I came down hard on him. We landed with an *oomph*, and the gun in his hand went flying. I lurched off him and pushed to my feet, slightly disoriented from the impact.

Cooper rolled and sat up.

The gun was a few feet to my left. Cooper was looking in its direction. Simultaneously, we went for it.

Two quick steps in that direction, and then I lunged, pushing off the ground to get air. I landed on my belly and skidded forward. I grabbed the gun as I slid over the spot where it landed. I flipped onto my back and sighted Cooper. He froze mid-stride.

"Put the gun down," he said.

Because I sucked with little pistols, I aimed more to the left. I'd been off at the range with Leo, and I was hoping that when I pulled the trigger, I would hit something. It was that moment that accepted I could kill Joseph Cooper. Only because if he got the gun from me, he'd not waste one second killing me. He wanted those thumb drives because they had the potential to destroy him. No matter how much he denied it.

Cooper knew the drives were at the bank. He needed me to get the drives, and then I was useless to him. In fact, I was a blight to his reputation.

"Leo," I yelled. "I have Cooper covered."

"Your friend is dead," Cooper said mercilessly.

I clumsily racked the slide.

He gave an odd laugh then lunged at me. I squeezed the trigger and lost count of how many shots I fired.

He crumbled at my feet, blood pouring from a wound in his leg. I couldn't see the others.

Suddenly, Leo was at my side. "Are you hit?" he asked, his hands patting me down. I sat up on my elbows. Leo took the empty gun from me.

"No, are you?"

"Your two-eyes man shot at me but grazed my shoulder. I shot him in the shins. Got him from underneath the SUV when I dove sideways to avoid getting hit." He gestured with his gun. "This one got away from me."

Leo approached Cooper with caution, then rolled him to his back.

The creep groaned and grabbed at his upper thigh. "It hurts," he said weakly. "What happened?"

Apparently, Cooper had a low pain tolerance.

When Leo jerked him up by gripping under Cooper's armpit, Cooper screamed and got wobbly in the knees. "You were shot, asshole. That's what happened. And then you passed out."

In the distance, sirens wailed.

"Hey," I asked Leo as I used a tree trunk to help me stand. "Was that true what you said about the eagle and the wind?" I'd always loved a good Native American story.

"Nope," Leo said with a chuckle. "Made it up. Just wanted you to kick dirt in his face." His grin was wide, and the corner of his eyes crinkled with merriment.

I caught his eye and laughed.

"Hey," Leo said, looking at Cooper. "You did a nice job with your shots, Sam. Wounded but not seriously. This guy can face the consequences of his actions."

I was doubtful. Cooper would likely buy his way out of trouble. "Yeah, well, I was aiming for his heart."

38

ONE WEEK LATER

D ad's story ran and was picked up by the Associated Press. Apparently, Senator Fulton had something to do with that. Fulton also made sure the video circulated through the right crowds just in case they didn't see it on the news.

Dad said Senator Fulton called him during Carson's celebration of life ceremony and offered his help with breaking the story wide open. The two concocted an additional plan to what was already in motion. Dad had been right; a parent would seek justice, and Fulton was no different. Joe Cooper's attempt at tricking the senator with a video had only fueled the senator's need for justice. And never mind that Cooper had attended Ben's wake.

Last I heard, Fulton was making sure he could rack up as many charges against Cooper and Bolt as possible. We later learned the DEA had been watching Bolt's resorts, fully aware of their drug trafficking proclivities. When the story broke, they stormed Bolt's resorts and caught the employees trying to scrub evidence. Leo, who'd been running late to the ceremony, had arrived in time to see them force me into the SUV. A building fire on the other side of Wind River had required all the Wind River cops to clear the area. The fire turned out to be my office building and Ruby's yoga/dance studio. One more thing to feel guilty about. My guess was Cooper started it to get the cops out of town.

I stretched out on a blanket on the lawn overlooking the river. The sun was bright and beautiful. The temps not so hot it was unbearable. Which was good considering I couldn't wear clothes that touched my body in certain areas due to the road burns I got when I tumbled from the car. So it was dresses for me. And short-sleeved ones at that.

Lockett, sitting next to me, sighed then said, "I'm sorry I let you down."

"How do you figure?"

"I should have stuck to you like glue at the ceremony. We knew they were going to come to town. I only looked away for a second." He slapped his knee in frustration.

"I took out the trash, but I could've had someone else do that. Like an employee. This isn't on you. Cooper would have done what he had to at any time. I gave him the opportunity." I shrugged. It was behind us now. Or at least I hoped it was.

I supposed I'd never truly know if I was targeted by Carson. Reconciling how he treated me as a spouse with his intentions when he came to our area was too hard for me. But I was okay accepting not everything could be cut and dry, black and white.

One question lingered. "Why me and not you? Why send me the bank code and the video if you were such good friends?" I was propped up on my elbows, and I let my head fall back so the sun could kiss my face.

"I was the obvious choice. Cooper knew Jake would come to me so he set me up to be disbarred. Being under review really hogtied me. Any misstep in Cooper's direction would have worked against me. Had I tried to discredit Cooper, it would have looked like an attempt to deflect what was happening with the bar association."

"But Carson came to you anyway?"

"Yeah, but not for the reasons Cooper thought he would. Jake knew Cooper better then Cooper knew himself. He came to me to help set up contingency plans. Like signing your PI license." He gave a wry smile. "I never knew about the video or what Jake had in his back pocket. I didn't even know about Ben Fulton."

"How do you think Cooper learned there was an incriminating video?" This was an unanswered question that bugged me.

Lockett shrugged. "I'd only be guessing. Maybe from spying on a meeting Ben and Carson had. Dumb luck. I don't know. But whatever it was that tipped off Cooper lead him straight to you."

For all the anger I had toward Carson there was an ache of sadness, too. On the day he'd sent me his backpack and fake identification he knew there was a chance he wasn't going to live. I couldn't imagine what that must have felt like.

"You think Cooper told wife number one about me to get the estate to move so quickly?"

Lockett nodded. "For sure. He was looking for that video. When I learned of Carson's death I figured it was only a matter of time before they learned about you."

"We were all part of some crazy plan of revenge. Just pawns." I said.

Lockett shook his head then did a one-shoulder shrug. "Maybe at first. Carson was enraged when he lost the company. I think you all started out as a means to an end, but there was a change in him these last few months." He held up a hand before I could ask questions. "What you don't know was that Jake's wife Cynthia's dad was a brute, the worst kinda guy, and Jake and I spent most of our youth protecting her from him. Jake enlisted in the Marines right after high school. Cynthia forged her dad's signature, and they got married immediately following boot camp. I think once Jake was making money, she wasn't going to let go, and he...well...he'd always taken care of her. They'd drifted apart a long time ago. I don't know why or how Cynthia became such a bitter woman, but she kept stalling the divorce. They were living separately for at least a year before he moved here. He didn't come here to marry you if that's what you're thinking. You guys took that trip to Vegas..."

"And we had too much to drink and got married," I finished for him.

He nodded. "Yeah. You'll have to take my word for it,

but toward the end there, I was seeing the old Jake I knew. Not the bitter Jake. I know that's because of you."

Processing everything was almost too much. Still little tidbits stuck out. Like this whole plan was convoluted and unnecessary.

"How can you be so sure? That he was changing because of me?" There was comfort knowing my man barometer wasn't fully broken. Maybe just needed calibrating.

"Because about a month before all this happened, he came to me and had me set up an account in your name."

"What?" I sat up.

"I think he knew he wasn't going to make it out alive." His voice cracked, and he cleared his throat. "He asked that if something should happen to him, then wait a month and give you the information about the account."

I calculated dates in my head. "It's not been a month."

Lockett gave me a look that said he thought I was being ridiculous. "Okay, I suppose I'll wait then."

I punched him in the arm.

"I emailed you earlier all the information. It's not much, a savings account with ten thousand dollars in it. But it's something, right?" Lockett gave a half smile.

I took his hand. At first I held it, but then I squeezed, pressing his thumb back. "Why didn't you tell me this before?"

He yelped and pulled his hand away. "The rules said I couldn't for a month. We're way closer to that now then we were when we first met."

I flopped back on the blanket and covered my eyes.

Ten thousand. At least I would have a small cushion, for a while.

I looked at him from under my hands. "I can forgive you for following the rules."

"That's good." He chuckled.

"I suppose you'll be returning to Seattle now? I heard the disciplinary board threw out your case in light of Cooper's actions."

Lockett nodded. "I kinda like it down here. Maybe I could open a satellite office. Jake used to admonish me for working too hard, not having a life. I see now he had a point." He glanced over to Precious who was sitting by my parents and hers.

"She has an off again-on again boyfriend. Just so you know. But I don't think she'd turn you down for a date. Maybe don't expect much after that," I said.

"I believe I'll accept that challenge," he said with a wide smile.

I snapped my fingers and pointed at him. "Carson talked about Precious, didn't he? That's how you knew who she was that day you told me he died."

Lockett gave a toothy smile. "Noticed that, did you?"

I shook my head in wonder. How we survived was anyone's guess. Dumb luck, I supposed. "I have a question for you. What was up with the no shoe thing when I saw you at Ralph's?" I nodded to his bare feet.

He laughed. "I'm a black belt. I have to be prepared to fight at any time. I can't afford to kick off my shoes when I need to take someone on."

"Ricci was nearby that day, wasn't he?"

Lockett looked away briefly then back at me. "I did what I could to keep you safe but sometimes you made it really hard. I knew you were being followed but not by who. Maybe if they saw you talking to a black belt, it might have helped you."

I side-hugged him. "Look me up when you're in town. I'm moving to the apartment over my dad's paper." I was letting go of the life I'd started with Carson. I didn't feel safe in the townhouse, and my good memories there were clouded with bad ones. I was taking what I had left of Carson and keeping those items and memories in a place where I felt safe. The townhouse was simply that, a house.

Lockett playfully pushed me away. "What are you going to do about the business? I kinda think you have a knack for this private investigator thing."

"Well, up until a few minutes ago, I was seriously broke."

"You can start your own photography studio," Lockett suggested.

See, here's the thing. Taking studio pictures on a regular basis was an instant snoozer. Such a boring idea. I liked using my camera for money shots. "We'll have to see. With the business burned to the ground, I'll have to see if any clients come to me," I said.

"I had Toby make you a website. You can deactivate it at any time."

We sat in a comfortable silence.

"I suppose we get back to the business of being normal again. No drama or chaos," I said, a bit woefully.

Lockett chuckled. "You know, this is going to sound crazy, but sometimes I think he's still alive."

I sat up wide-eyed. "What? Why?"

He gave a gallant shrug. "Dunno, but it's totally something Jake would do. Fake his own death."

I took in my surroundings, people milling about through the park. A man in dark shades and a ball cap lingered by the river's edge. He was watching us. Or maybe he felt me watching him and turned in our direction. I squinted, trying to see him better. My imagination was getting away from me. He touched the bill of his cap, then hopped into a speedboat and zoomed away. He was the right height and build for Carson. But he'd been too far away for me to be sure. He was probably just a guy who saw a weird woman staring at him.

"You're kidding, right?" What I'd seen was just a man with similarities. That was the logical explanation.

"Mostly."

"If Carson isn't dead and resurfaces, I will kill him myself."

Enjoyed this story? Want to know if Carson is still alive? Or maybe what Samantha will have to face next? Is something brewing between her and Leo?

There's more Samantha True coming up. Make sure you sign up for my Read & Relax community to be first to learn of when *BEST LAID PLANS* is schedule for release. Go to www.kristirose.net

BOOKS BY KRISTI ROSE

Samantha True Mysteries

One Hit Wonder

All Bets Are Off

Best Laid Plans

The Wyoming Matchmaker Series

The Cowboy Takes A Bride

The Cowboy's Make Believe Bride

The Cowboy's Runaway Bride

The No Strings Attached Series

The Girl He Knows

The Girl He Needs

The Girl He Wants

The Meryton Brides Series

To Have and To Hold (Book 1)

With This Ring (Book 2)

I Do (Book 3)

Promise Me This (Book 4)

Marry Me, Matchmaker (Book 5)

Honeymoon Postponed (Book 6)

Matchmaker's Guidebook - FREE

The Second Chance Short Stories can be read alone and go as follows:

Second Chances

Once Again

Reason to Stay

He's the One

Kiss Me Again

or purchased in a bundle for a better discount.

The Coming Home Series: A Collection of 5 Second Chance Short Stories (Can be purchased individually).

Love Comes Home

MEET KRISTI ROSE

Hey! I'm Kristi. I write romances that will tug your heart-strings and laugh out loud mysteries. In all my stories you'll fall in love with the cast of characters, they'll become old, fun friends. **My one hope** is that I create stories that *satisfy any of your book cravings* and take you away from the rut of everyday life (sometimes it's a good rut).

When I'm not writing I'm spinning (riding a stationary bike- I'm obsessed with having smaller calves. Mine Are HUGE- and not in a good way, ya'll), repurposing Happy Planners, or drinking a London Fog (hot tea with frothy milk).

I'm the mom of 2 and a milspouse (retired). We live in the Pacific Northwest and are under-prepared if one of the volcanoes erupts.

Here are 3 things about me:

- I lived on the outskirts of an active volcano (Mt.Etna)
- A spider bit me and it laid eggs in my arm (my kids don't know that story yet)

- I grew up in Central Florida and have skied in lakes with gators.

I'd love to get to know you better. Join my Read & Relax community and then fire off an email and tell me 3 things about you!

Not ready to join? Email me below or follow me at one of the links below. Thanks for popping by!

You can connect with Kristi at any of the following:
www.kristirose.net
kristi@kristirose.net

CPSIA information can be obtained
at www.ICGtesting.com
Printed in the USA
BVHW070549130819
555662BV00010B/1611/P